He gazed into her eyes so intently, she felt he burned away the mask and could see straight to her heart. Instead of answering, he lowered his head and kissed her.

His lips rested so lightly against hers that she felt no fear. They were soft, gently caressing. She could not help parting her own lips to more fully enjoy the delight.

When he raised his head, his mouth curled at one corner. "You mustn't blame me, for we are sitting beneath a kissing bough."

"I am not angry, my lord." How could her voice sound so calm when she trembled inside?

A REGENCY CHRISTMAS

An Anthology

"GREETINGS OF THE SEASON"
by Barbara Metzger

"HOME FOR CHRISTMAS"
by Jennie Gallant

"LOVE À LA CARTE"
by Joan Smith

"THE CHRISTMAS BALL"
by Leslie Lynn

FAWCETT CREST • NEW YORK

A Fawcett Crest Book
Published by Ballantine Books
"Greetings of the Season" copyright © 1994 by Barbara Metzger
"Home for Christmas" copyright © 1994 by Jennie Gallant
"Love à la Carte" copyright © 1994 by Joan Smith
"The Christmas Ball" copyright © 1994 by Elaine Sima and Sherrill Bodine

Library of Congress Catalog Card Number: 94-94406

ISBN 0-449-22267-5

Manufactured in the United States of America

First Edition: November 1994

10 9 8 7 6 5 4 3 2 1

Contents

GREETINGS OF THE SEASON

by
Barbara Metzger

1

"Dashed if I can figure why everyone gets in such a pucker over this Christmas shopping nonsense." Bevin Montford, the Earl of Montravan, paused in the act of putting the last, critical fold in his intricately tied neckcloth. His valet, standing by with a second or—heaven forfend his lordship be struck with a palsy or such—a third starched cravat, held his breath.

"Why, the park was so thin of company this afternoon, you'd think the ton had packed up and gone to their country places weeks early," the earl complained to the mirror. "Where was everyone? Traipsing in and out of shops as if the British economy depended on their spending their last farthings."

The earl finally lowered his chin, setting the crease in his neckcloth. Finster, the valet, exhaled. Another perfect Montravan fall. He tenderly draped the reserve linen over the rungs of a chair and reached for his lordship's coat of blue superfine, just a shade darker than the earl's eyes.

"And now here's Coulton, crying off from our dinner engagement," Montravan went on, shrugging his broad shoulders into the garment. No dandy, the earl refused to have his coats cut so tightly that he'd require two footmen to assist. He made sure the lace of his shirt cuffs fell gracefully over his wrists while Finster straightened the coat across his back. "I never thought I'd live to see Johnny Coulton turning down one of Desroucher's meals to go shopping. Haring off to an Italian goldsmith in Islington, no less."

Finster was ready with the clothes brush, making sure no speck of lint had fallen on the coat between his final pressing and his lordship's occupancy. "I understand Lord Coulton is recently engaged," Finster offered, more relaxed now that the more crucial aspects of his employer's toilette were complete.

"What's that to the point? The chit's blond with blue eyes. Sapphires, obviously. Rundell and Bridges ought to be sufficient for the purpose."

"Ah, perhaps Lord Coulton wished to express his affection in a more personal manner."

"More expensive, you mean. Deuce take it, he's already won the girl's hand; there's no need for such extravagance."

"If the viscount is indeed visiting goldsmiths, he might wish to design a bit of jewelry himself to show his joy at the betrothal."

"Claptrap. You've been reading the housekeeper's Minerva Press novels again, haven't you?" The earl turned from the mirror to catch his longtime servant's blush. "Ah, Finster, still a romantic after all these years? I must be a sad trial to you."

"Not at all, my lord," the valet said with a smile, thinking of all the positions he'd been offered and had turned down. There could be no finer gentleman in the ton to work for, none more generous and none who appeared more to his valet's credit than the nonpareil earl. Of course, Lord Montravan was a bit high in the instep, his valet admitted to himself, but how not, when he'd been granted birth, wealth, looks, and charm in abundance? No, Lord Montravan's only fault, according to the loyal Finster, was a sad lack of tender emotions. Still,

4

the valet lived in hope. He passed the silver tray that contained the earl's signet ring and watch fob, the thin leather wallet, and the newly washed coins. He also proffered, by way of explaining Lord Coulton's defection, *"L'amour."*

"Larks in his brainbox, more likely, getting himself into a pother over a trinket for a wench. And those other clunches, the ones who were too frenzied for a hand of cards at White's yesterday, nattering on about where to find the perfect fan, the best chocolates, the most elegant bibelot for madam's curio. Gudgeons, every last one of them, letting their wits go begging over this nonsensical holiday gift giving."

Finster cleared his throat. "Ah, perchance the gentlemen find the difficulty more in the expense than in the selection. The ladies do expect more than a bit of trumpery at this time of year," he hinted.

The earl sighed. "What, dished again, Finster?" He casually tossed a coin to the smaller man, who deftly caught it and tucked it out of sight in one of his black suit's pockets. "You'd think you'd have learned after all these years either to save your shillings or not to fall in love at the Christmas season. What female has caught your eye this week?"

"The new French dresser at Lady Worthington's. Madeleine." Finster whispered the name and kissed his fingertips.

"French, eh?" Montravan tossed another coin, which followed its brother, then shook his head. "Next I suppose you'll be wanting the afternoon off to do your shopping."

"The morning should be sufficient, milord, thank you." Finster smiled. "After milord returns from his ride, naturally."

"Naturally. I suppose I should be thankful my own valet is not abandoning me in favor of the shops." The earl gave a final combing through his black curls with his fingers, setting them into the fashionable windswept style. One curl persisted in falling over his high forehead. He shrugged and left it.

"Though it would be all of a piece with this wretched week. What gets into everyone mid-December that their attics are to let? There must be some brain fever that scrambles perfectly normal minds into this mush of indecision, this urge to outrun the bailiffs, this agony of self-doubt over a bauble or two. Just look at you, the most fastidious person I know." He waved his manicured hand around his own spotless bedchamber, where not a towel remained from his bath, not a soiled garment was in sight, not a loose hair reposed on the Aubusson carpet. "Then comes Christmas shopping. You are ready to desert your post in order to wait for some caper-merchant to deign to assist you in spending your next quarter's salary. Mush, I say. Your brains have turned to mush along with everyone else's."

Finster smiled as he polished the earl's quizzing glass on a cloth he pulled from another pocket. "There is no other way, milord."

"Of course there is," said Montravan, surveying his person through the glass. "Organization, efficiency, an orderly mind—that's all it takes to keep this idiocy in proper perspective. You don't see me chasing my own shadow up and down Bond Street, do you?"

"No, milord, your secretary does that for you."

The earl chose to ignore that home truth. "Humph. The diamond or the black pearl?" he asked, nodding toward the velvet-lined tray holding his stickpins.

Finster surveyed the earl, the muscular thighs encased in black satin, the white marcella waistcoat with silver embroidery. "The ruby, I believe, will be more festive. 'Tis the season, after all."

Montravan frowned. "Blast the season."

Still, he affixed the ruby in his neckcloth, told his man not to wait up for him, and stepped jauntily down the stairs.

Ah, the season. Just a few more weeks and his own perfectly ordered existence would be even more satisfactory. He'd have satisfied his filial duties with a trip to Montravan Hall in Wiltshire and fulfilled his more pressing familial obligations with the selection of his future countess. If Lady Belinda Harleigh proved satisfactory during the visit she and her parents were making to the ancestral pile, Montravan meant to offer for the duke's daughter before the new year. Then he'd be free to return to London and his new mistress. First, of course, was this minor trifle of Christmas shopping to be gone through. The earl consulted the pendulum clock in the marble hallway. Yes, there was an hour before dinner; that should do the trick.

2

The library at Montford House, Grosvenor Square, was larger than Hatchard's Bookstore and likely contained more volumes. Unlike the bookseller's, what it did not contain—and would never contain, if Bevin Montford had any say in the matter—was any gaggles of chattering females or any of those gothicky romances so beloved of polite society and its servants. The library was quite Lord Montravan's favorite room in the house, with its precise shelves of both old tomes and new editions, all neatly cataloged and in their proper order. Situated toward the rear of Montford House so no street noises could intrude, and thickly carpeted to muffle any interior sounds, the library was a quiet haven of dark wood and old leather.

What did intrude, and did offend the earl's usual feeling of contentment in this private place, was the young man standing next to the large desk. Wearing yellow cossack trousers, ear-threatening shirt points, buttons the size of dinner plates, and a puce waistcoat embroidered with cabbage roses, Vincent Winchell was not of an appearance to appeal to the austere earl. Happily Vincent was a better secretary than a fashion plate.

The son of Bevin's mother's bosom bow in Bath, young Winchell had arrived in London with a note from Lady Montravan imploring the earl to do something for dear widowed Bessie's fatherless boy.

Unfortunately dear Bessie's boy had no prospects. He also had no aptitude for the law, the church, or medicine. Bessie, according to Lady Montravan, would go into a decline if her baby took up colors, and likewise if he took one breath of India's insalubrious air. The young cawker's ambition, Vincent revealed upon questioning, was to become a man-about-town. Like the earl.

Trained since birth to the duties and responsibilities of his position, Lord Montravan was not about to feed and house some useless unlicked cub. He had enough pensioners as it was without adopting able-bodied layabouts only eight years his junior. The best solution, of course, was to find the lad a rich wife. But with no fortune, the doors to the polite world were closed to the son of Bessie Winchell of Bath, and with no title, wealthy cits were more likely to offer him a position rather than their daughters. Or they would, Bevin acknowledged, if the chawbacon showed any potential for hard work. Instead, in the fortnight the earl took to think about young Winchell's future, the nodcock had gambled away his pittance and signed himself into debt, come home drunk thrice, and hadn't returned at all once, sending Montford House into a furor. He'd had his nose broken in a taproom brawl and been taken up by the watch until Montravan paid his fines. So Bevin made the pup his secretary.

Three years later the earl was satisfied with his gamble. He had an aide who knew how he liked things done, who didn't look askance when asked to lease a house for his latest light-o'-love or to place a bet at Newmarket. As for Vincent, he had a steady income, a fine address with servants to provide for his every need, ample free time to enjoy London's pleasures—and all for a few hours of paperwork and a promise to stay out of trouble. To the earl's gratification and Vincent's surprise, they

9

even discovered that young Winchell had a knack for pesky details, like Christmas lists.

"I have sent your instructions to Montravan Hall," Vincent now reported, consulting his pages of notes, "along with the proper number of presents for the tenants' children, dolls and hair ribbons for the girls, tops and pocketknives for the boys. I have also sent directions and a bank draft for Boxing Day gifts for the staff, along with last year's distributions. Everything will be arranged before your arrival next week, according to Miss Sinclaire. Mr. Tuttle will oversee the London staff's holiday gratuities."

"Excellent, Vincent. I know I need not concern myself whilst you are in charge." The earl sat behind his desk and lit a cigarillo. "When do you leave for Bath?"

"Oh, not till after you depart, my lord, in case there are any last-minute changes in your plans."

Montravan blew a smoke ring and smiled. "That's a relief. Sometimes I wonder how I got on without you."

"Poorly, I imagine." Vincent ruffled his pages, bringing Bevin's attention back to the matter at hand, and unfortunately back to the multitude of rings on the same hand. The earl winced and looked away.

"Do go on. I surmise you are in a fidge to be off for the evening."

"Drury Lane, my lord. There's a new production of *Othello*."

"And a new farce, with the chorus girls showing their ankles, I hear tell."

"I could not say, my lord." The secretary hurriedly turned and pushed forward a stack of calling cards from the corner of the desk. "I had these printed up special for your holiday messages, if you cared to include a personal note to any of the employees or tenants, and, of course, for your relatives and, ah, close acquaintances." He cleared his throat and scanned another list. "The gifts for those, ah, family and friends are here on the side table, awaiting your final selection."

The earl got up and followed the younger man to the table, where parcels were displayed, two by two, with an elegantly printed name card in front of each pair. Bevin took out his quizzing glass to survey the groupings before once again declaring his secretary invaluable.

"You toddle off now while I scribble my compliments to Lady Montravan and the rest. I'll place my card and the name plaque by the gifts I choose, and you can send them off on the morrow, except, of course, the ones I'll be taking with me to the Hall."

"If you are sure, my lord. I could stay to advise—"

"No, my dear boy, you've done enough. I can surely sign my own name. Have a pleasant evening. Oh, and, Vincent, do remember to give yourself a generous Christmas bonus. You deserve it. Perhaps you'll even purchase a new set of clothes before you give your mother palpitations in those."

"They're all the crack, my lord," Vincent said, bowing his way out of the library. "Bang up to the mark."

"I'm sure they are," the earl whispered to the closing door, feeling considerably older than his thirty-two years.

Bevin returned to the desk and poured himself a glass of sherry from the cut-glass decanter there. He sat and took up a quill—neatly sharpened—and one of the new cards. At least Vincent had learned to restrain his flamboyant taste when it came to his employer's business. The cards merely held Lord Montravan's name and title, under the simple inscription "Greetings of the Season" in raised black letters. The whole was edged in a thin border of holly, with hand-tinted leaves and berries. No gilt edges, thank goodness, or flowing script or flowery prose. The earl nodded, sipped his drink, and began his task, adding a salutation here, a New Year's wish there, knowing his dependents counted on the monetary rewards yet still appreciated the personal touch.

Half a glass of sherry later, Bevin was ready for the challenge of selecting gifts and writing warmer messages. He carried a handful of cards and his glass to the other table, where another inkstand was positioned, another quill perfectly pointed. Raising his glass, he silently toasted the absent, efficient secretary.

For the dowager countess, Vincent had laid out a diamond pendant and a ruby brooch. Montravan chose the brooch. It was larger, gaudier, and more expensive, just the thing to appeal to his flighty mama. Vincent should have been her son, their tastes were that similar. No matter, the earl told himself, Mama's real Christmas present was Lady Belinda Harleigh. Hadn't the dowager been nagging at Bevin since his twenty-first year to find a bride and assure the succession? She must be in alt over the visit of Lady Belinda, ducal parents, handsome dowry, and all. He penned a short message about fulfilling obligations and moved on to his baby sister's gift.

Following the earl's instructions, Vincent had purchased, on approval of course, the set of pearls proper for a young miss about to make her comeout, and a tiara. A gold tiara was totally unsuitable for a chit just out of the schoolroom, of course, even without the diamonds Allissa wanted, but the minx had been begging for one this last age. Allissa was growing into the type of spoiled, grasping featherbrain Bevin most disliked, but he recalled her cherubic infancy and put his card atop the tiara. The pearls could wait for her official presentation in the spring, he decided, when the budding beauty was bound to set London on its ear no matter what she wore. He groaned to think of all the young sprigs haunting Montford House and the idea of having to listen to their petitions for Allissa's hand. Gads, he wasn't that old, was he, that some spotty youth might come quaking into this very library? He downed another swallow of sherry. Mayhap he could get the prattlebox buckled to some country lad before the time, or a beau from Bath, where she and his mother were going after the holidays. Ah, well, at least Miss Sinclaire would not let the rattlepate wear the tiara to any of the country gatherings, so none would know what an expensive bit of fluff she'd be. And in the spring he'd have Lady Belinda to help with the presentation.

For Squire Merton, his mother's faithful cicisbeo, Bevin choose the riding crop over the snuffbox with a hunting scene on the cover. The old fool would only spill the snuff on Montravan's own furniture. Lord Montravan quickly scrawled "Happy hunting" on the card and moved on.

The next grouping was labeled *Miss Corbett*. Ah, Marina, the earl thought fondly, but not so fondly that he was tempted to keep the raven-haired actress on as his mistress. She was exquisite, voluptuous—and boring. She hadn't always been, of course, so he designated the heavily jeweled bracelet as her Christmas present. The extravagance alone would tell her it was also a parting gift, but he added a few words to the card to ensure Marina knew he would not be returning to her when he returned to London after the holidays. Vincent could deliver the package, saving Montravan an unpleasant scene when Marina received her congé. Not that he was a coward, he told himself, just discreet.

And wise. Too wise to leave town without securing the affections, or attentions, at any rate, of the latest highflier to soar over London's demimonde. He tucked his message under the card addressed to Mademoiselle Bibi Duchamps and put both alongside the pair of diamond earbobs, setting the matching necklace aside for another occasion, such as the formalization of their arrangement. Bevin had no doubt there would be such an understanding, not when his note expressed his intentions. Bibi was no fool; she'd wait until Montravan came back before selecting her protector. He was bound to be the highest bidder, even if the earl modestly refused to consider his other attractions. No woman had turned him down yet.

Bevin had never asked a woman to marry him, but he did not expect Lady Belinda Harleigh to refuse him either if he decided to make the offer. She was an acknowledged beauty, well educated for a woman, and two years beyond that first giddy debutante stage. The on-dit was that her father, the duke, was also holding out for the best offer. A wealthy earl was like to be the best, or they would not have accepted his invitation to Wiltshire, where Montravan wanted to see firsthand how Belinda reacted to his home, his tenants, and his ramshackle family. He also wanted to have some private conversation with her, impossible in Town, and at least one tender embrace before deciding to spend the rest of his life with the young woman. Besides, he wanted to get a better look at her mother, to extrapolate the daughter's future.

The Harleighs were not arriving at Montravan until a day or two before the New Year's ball, so a gift for the earl's almost-intended would have to be delivered here in London. The present could not be too expensive and personal, such as jewels or furs, without being a declaration; it could not be too trifling without giving offense. Vincent had done well again, presenting the earl with a choice between an exquisitely filigreed fan and a pearl-studded jewel box. He selected the fan, which Belinda could carry at the ball, indicating her approval of his suit, instead of the jewel box, lest she and her father get the notion he was bound and determined to fill it with the family betrothal ring, now in the vault in Wiltshire. He wrote about looking forward to her visit, then considered the next and last pile of gifts.

Miss Petra Sinclaire. Now there was a problem indeed. The earl went back to his desk and refilled his glass. Then he paced between the desk and the table, undecided. Petra was an employee. She was also an old friend, the orphaned daughter of his old tutor. When Vicar Sinclaire passed on, Bevin had paid for her schooling. Then it was natural for Petra to take up residence at Montravan, where the countess could take her around and find her some likely parti among the local gentry. She had no other connections, no great beauty to attract suitors, and only the modest dowry the earl insisted on providing. Only Petra had not accepted any of the offers and refused to live on charity. She threatened to accept a paid position in London, until Bevin was forced to hire her on as his mother's companion, a position she'd been filling anyway, as well as mentor to his hoydenish sister, surrogate chatelaine of Montravan Hall for the vaporish countess, and general factotum in Bevin's absence. If Vincent was indispensable in London, Petra Sinclaire was the earl's lifeline in Wiltshire. Still, he was determined to see her established in her own household before she was more firmly on the shelf than her five and twenty years dictated. When she accompanied Allissa to London for the

Season, Miss Petra Sinclaire was also going to find herself presented to every respectable gentleman Bevin knew, whether she wished it or not. He owed her that much, and more.

Unfortunately he could not express his gratitude for her loyalty and calm good sense in his Christmas gift. It simply wasn't done. He was already paying her the highest wage she would accept, and money would only place her more firmly among the ranks of servitors. He looked at the heap of rejected jewels from his mother's and mistresses' gifts, even the pearls for Allissa's comeout, and had a mad urge to fill the pearl jewel box with the pirate's treasure, for Petra. She was the only one of the bunch deserving of his largesse, the only one without a relative or other protector to satisfy her every whim, the only one not expecting an exorbitant present. And the only one he must not be lavish with.

Vincent had selected carefully: a volume of Scott's ballads, because Petra was of a serious mind, and a set of mother-of-pearl hair combs, which would look well in her long brown hair. Perfectly acceptable, perfectly tasteful, and perfectly awful.

Bevin paced some more, then sat at his desk, thinking that a warmer greeting might better express his appreciation, since his gift could not. He disarranged his hair by threading his fingers through it in thought as he crumpled one card after another. Finally, just as the dinner gong reverberated through the halls, he had a message that met with his approval. He waved the card about to dry the ink, then put it on top of the combs. No, the book.

"Hell and the devil take it!" he swore, putting the combs and the book together and slamming his card and Petra's name on top of both so there was no mistake.

Satisfied, the Earl of Montravan went in to dinner, whistling. This Christmas shopping was child's play.

3

"Christmas gifting should be just for children," Lady Montravan declared. "Gingerbread and shiny pennies and no bother to anyone else. This fustian of bestowing presents on everyone for miles around is too fatiguing for words," she stated from her reclining position on the love seat, a pillow under her feet, a lavender-soaked cloth on her weary brow. The dowager countess credited her enervation to bearing her daughter so late in life. Others, such as her dresser, Travers, blamed it on sheer miserliness. Lady Montravan was so cheeseparing, she wouldn't expend a single groat or an ounce of effort more than she had to. "Besides," she went on now, sighing with exhaustion, "all these gifts take away from the religious celebration." Which cost her nothing except her son's donation to the church.

"Oh, Mama, you cannot mean you wish for a Christmas without presents! Just think of all the treats you'd miss and the surprises you have to look forward to." At seventeen, Allissa Montford was still young enough to shiver with anticipation, tossing her blond curls. Allissa's fair hair was her heritage from the father she barely remembered, while Bevin's coloring came more from his mother, whose own dark hair was now gone to gray—from frailty, the dowager swore.

"Do sit still, Allissa. Your restlessness is agitating my nerves."

17

"Yes, Mama." Lady Alissa dutifully picked up the fashion journal she'd been studying, but she couldn't drop the subject, not with Christmas just a week or so away. All the cooking going on below-stairs, all the baskets being readied for the tenants, and all the greenery being fetched in for decorations kept her normally high spirits at fever pitch. "Only consider, Mama, Squire Merton is coming for Christmas dinner. He is sure to bring you something pretty, and you know Bev always delights you with his gifts. I'm sure this year will be no different. Except," Allissa said with a giggle, "this year he can buy me extravagant jewelry, too."

"Oh, dear," spoke a quiet voice from the window seat, where the light was better for her embroidery, since too many lamps bothered Lady Montravan's eyes and used too much oil. "You haven't been pestering your brother about a tiara again, have you?"

"Oh, no, I merely wrote to Vincent about it."

Miss Sinclaire clucked her tongue and went back to her needlework. If Lady Montravan did not find fault with Allissa's manners, surely it was not Petra's place to correct the forward chit. Besides, she'd only be wasting her breath. Petra smiled to herself, a smile that softened her rather common-place features into loveliness, to think that she was growing as stingy with her energy as her employer. She knew what Travers and the others thought of Lady Montravan: that she would let her son's house burn down around her ears without lifting a pudgy, beringed finger, so long as her jewel box and bankbook were safe. Why, the abigail was fond of repeating, before Miss Sinclaire came to the Hall, the place was a shambles and Lady Allissa was running wild through the countryside with none to naysay her. 'Twas doubtful she even knew her letters before Petra took her in hand, the little savage. The staff adored the little hoyden—that was

18

half the problem—but not one of them misdoubted that she'd make micefeet of her reputation ere long.

The tiara was *not* Petra's problem, she tried to convince herself. Bevin couldn't be such a gudgeon as to forget what was suitable for such a young miss. Then again, it would be just like the generous earl to cave in to Allissa's demands, then leave it up to Petra to forbid the peagoose to wear it. And it would be just like Lissa to want to flaunt a diamond tiara at the small local assemblies before her less fortunate friends. At least Bevin would be at Montravan for the New Year's ball. If he wanted to see his little sister make a cake out of herself in front of his ducal guests, or be labeled "coming" by the neighbors, even before her presentation, that was *his* problem. Christmas was Petra's.

"You know, dearest," she hinted, "you might think a bit more of others at this special season."

"Oh, I do, Petra!" Allissa jumped up. "I wonder if Squire Merton will bring me a gift as well as Mama."

"He can well afford it," her fond mother commented, popping another bonbon into her mouth, then sucking on it as if the effort to chew was just too great. "If he ever gets his nose out of the smelly stables and kennels long enough to go shopping. And not in the village, either. There is nothing but pinchbeck stuff in the local shops. He'll send to London if he has any sense."

If the squire had any sense, Petra thought, he wouldn't be hanging around Lady Montravan. The hunting-mad squire was going to see his carefree bachelor days ended, if Petra was any judge, as soon as Bevin brought home his bride. Lady Montravan had declared often enough her refusal to take up residence in Montravan's pawky dower house. And why should she, spending her own join-ture on its upkeep, when Merton had a perfectly fine manor house just waiting for a mistress?

The dowager had finally swallowed the sweet, but not the bitter thought of Merton's coming the lickpenny with her present. "He'd better come down handsome, I say, after all the trouble I have gone to for his gift."

The squire's gift was to be the needlepoint pillow with a portrait of his favorite hunter on the cover, the one that Petra was currently embroidering.

Lady Montravan believed that handmade gifts showed greater feeling than mere monetary expenditures. "Why, giving Merton a gift he can jolly well go purchase for himself is foolish beyond permission," the dowager had declared. "And as for buying Bevin a present, la, I am sure the boy has five of everything he could ever want or need. And doxies to provide the rest. Buying gifts for nabobs is like bringing coals to Newcastle."

Still, he was her son, so after much deliberation Lady Montravan decided on a burgundy velvet dressing gown with satin lapels and sash, with his initials embroidered on the chest and the family crest embroidered on the back. By Petra. A lion, a scepter, and a hawk, in gold thread.

"Now that Mama is giving Bev such a marvelous surprise," Allissa had mused to Petra, "I need a really special gift for him, too, to thank him for the tiara."

"What if he gives you something else, something equally nice, just more suitable?"

"Then I'll still want to give him something wonderful, so he feels guilty. My birthday is soon." She twirled a golden lock around her finger, thinking. "Mama says handworked gifts show heart." So Lady Allissa designed a pair of slippers to match the burgundy dressing gown, with a lion on the

20

right shoe, a hawk and a scepter to be embroidered on the left. By Petra.

Miss Sinclaire kept sewing, turning to catch the afternoon light. Lady Montravan was still exhausted from reading Vincent's lists out loud to her companion. "I swear," she said, "this doling out of money to the servants is another ridiculous tradition. Heaven knows we pay them a good enough wage. Why should we have to reward them extra simply for doing their jobs?"

"Because they work harder at Christmastide, with all the extra company and such, my lady," Petra offered. "And so they might have more joy in the season, buying gifts for their loved ones, too."

Allissa looked up from her magazine. "And you know servants can never manage to save any money. Besides, Mama, you shouldn't say such things. Petra is a paid employee, too."

"Nonsense," Lady Montravan stated, without lifting the scented cloth from her eyes to see Petra's blush. "Petra is one of the family. Bevin explained it to you ages ago. We are not paying her a wage to make herself useful; we give her an allowance, the same as we give you one."

Except that Petra could not refuse to make all the arrangements for the ball, the household's celebration, and the arrival of the ducal party. She couldn't say she was too busy to wrap and pack all the baskets for the tenants, and she could not choose to work on her own Christmas gifts instead of embroidering scepters, lions, and hawks! She certainly could not go spend Christmas with her sister and Rosalyn's curate husband at their tiny cottage in Hampshire—no, not even if there was a new niece she had never seen, not with such an important event in the offing, the heir's bringing home a prospective bride.

And as for her allowance, why, Allissa couldn't pass

through the nearby village with its two insignificant shops without spending more than Petra's quarterly income. Not that Petra complained, ever. She was nothing to Lord Montravan, no obligation, no relation, no debt of honor, yet he supported her, and handsomely. He even insisted that her clothes money come from the household accounts, not her "allowance." The dowager agreed, not surprising since the bills were on Bevin's tab, and since a well-dressed Miss Sinclaire was a suitable enough companion to send out with Allissa on her rounds of the neighbors, saving Lady Montravan the stress and strain of carriage rides and morning calls. Besides, the dowager liked to show Petra off to the local gentry and her Bath cronies as a symbol of her generosity.

Lady Montravan *was* generous, in her way. She treated Petra like a daughter—just as negligently as she treated Allissa.

That night, long after the other ladies were abed, Petra sat up reflecting, not for the first time, on Lord Montravan's generosity.

It was not enough. Her quarterly payments, her life savings, and all the coins she'd managed to squirrel away in a more frugal fashion than even Lady Montravan espoused were not enough for her Christmas shopping. So Miss Sinclaire sat up sewing through the night on her own Christmas gifts.

A gift from the hands was a gift from the heart, she tried to convince herself, echoing Lady Montravan's oft-repeated sentiments. The recipients would appreciate Petra's laboriously worked handkerchiefs more than some store-bought bauble. And pigs would fly. Petra tried to imagine Allissa preferring the lace-edged, monogrammed linen squares to a diamond tiara. Instead she pictured Squire Merton wiping the manure off his boots with his initialed handkerchief.

No matter, she thought, yawning but still setting

neat stitches in the bib for her new niece, she could not afford to squander her ready on gifts for people who wanted for nothing. Oh, she set aside coins for the vails for the servants; that was different. And there'd be a coin wrapped in the handkerchief for her sister, and another in the toe of the socks she'd knitted for Rosalyn's struggling husband. But that was all. Not another brass farthing was going to leave her hands, not even if those hands were so needle-pricked, they snagged on her stockings. She looked over at the considerable pile of handkerchiefs. Rosalyn, Cook, and Mrs. Franklin, the housekeeper, were all getting some, as well as Allissa, the squire, and Lady Montravan. And his lordship . . .

When the tiny stitches blurred in front of her weary eyes, Petra set her sewing aside and stretched her stiff muscles. Then she went to her bureau and reached under her gloves for the old reticule that held her fortune. It was heavy. Pound notes rustled and coins clinked. Petra could almost hear the devil whispering temptations in her ear. If it weren't the middle of the night, she'd take all the money and go buy him the most lavish, stupendous, one-of-a-kind gift she could ever hope to find, something a lot more worthy of the Earl of Montravan than another handkerchief or another embroidered lion, hawk, and scepter.

But it was the middle of the night, and Petra did know that she needed every last pence of her savings if she was going to make her own way in the world. Who knew if Lady Montravan would even write her a reference if she left? Or how long before she found another position, or how much a decent lodging would cost until she found one? Rosalyn and her curate were barely surviving, so Petra could not add to her sister's burden, even if they had room in their tiny cottage.

For certain she could not stay on at Montravan Hall much longer. The earl was bringing home a bride. It was not official yet, but it was all anyone could talk of, and a sure thing, according to the kitchen wagering. She was known to be a peeress with fortune and face, manners and a mind. Lady Belinda Harleigh. Petra said the name over to herself. Belinda. Belinda and Bevin. Perfect.

Lady Belinda would have been brought up to manage a household like Montravan; she'd be an experienced guide for Allissa through the shoals of a London Season; Lady Montravan was already calculating the settlements.

So there was no reason for Petra to stay, nothing here for her except more heartbreak. Could a heart keep breaking eternally, or would it just crumble into dust and blow away?

Petra had loved the earl forever, it seemed. When the wiry thirteen-year-old had ridden over for his Latin lessons and offered a nut brown hobbledehoy six-year-old a ride, she was lost. When he sat by her ailing father, sent her macaroons at school, trusted her with Montravan's running, she loved him the more. Loving Bevin Montford was like loving the hero in a romance novel—from a distance. Bevin was more handsome, more dashing, more caring than any hero—and just as unattainable for a poor vicar's daughter who had to earn her living.

Petra looked over to her wardrobe door, where the burgundy robe hung, the slippers placed neatly on the floor in front, almost as if the earl would walk into her bedroom at any minute. And pigs would not just fly; they'd start teaching astronomy at Oxford. Earls did not look at impoverished nobodies except in charity. And charity was cold comfort indeed when a heart ached for a much warmer touch.

4

White's was fairly thin of company that evening, most of the members having already left town for their far-flung estates or country parties. Some young sprigs were in the dining room, drinking their suppers, and a few of the old gents were snoring in the reading room with newspapers over their faces. After handing his hat and gloves to the footman at the door, Montravan looked into the game room for his own particular cronies, gentlemen past their callow youth but not yet settled into sedentary respectability. They were more Corinthians than Tulips, and generally well breeched enough to pursue avidly the two favorite pastimes of the more raffish section of the aristocracy: wagering and womanizing. Happily there were enough of Lord Montravan's set at the club tonight for a decent hand of whist and congenial conversation. Or so he thought.

After the current war news, talk turned to homely Lady Throckmorton and her handsome footmen, thence to the new bareback rider at Astley's Amphitheatre: her bare legs, her nearly bare chest. Then Lord Coulton came in, rubbing the chill out of his hands.

"Ah, the very gentlemen I was hoping to see," he said, fitting his large frame into a chair near Montravan and the others. "I have just consigned my fate to River Tick and need your heavy purses to bail myself out. Cards, anyone?" A wide grin split his freckled face as he started to deal. The earl called for another bottle.

"'Tis the least I can do for a friend who is so badly dipped," he told his other companions. "Besides, the cognac might dim that avaricious gleam in our Goliath's eye, so we poor Davids have a chance."

For a while the only sounds were softly spoken bids and answers, the slap of cards on the baize, and the clink of glasses. Then the group of younger men strolled in from the dining room, carrying their bottles and glasses. Most sauntered; a few staggered. They took up chairs at a nearby table but immediately started arguing about the stakes. One of the players at Bevin's game glared in their direction, without affecting their raucous noise in the slightest. Finally Viscount Coulton put his cards on the table, stood up to his considerable height, and walked over to the other group.

"Gentlemen, I truly need to win tonight. In order to win, I need to concentrate. In order to concentrate, I need quiet. In order to get that quiet, I'll bash your bloody skulls in." He bowed, smiled his boyish grin, and took up his own seat.

Not only was Lord Coulton larger than any of the young blades, he was Gentleman Jackson's own sparring partner. Furthermore, while the viscount might smile, leaving his intentions in question, the Earl of Montravan had his dark brows lowered in a scowl. No one doubted Montravan's disapproval, and no one wanted to challenge the devil's own temper. The argle-bargle subsided. Two of the Bartholomew babes decided on a hand of piquet, and another came over to observe the earl's game. Nessborough's heir and his chum Rupert Haskell lurched over to where the betting book was kept.

As usual, Lord Montravan figured largely in the current entries.

"Just look at this: Calbert Hodge put twenty pounds on Lady B——H——," Nessborough whispered, loudly enough to rouse the snorers in the next room. "I put down only five." He jerked his head toward the earl. "I wish he'd put us out of our misery before we leave town. I could use the blunt."

Haskell curled his lip and didn't even attempt to lower his voice as he asked, "What was the wager, that he'd offer or that she'd accept?"

Nessborough hooted, forgetting to whisper. "No one'd take you up on the last bet, you nodcock. No woman in her right mind would turn down such a title and fortune."

"And the duke wouldn't let her even if she had other inclinations." Haskell spoke bitterly, then downed another glass of liquor. "I need her fortune a sight more than Montravan does, but, no, it's always the rich swells who get everything."

Some of the earl's friends were beginning to look uncomfortable, while Johnny Coulton's florid complexion was turning redder. Bevin took up the cards. "My deal, I believe."

Haskell did not drop the subject. "I'd bet a monkey she wouldn't have him without the blasted title."

Nessborough scratched his head, leaving greasy pomatum on his fingers. "I don't know. There's still the blunt, and the fellow *is* a top-of-the-trees Corinthian. I mean, she ain't like to find a better shot or a better eye for horseflesh. And everyone knows he's a regular prime 'un."

"A veritable paragon," Haskell sneered. "Why, he's—"

Before Haskell could complete the thought, a graceful, manicured hand reached out and slammed the betting book shut. "You are putting me to the blush, gentlemen," Lord Montravan quietly explained in a silky voice with the edge of steel. "I hadn't realized that your lives were so empty, you had to rely on mine for titillation. I *do* wish you'd find a—"

Nessborough recalled a previous engagement. Haskell ordered another bottle, but he did wander over to the piquet table. Montravan returned to his own play, where Lord Coulton was quick to joke about the cards growing cold in Bevin's absence.

Rupert Haskell was such a dirty dish, his own mother didn't invite him home for Christmas. He was mean and dumb at the best of times. Drunk, he was dumber; disappointed, he was meaner. Having suffered a rebuff from Lord Harleigh after three disastrous days at the track, he'd been drinking steadily for the last fourteen hours. Upon muddled reflection he was not about to let some toff on his high horse send him to the corner like a misbehaving schoolboy. He reeled back to the betting book and began flipping pages, mumbling to himself until he reached an interesting entry.

"Ain't that a coincidence?" he asked the room at large. "Here's the Earl of M——again. Lemme see what it says this time." He peered closer at the book, then stood back, attempting a whistle but spraying spit instead. "A golden boy on the golden boy. Too bad his hair ain't blond, Nessborough'd make him out to be some Greek god." He read the wager again. " 'A golden boy that the Earl of M——will be first out of the gate with the new French filly.' According to Nessy, there'll be no race." He took another swig and addressed the earl directly: "Unless you're even more of a nonesuch than they say, I suppose that'll leave the beauteous Marina available to us poor mortals."

The card game had stopped, but Coulton had his hand on the earl's shoulder, keeping him in his seat. "Never, to the likes of you," Bevin muttered through gritted teeth.

"That's right, m'pockets are to let."

"Your attics are to let, boy." Sir Cedric laughed from Montravan's other side.

"You going to explain that remark?" Haskell took a belligerent step in Sir Cedric's direction, but Bevin drew his attention again. He cleared his throat and said, "What my friend means is that you are dicked in the nob if you think the lady would entertain you at any price. Miss Corbett is too refined in her ways. She never lets slime cross her threshold."

"Slime? You're saying your doxy's too good for the likes of me?" Haskell shouted.

Never raising his voice, the earl answered: "No, I am saying the lady is under my protection, and I'll have your liver and lights if you so much as mention her name again."

"Why, you—"

Haskell lunged toward the seated nobleman, but the piquet players grabbed him by the coattails and wrestled him into a chair. One of the vigilant footmen immediately came by with a dice cup and suggested a game.

Some other late-arriving members wandered into the card room, attracted by the yells. A few stayed to bet on the first roll, surrounding Haskell and his chums with a hum of conversation.

Having tossed down their cards in preparation for battle, Montravan and his friends declared the game over and undecided. Before dealing out the new hands, Bevin turned to Lord Coulton. "I take it you've found the perfect gift for Miss Framingham at last, Johnny, since you're suddenly so badly dipped."

"The fairest for the fair," the viscount said with

one of his ready grins. "And likely paid three times too much for the gewgaw."

"It's worth it, to have you returned to our ranks. Now you can come with me to Tatt's tomorrow. I hear Adderly's chestnuts are going on the block."

Lord Coulton shook his head. "Sorry, old chap. Elizabeth's was the easy one. Now I have to find something for my four sisters and my mother, to say nothing of the governor. When I think of all the ready I'll have to spout, I could thrash that muckworm Haskell. I was winning that last round, I know it. If I don't win this next one, I'll be handing m'sisters vouchers."

Sir Cedric groaned. "Don't remind me. My wife will comb my hair with a footstool if her sister's husband is more openhanded or original." No one disagreed with him, knowing how Lady Margaret had her spouse so thoroughly cowed, which was why he was so often to be found at White's. "Whatever happened to the days of shiny apples and a ha'penny?"

"Gone the way of perukes and farthingales." The earl finally unclenched his jaw and relaxed back in his seat. "My friends, you make too much of a simple thing."

"Simple for you, Bev. You're as rich as Golden Ball."

Montravan gestured toward the dice game. "You're sounding like that rum touch over there. Money isn't everything. You'd be dithering over baubles at half the cost."

"I suppose you've got all of your shopping done, eh, Bev?" Lord Coulton asked, winking at Sir Cedric.

"But of course." The earl tried not to sound too smug, but his blue eyes crinkled at the corners.

"Dashed if I know how you do it," Sir Cedric complained. " 'Something thoughtful,' she says. Balderdash, I say! Blister me if I can figure where to start."

"Come on, Bev," Lord Coulton urged, "give us poor sods some hints. The dowager cannot be an easy one to shop for, and you've got a sister the same age as one of mine."

Lord Montravan steepled his fingers in front of him and closed his eyes in serious contemplation. Then: "Very well. There are two basic steps. First, make a list. Second, hand the list to the brightest, most efficient and reliable person on your staff."

They all laughed, until Haskell's slurred voice rose above the room's chatter. "Tha'sh right, Montravan. Says so right here." No one had noticed him stagger away from the dice table. Now everyone turned to stare in his direction, back at the betting book. "Says you have the most effemin—no, efficient secretary in all of London."

"Oh, take a damper, man," Sir Cedric called, while Lord Coulton mumbled, "We're in for it now."

The earl looked to his friends, who were desperately trying to get his attention, asking about his stable's latest acquisition or inviting him into the adjoining room for a late supper. Then he looked back at Haskell, who was rocking back and forth on his heels, his mouth trailing saliva, his clothing rumpled and soiled. Bevin casually leaned back in his chair until the front legs tipped up, and just as casually he drawled, "Found another bone to chew, have you, Towser?"

Someone's laughter was stopped midsnicker by the earl's one raised black brow. He fixed his unflinching gaze back on Haskell, who was too castaway to realize his days at White's were numbered, if not his days on earth.

"Leave it be, Bev," Lord Coulton appealed to his friend. "The dirty dish ain't worth soiling your hands over. You can see he's just an unlicked cub who can't hold his liquor and is spoiling for a fight."

"Then perhaps you'd care to explain that bet, Johnny." The viscount looked away. "No? I thought not. I myself always believed Vincent Winchell was a prince among secretaries, but I never thought anyone would lay blunt on his capabilities, did you, Johnny?"

"It's just a foolish joke, Bev, blown out of proportion by this addlepated tosspot. Let it go."

"Perhaps the makebate would care to explain the joke to me, for you can see I am not laughing." He tipped his chair forward again. "You, Haskell, suppose you tell me the point of that entry you're so fond of."

"The point, your stiff-rumped lordship, is what everyone knows. Your blooming secretary is so efficient, it's a wonder he doesn't wipe your nose. And he's so efficient, he even beds your women for you! Your bits o' muslin may not share their favors with poor gentlemen like me, but it seems they can give 'em away free to—"

Haskell swallowed his next words, along with his two front teeth.

"He is no gentleman" was all Lord Montravan said as he wiped his hands on a napkin, while footmen carried Haskell's prone form from the room. Then Bevin turned to Lord Coulton. "Is it true, Johnny?"

The viscount couldn't meet his friend's eyes. "I don't know, Bev. I heard rumors, that's all. Don't even know who put it in the book—there were no initials—so I didn't think it was worth mentioning."

His nose wasn't worth mentioning either, after Lord Montravan's right fist connected with it.

5

The first thing Bevin did on his return to Montford House was collect the pearl-decorated jewel box from the library. He placed one of his holiday calling cards under the lid, then thrust the box into the hands of Tuttle, the butler at Montford House since before the wheel was invented.

"Here, Tuttle, since you insist on waiting up for me, make yourself useful. Wrap it."

The white-haired servant blinked at the box on his outstretched, gloved palm. He couldn't look more surprised than if a particularly hairy spider had suddenly landed there. "Wrap it, my lord?"

"Yes, blast it, wrap it. It is a gift. You know, paper and ribbons, that sort of poppycock. Then rouse one of the footmen and have him deliver it to Miss Elizabeth Framingham."

"Miss Framingham?"

"B'gad, are you going deaf on me, Tuttle? Yes, Miss Elizabeth Framingham, who resides three houses away, in case you have forgotten. Lord Coulton's fiancée. The footman is to say that it comes with my most sincere apologies."

"But . . . but, my lord, it is the middle of the night."

"I didn't say he should deliver it to the young lady in her bedchamber, dash it. In fact, I *forbid* him to deliver it to her bedroom altogether. He's to leave it with the butler or night guard or whatever, as long as she gets it first thing in the morning. Is that clear?"

As clear as the air over London town. Tuttle nodded.

"Oh, and fetch me some ice."

"Ice, my lord?"

"Ice. These are the 1800s, man, and it's winter. Somewhere in London there must be an icehouse. I need some upstairs in a bowl. And the good cognac."

Now the stately majordomo was really shocked. Master Bevin wished to chill the Bouvelieu? Never. Tuttle carried up the ice in a silver bucket and hot coffee in a silver urn. More of the latter than the former.

Lord Montravan sprawled on a chair before the fire, his shoes kicked off, his coat lying in a heap near the wardrobe, his cravat draped over a bedpost, and his right hand soaking in a bowl of cold water.

Life was hard, he lamented. A fellow just couldn't trust anyone. Not his best friend, not his faithful servant, not his mistress. Bevin was glad he didn't have a dog; it would most likely bite him. He couldn't even trust the old family retainer to bring him a brandy, and the bellpull was so confoundedly far away. What good was coffee going to be in keeping infection from the cut Haskell's teeth had opened across Bevin's knuckles? What good was coffee going to be in dulling the pain of betrayal?

Hell and damnation, Vincent and Marina. Unless . . . No, it couldn't be. That peacocking twit of a nobody *couldn't* be tupping Bibi Duchamps while he, the Earl of Montford, was still trying to fix her interest. Life couldn't be that hard, could it?

No. There was still some softness in the world, some tender honor a man could trust. His mother? If she never played his father false, it was because

34

she was too lazy. His sister? Allissa was growing into another avaricious, manipulative harpy. But there was Petra, sweet and pure. Petra, who had never let him down, never went back on her word.

Bevin laughed at himself. He hadn't seen Petra since the summer. For all he knew she'd have some local swain just waiting for the earl's arrival to declare himself. Hell, Petra was only a woman; there was no justification for putting her on a pedestal. For all Bevin knew she already had some gent's slippers under her bed.

The next morning did not start until nearly noon. Finster took one look at his master, asleep in the chair, and called for the sawbones. That worthy poked and prodded, only to declare that perhaps the knuckles were broken, perhaps not. As if Lord Montravan could not have figured that out for himself. At least the cabbagehead put basilicum powder in the open cuts and wrapped the hand—in enough linen to shroud a mummy.

He couldn't tie his own neckcloth. He spilled coffee on the one Finster had fashioned, trying to breakfast left-handed, and had to have the thing done again. At last, in an even more foul mood, the earl was ready to confront his secretary.

According to Tuttle, Mr. Vincent was in the library wrapping gifts. This last was said with a sniff, indicative of the butler's opinion of such a lowly occupation. Vincent obviously did not mind, for he was whistling in a welter of silver paper, tissue, and bright ribbon. Nothing was quite as bright as his parrot-embroidered waistcoat. Montravan paused in the doorway to let his aesthetic sense acclimate itself gradually.

"Good morning, my lord," Vincent called cheerfully. "I'll be finished here in just a bit unless you needed me for something immediately. I heard you had the doctor in to see about your hand, so I wanted to get this done in case you had any additional chores for me. I hope it's nothing serious, whatever happened."

"Marina," Montravan stated, striding farther into the room and skipping all preliminaries.

Vincent's mouth hung open. "Miss Corbett did that to you? Good grief, what did she do? I mean, pardon me, my lord. None of my affair, of course."

"Precisely!" Bevin was across the library's expanse, almost nose to nose with the younger man, and was about to take Vincent by the ridiculously high shirt collar and shake him as a terrier would a rat. Except that he couldn't bend his swollen, throbbing fingers in their wrapping. "Blast! Have you been seeing Marina, sirrah?"

"My lord?" Vincent took a step back, dropping the scissors. Then he seemed to reconsider, what with his employer running amok right in front of him. Picking the scissors off the table, he cut a length of ribbon.

"Answer me, damn you! Have you been seeing Marina?"

Vincent's hand started to shake. "I saw her last night in the play. Remember, I told you I was going?"

"And otherwise?"

"I don't know what you mean, my lord. I took her home that night last week when you had to attend the reception at Carleton House. Recall, you asked me to?"

"And did you see her in?"

Vincent squared his padded shoulders. "Naturally. You charged me with her escort. And she asked me to have a glass of wine," he said with a tinge of defiance. "She is a very gracious lady."

"And what about Bibi Duchamps?"

The bow Vincent was tying became knotted

around his finger. "Drat." He tossed the ribbon aside and cut a new one, not half the length needed to go around the box he was wrapping. Sweat was starting to bead on his forehead. "I . . . ah . . . have seen Mademoiselle Duchamps only once, outside of the opera house."

The earl was seated at his desk, hefting the weight of the silver letter opener in his left hand. Vincent swallowed audibly and continued: "The one time when you had me send her flowers after her debut."

"Send. I said *send* her flowers, not bring her flowers, you lobcock!"

"I . . . ah . . . thought she'd be more impressed that way. 'Twould show your interest more personally than having the flower seller's boy just drop off another bouquet."

Bevin scowled; Vincent trembled.

"I swear, my lord, I have done nothing without your direction or your interests at heart. Neither lady has cause for complaint at my conduct."

"Well, somebody does. Something you've done has given rise to the most damnable rumors, and that's a fact."

"That's impossible. No one saw us. That is . . . ah . . . what rumors, my lord?"

"No one saw you and . . . ? Great Scott! Belinda? You've been sniffing around my intended?" the earl thundered.

"No, no," Vincent cried. "That's not how it was. I never intended . . . that is, Lady Belinda is . . . You see, it was the invitation."

"No, you miserable mawworm, I do not see. What bloody invitation?" The papers on the earl's desk went flying, from the gale winds of his rage.

"The . . . the one to the house party for New Year's," Vincent stuttered. "I thought I should deliver it in person, like the flowers. Only no one was

home except Lady Belinda. The footman mustn't
have realized, for he showed me into the music
room, where she was practicing. I would have given
the invitation over and left immediately, I swear.
Young lady with no chaperon and all, I knew it
wasn't seemly."

"Then why the hell didn't you?"

"Lady Belinda asked me to stay, to tell her about
the house party, who else was invited, what activi-
ties were planned, that type of thing. I suppose she
wanted to know what to pack. I never even *thought*
of . . . of . . ."

"Yes, I know what you never thought of: what every young man spends every waking hour trying
not to think of. Go on."

"It was the mouse, you see. This mouse ran
across the room, and Lady Belinda started to
scream and jumped up on the sofa. I jumped up,
too, thinking she might fall, and I accidentally dis-
lodged one of the sofa pillows. Did I say we were
sitting on the sofa? Well, the pillow hit the mouse
and must have stunned the poor thing, because
there it was, just lying there, with Lady Belinda
starting to turn greenish, so I scooped it up with
the coal scuttle and tossed the little blighter out
the window."

"Lancelot to the rescue," Montravan commented
dryly.

"I thought I'd done a neat job of it myself. But
then—"

"Ah. The denouement. I am all aflutter to hear
the outcome. Do go on," he urged, rising. " 'But
then'?"

"I promise you I never meant to . . . Lady Belinda
was thanking me, and I was looking around for
some brandy or something, a restorative, don't you
know."

"For you, the lady, or the mouse?" Bevin asked sarcastically, knowing full well what was coming.

"Then suddenly she was in my arms, and it seemed only natural, and she didn't tell me to stop, and suddenly we were back on the couch."

"And then?"

"And then the butler came in. But Belinda swore he'd never tell a soul. And . . . and I am terribly sorry, my lord."

"Sorry? You're sorry you were caught making love to the woman I am going to marry?" Bevin pounded the desktop in fury, then had to catch himself on the edge of the table as the pain made him almost light-headed enough to faint.

Words failed Vincent. He could only hang his head, staring at the elaborate buckles on his shoes.

When Bevin caught his breath, he corrected himself. "No, Lady Belinda is the woman I *was* going to marry. I'd never have the jade now. By Jupiter, did she think she'd play me false with my own secretary? My God!"

"It wasn't like that, my lord! Belinda is a lady! We didn't . . . That is, the butler . . ."

"No? Were you waiting for after the wedding to plant horns on me? Should I be thankful? Or were you going to take up with Marina where I left off once *Lady* Belinda and I were leg-shackled? Or was it Bibi whilst I was honeymooning?"

Montravan sank wearily back into his seat. "No, don't answer. I wouldn't believe anything you'd say." He toyed with the letter opener again, making Vincent anxiously measure the distance to the door while his lordship pondered his fate.

"I would thrash you to within an inch of your life, you know," Bevin told the other man, speaking conversationally now, "were my hand not already knocked to flinders. Instead I'll give you until dark to gather your things and get out. If I see you after, or if anything but your own possessions is missing tomorrow, there is no answering for the consequences, for I still have my left hand, by Jupiter. You'll have no references out of me, not that it makes much difference; your name is already a byword in town. No sane man would ever hire you, not if he had a wife, daughter, or mistress."

The earl reached into a desk drawer and pulled out a purse, which he tossed onto the table amid the ribbons and wrappings. Standing, he said, "Go as far as this takes you and don't come back. Consider it an early Christmas gift. Greetings of the season, you bastard."

Vincent hadn't wanted to be a secretary anymore anyway, he told himself after the library door slammed behind the earl. He wanted to be a gigolo. Now he had the wherewithal. He lifted the purse, thinking. He'd need a new name, of course. Perhaps a mustache for a disguise. Yes, a military-style mustache, with sideburns, maybe even a hussar uniform. Women couldn't resist a man in uniform, especially if he had a slight limp or a scar for sympathy's sake. Besides, he would look a handsome devil in the scarlet regimentals, if he had to say so himself. Who'd ever check the rosters for a retired captain? No, a major.

The future was not dim at all, but the present certainly had a shadow over it. This was no way to treat a chap after all those years of faithful service, booting him out on his ear the week before Christmas. Vincent poured himself a healthy dose of the earl's brandy. He *had* done a deuced fine job for old sobersides. He really was quite good at all the details that made Montravan's life much simpler, and he never left a task uncompleted. Vincent simply hated to leave a job undone, so he finished wrapping the earl's gifts, then regretfully locked the unchosen jewelry et cetera away in the earl's desk. He carefully printed each recipient's address on the outer wrapping, matching direction to gift, and just as carefully switched all of the cards.

He handed three to a footman to be delivered that very day in London. Then Vincent ordered a groom to set out for Montravan Hall immediately with the rest of the parcels, saying that the earl might delay his departure because of the accident to his hand and wished to make sure the presents reached his family in time.

Now Vincent was ready to go upstairs and pack.

And greetings of the season to you, too, my lord.

Lord, what was he to do now? Bevin could only think of things he *couldn't* do. He couldn't write to the Harleighs claiming their visit had to be canceled due to an influenza epidemic or such. They'd be sure to twig that faradiddle. Besides, he couldn't write at all with his hand all swollen, and he had no blasted secretary to write for him! And Bevin couldn't let Miss Harleigh's name be bandied around town—he was a gentleman, after all—as would be sure to happen if he suddenly claimed an emergency at his Scottish property. He'd be lucky if Harleigh didn't get a hint of the current gossip and come demanding an explanation.

If not, Belinda and her family would be off for the ducal seat in Dorset in a day or two; from there they'd travel on to Montravan Hall to wait for the earl's offer, an offer that he couldn't, wouldn't make. Zeus, what a house party that should be! What a damnable coil.

And he couldn't stay drunk for the rest of the century either. His innards were already protesting. Besides, he had to hire a new secretary. An old, ugly secretary. Vincent had seen to the Christmas gifts, heaven be praised, but there was new mail every day that needed answering: invitations, bills, and personal letters, to say nothing of the household accounts and all of the correspondence appurtenant to Montravan's vast and varied holdings.

The first man the agency sent over was so old, he could have transcribed the Ten Commandments. Bevin was afraid he'd expire before the sennight.

The second smelled so bad, the earl knew he couldn't share the library with this man, much less his personal life.

When the third man spoke, he whistled through ill-fitting false teeth, and the fourth took a coughing fit and nearly fell off the chair. Bevin felt guilty over not hiring one of the decrepit oldsters, but he sent each home with hackney fare after a snack in the kitchen.

And he canceled his previous specifications for prospective employees, this time requesting a middle-aged misogynist. The first man smelled of lavender, and the second man lisped.

What about a scribe who was happily married? the hiring agent wanted to know. Bevin doubted that there was such a thing, but he said he would consider the applicants, who would have to be paid more, living out. Mr. Browne blanched at the idea of handling love-nest leases, and Mr. Faraday was newly wed; he couldn't leave his bride alone in the evenings. Stedly had shifty eyes and four sons who were willing to do any manner of work, most likely including purse snatching and housebreaking. The earl made sure Tuttle escorted this last applicant out the door.

"Damn and blast," Lord Montravan exclaimed when Tuttle returned, this time alone. "This should be Vincent's job."

"Ahem." Tuttle stood in the doorway of the library, looking more disapproving than ever.

"Whatever it is, I don't want to hear it. There must be hundreds of other employment services, or I can put an advertisement in the newspapers."

Tuttle cleared his throat again. "If I might be so

43

bold, my lord, may I suggest you ask Miss Sinclaire?"

"What, ask Petra to move into Montford House and become my secretary? Have your wits gone begging altogether, old man? You mustn't go senile on me quite yet, Tuttle. I couldn't face having to hire a new butler, too."

"What I meant, my lord," Tuttle continued as if Lord Montravan had not spoken, "was that Miss Sinclaire most probably knows of some likely lad from Wiltshire, a young man on the scholarship lists at Oxford that you support, or perhaps one of the tenants' sons returning from the war. You must already have their gratitude and loyalty, and knowing their families have roots in your holdings should keep the young men from overstepping the boundaries."

"Tuttle, you are brilliant!"

"Thank you, my lord. I find that younger men are easier to deal with, more comfortable about taking advice."

"I am convinced, Tuttle. Petra will know just the right man, and if not, her brother-in-law, the curate, might. He's not that long out of university." Lord Montravan was delighted. His problem was as good as solved, once he dumped it into Petra's lap. Not that he was ungrateful, nor that he thought Petra would consider his difficulty another burden. Petra would see the situation as a welcome opportunity to help some worthy lad. She was just like that. And he'd make it up to her. Why, he'd find her the finest gentleman in town to wed, not one of his own rakish friends.

"That's what I'll do, Tuttle. I might even travel to the Hall a day or two early. There's nothing pressing here, after all, so close to the holidays." And it just might be politic to stay out of Johnny Coulton's proximity for a while, and to give the gabble-

44

grinders a chance to find another juicy morsel. Devil take it, soon enough after New Year's they'd be talking about the ring that was not on Belinda's hand. Perhaps, the earl mused when Tuttle went to advise the agency that no more applicants would be interviewed, he could stay on at Montravan after his mother and sister left for Bath, sit by the fire, read books, ride around the countryside, and talk to Petra. He was tired of this drinking, wagering, and wenching. Then again, Petra would travel to Bath with the others, and Bibi would be waiting for him here in London. Country pursuits palled so quickly. Still, the sooner he left, the sooner he'd have a competent secretary. He almost rang for Vincent to make all the arrangements. Hell and confound it!

Then Tuttle came back wearing a censorious frown and bearing a letter on a silver salver. The smell of jasmine wafted halfway across the room, identifying the sender even before Montravan recognized the curling script on the address. He waited for Tuttle to remove his condemnatory but curious phiz before slitting the wafer to see what Marina had to say.

"What the bloody hell?"

The second reading made no more sense than the first. Marina was effusively grateful for his gift and his note. What had he written? Montravan tried to recall. Something like "Thank you for our past association and the pleasant times, and best wishes in your future relations." How could that send her in alt unless she was happy to be shut of him? But, no, she wrote that she couldn't wait to see him, just knew he'd be calling on her after the theater tonight since they had so much to discuss. For the life of him, Montravan couldn't think of one thing a cove discussed with his discarded mistress.

He went anyway. He was too much the gentleman to keep a lady waiting, and too curious. Marina met him at the door of the neat row house in Kensington and instantly threw her arms around him. One of those arms wore the multigemmed bracelet he had picked as her Christmas-cum-parting gift, and it looked even more garish by the candlelight. Marina must have liked it, because she wore a diaphanous red robe with matching multicolored ruffles at the hem. That gown, what there was of it above the ruffles, could have made the devil blush. She also must have liked the bracelet, he deduced, from the enthusiasm of her greeting.

"Darling," she gushed, "I cannot wait."

With her lush curves pressed against him, Bevin's body was stirred despite his loftier intentions. "I can't wait either," he whispered in her ear, trying to free his arm to remove his coat.

"No, silly, I mean I cannot wait for the wedding."

"The wedding?" Those two words had more effect on Britain's population than any number of cold baths. He took a step back. "What wedding?"

"Why, ours, of course. Your card made me the happiest of women, darling. I mean, you could have knocked me over with a feather. I never would have guessed. I never dared let myself hope."

Bevin wiped at a nonexistent smudge on the sleeve of his bottle green coat. "Ah, what exactly did the card say, my sweet? I cannot seem to recall."

Marina chewed on her lower lip in a well-rehearsed seductive pout. "Now isn't that just like a man, forgetting something so important. The card is already tucked into my Bible, but I swear I'll remember the exact words to my dying day. I always did have a mind for memorizing, you know. That's real helpful in the theater. Anyway, 'Greetings of the season,' it said, only that was inscribed. And then: 'To a real lady, with respect and affec-

46

tion,' " she quoted with enough timbre for Lady Macbeth. "And then you wrote, 'Ware, I hear wedding bells in your future.' "

Which was, of course, the note he'd written to Petra, concerning her Season with Allissa on the Marriage Mart. Oh, God.

"I never thought you'd do it," Marina was going on, "so starchy you always seemed and all. The other girls said you were too toplofty by half, and here you've gone and proved them wrong in the most wonderful way. Respect and affection," she intoned as if they were her passport into heaven, "and a real lady. Just think, Mary Corby, a real lady. And not just a plain lady. I'll be a countess."

When hell froze over. Obviously there had been a horrible mistake. Obviously there was going to be a horrible scene.

Bevin could feel a droplet of sweat trickle down between his shoulder blades. He despised disordered freaks and disputations, so he damned the decamped secretary for the hundredth time. The chawbacon must have been so rattled at being found out that he mixed the cards by mistake. If Vincent wasn't already dismissed, he'd be turned off for the atrocious lapse. "May he rot in purgatory for the rest of eternity."

"My lord?"

Bevin took a deep breath. Following the hunting maxims of riding quickly over rough ground and throwing one's heart over the hurdle, he opened his mouth to speak, but all that came out was the whoosh of the same deep breath.

"Darling?" Marina—Mary—was ready to soothe his agitation the way she knew best.

Oh, no. Montravan couldn't let himself get distracted. Fully aroused, he might promise anything. He put more distance between her ample charms and his traitorous body. "No, my dear Marina, er,

47

Mary. There isn't going to be any wedding, at least not yours and mine. I am afraid there's been an error with the cards."

Then he was afraid there'd be a visit from the watch, the constable, and the local magistrate, so piercing were her shrieks, so loud was the sound of shattering bric-a-brac and furniture bouncing off walls.

Marina threw everything at him but the sofa, which was too heavy, and the bracelet, which was too valuable. She was too downy to act the fool twice in one day.

Montravan tried to appease her with cash, which was a foredoomed effort, since what he had in his pocket couldn't possibly compare to what he had in the bank, all of which would have been hers along with that title. "But, Marina, you must have known the Earl of Montravan couldn't marry a wh—an actress."

"Stranger things have happened," she insisted, emphasizing her point with a china shepherdess that missed his head by scant inches.

Not in his family, not in his lifetime, Bevin vowed, but was wise enough to keep that thought to himself. He gave up trying to placate the raging woman when she dashed for her little kitchen and returned with a carving knife. The heretofore dauntless earl daunted himself right out the window onto a bare-branched rosebush.

Shredding his inexpressibles away from the prickers, Bevin had time to think about the second half of the disaster. If Marina had Petra's note, then come Christmas morning, Petra would be receiving that tripe about past attachments and future plans. Petra was needle-witted enough to recognize the note for what it was—and what type of woman it was meant for—but she was a trump. She'd not fly into the boughs like some others. He'd explain about the mix-up, they'd have a good laugh, and that would be the end of it, except that he'd look the fool in Petra's eyes. No, things never need come to such a pass that he had to explain about errant secretaries and discarded mistresses to an innocent girl. He'd simply travel to Montravan a bit earlier, as he'd planned anyway, intercept the gifts, and write a new card to his mother's companion. No one would ever be the wiser, except Bevin, who had instantly learned not to leave everything up to the servants.

7

White's was more a habit than a destination. Bevin's fuddled brain just took him there, not in hopes of having a convivial evening—it was too late for convivial, convenient, or comfortable—but just a way to pass this wretched night until he could set out for Montravan Hall in the morning.

The majordomo kept his usual imperturbable expression, but some of the members visibly started to see the earl's condition. The black look on his face kept any from commenting, however. A few of his usual associates, in fact, suddenly started yawning with the need to make an early night of it, with their own journeys to the country soon to commence.

Bevin walked through the rooms until he spotted his friend Coulton, who looked as if an ale barrel had rolled across his face. The earl winced but gamely took a seat next to the viscount. Johnny raised his quizzing glass and painstakingly surveyed the porcelain shards on Bevin's shoulder, the pillow feathers in his hair, and the scratches on his cheek, scratches the earl was only now beginning to feel.

The viscount held out a clean handkerchief. "I'd beat you to a pulp, my erstwhile friend, but it appears someone has been there before me."

"No one up to your weight, so go ahead, take your

shot. You're entitled." Bevin held up his bandaged hand. "I won't put up much of a fight."

Coulton nodded toward the bandage. "My nose do that?"

"Your nose or Haskell's teeth. Makes no nevermind which. You've got my apologies, for what they are worth."

"'Twas a flush hit."

Bevin lifted one corner of his mouth. "That it was." He waited to see if the big man smiled back, or if it was to be pistols for two and breakfast for one, unless Johnny decided on more immediate, brutal, and bloody retribution. Bevin was debating whether he should throw the first blow or just go down quietly, when the Duke of Harleigh walked into the room, leaning on his cane.

Bevin stood to offer his gouty grace a seat, pleased that Coulton's revenge would at least be postponed by the presence of the august peer. The duke looked at Montravan, then through Montravan, and limped on to greet an acquaintance at the next table without even a nod for Montravan.

The cut was direct, and right in front of half of White's members. Now that was sure to set the cat among the pigeons. A few of the gambling men were already scrambling for the betting book to change their wagers. The earl shrugged. He wasn't the one whose daughter was playing fast and loose with the servants.

"Not too popular tonight, are we?" Johnny asked, with more than a tinge of satisfaction.

Bevin waved his unbandaged hand. "His Grace must have heard of last night's debacle. He doesn't like gossip."

"Gammon. His Grace wouldn't turn his back on an eligible parti like you if your name was as black as Byron's. You must have done something beyond the pale for him to cut you that way."

"I merely dismissed his daughter's—ah, that is, I had to discharge Vincent. I believe the duke thought he was a coming lad with political possibilities," he temporized, "so His Grace might disagree with my decision. He is welcome to hire the blackguard."

"It sounds like you have some fence-mending to do before Harleigh and his family travel to Montravan Hall."

"No, I have never been good at manual labor. I think I'll let these fences stay broken."

"But the chickens might fly the coop," Johnny hinted.

"And that would be a shame," Bevin answered with a grin. "A veritable shame."

Lord Coulton gestured toward the betting book. "Then I can lay my blunt on the banty cock staying out of the parson's cook pot?"

"From the, er, rooster's mouth. If it will make your fortune, bet the farm. That particular little game pullet will never take up residence in my coop, the saints be praised."

"From your noticeable lack of regret, I take it that your heart was not involved." Newly affianced and deeply in love, Lord Coulton looked at his friend in pity. "Then you are better out of it."

"My thinking entirely. Of course, now I'll have to explain to Mama why I am not filling my nursery posthaste, and then I'll have to go through the whole tedious business of finding another suitably well-born bride. But I'll have to attend some of those debutante affairs with m'sister Allissa, at any rate, so I can kill two birds with one stone."

"Still in the barnyard?" Coulton shook his head regretfully. "There are other reasons for taking a wife, you know, besides begetting an heir."

"Of course, there's marrying for money. Luckily I

don't need a large dowry, so my choices will be that much wider."

"I would have offered for Elizabeth if she were penniless and a cit," Lord Coulton insisted.

"My dear romantic friend, you wouldn't even have *met* Elizabeth if she did not have entry to Almack's and the fashionable dos. You'd not have looked twice at her if she dressed in twice-turned gowns or dropped her aitches." Bevin suddenly recalled—with help from the additional color suffusing his friend's face—that he did not wish to antagonize the large man any more than he already had. "But, of course, Elizabeth is a gem who would possess the same beauty of soul no matter her social standing. You're a lucky devil, Johnny."

The angry blotches faded, except for the viscount's nose, of course, and his freckles. "And now you are free to find such a treasure for yourself, if you aren't blinded by that fustian of finding a 'suitable' bride."

"I take it Elizabeth has forgiven me, then?"

Coulton lifted his glass in silent toast. "She thinks I should have mentioned the rumors to you."

"A prize indeed. I'll keep your words in mind, after my narrow escape," the earl said, getting up to leave before Coulton had yet another change of heart. There was no reason to tempt fate.

And speaking of tempting fate, Bevin considered confronting the duke on his way out of the club, then gave himself a mental shake. He mightn't understand Harleigh's actions, but if they meant that dreaded house party was canceled, the duke could turn his back on Bevin five times a day for the next ten years.

The duke's behavior made more sense when Bevin reached Montford House and Tuttle presented him with a wad of tissue on a silver salver.

"This was delivered earlier from Harleigh House," the butler informed him.

Bevin eyed the misshapen lump with suspicion. "Was there any message?"

"I believe the item is self-explanatory," Tuttle said with a sniff of disapproval. "But there is a note."

Montravan gingerly pushed aside some of the paper to find a gilt-edged card with a border of angels playing improbable musical instruments like floating pianofortes, and inscribed with the message: *May the heavenly host make joyous music for you at this season of gladness.* At least Vincent hadn't committed that travesty. On the back of the card was written: *Her Grace, the Duchess of Harleigh, regrets that she and her family are unable to accept your invitation.* Short and simple, no flimsy excuses. But why? Dash it, *he* was the one who should have cried off; he was the wronged party, wasn't he?

Perhaps Belinda hadn't thought his gift was substantial enough for the almost betrothal, for surely that had to be the gold filigree fan returned in its crumpled wrappings. Odd, Vincent's taste was usually impeccable, and Bevin had thought the fan a charming token. Belinda must have thought otherwise, for each and every one of the delicate spokes was snapped in half. A trifle excessive, Bevin thought, for an unappreciated gift. Why, he accepted Petra's embroidered handkerchiefs every year with all the graciousness at his command, even though he had a drawerful by now. He didn't rip them up just because he rarely had the need to blow his nose. She went to the considerable effort to create the blasted things, just as he—or Vincent—had selected the fan expressly for Lady Belinda. That made three insults from the duke's family in one night, still without explanation.

Bevin was contemplating the ruined fan when Tuttle lifted a few shreds of silver paper and a bow to reveal his employer's own calling card, the one with its holly edge and simple message of season's greetings. This, too, was decimated, torn into halves and then smaller bits, but not so small that Bevin could not piece the thing together enough to read: *With fond thoughts of our past shared pleasures, and best wishes for better luck in your future relations.*

Marina's message. So the one for Petra and the one for his ex-mistress did not simply cross each other's paths. *All* of the cards were somehow confused.

This was so unlike the methodical Vincent with his attention to detail that the mingle-mangle had to be deliberate, the bounder. And what an unintentional favor he'd done, Bevin thought, freeing him of unwanted houseguests and an even more unwanted fiancée. The earl went up to bed, freer of dreary thoughts than he'd been in an age, he realized, or at least since he'd contemplated making Lady Belinda his wife.

As Finster was helping him remove his boots, however, Bevin suddenly recalled that the gifts to his entire family, gifts that the dastardly scribe had already sent on ahead, might also have mismatched greetings, not just Petra's. One of the boots and Finster went flying across the room. "The devil take it!" Heaven only knew what a mare's nest that would stir up!

Bevin still had a few days' leeway before his acquisitive sister would dare open the box to find her tiara, so he wasn't really worried. As long as he got to the Hall before Christmas Eve, with enough time to spare to rewrap the gifts, he'd be safe. And if he left tomorrow as planned, he'd have time to speak with Petra about finding a new secretary, too, before the festivities began. There, the dibs were in tune again, despite that gallowsbait, and the earl could finally rest easy, except for having his hand so swaddled, Finster had to button his nightshirt.

In the middle of the night Montravan woke with a start. Zounds! He'd forgotten all about Bibi! How in the world could he have forgotten that she might have another's message? He desperately tried to remember what he'd written and to whom, but he'd just dashed the things off, never suspecting anyone else but the so-discreet Vincent would ever see them. Now he'd have to wait until late afternoon to go make amends to the alluring demirep. He couldn't very well call on a woman at three in the morning, even if she was a Cyprian. She wasn't *his* Cyprian yet, and might never be if Vincent took it into his vengeful mind to wreak more havoc on his late employer. What if the cad had written his own message? What was to stop him from doing more than switching the cards, now that Montravan's bullet couldn't reach him?

Blast, he couldn't even call on the woman until after luncheon. Birds of paradise never strutted their plumes until the sun was well up. And what the bloody hell was Bibi's card supposed to read anyway?

Certainly not *Here's what you wanted, you greedy little hoyden. Next time I'll warm your backside instead.* That was meant for his sister Allissa and her tiara.

Bibi was not open to explanation or apologies. Bevin's ears were ringing to her screams of "I'm not that kind of woman," and his cheeks were stinging from the resounding slaps she'd administered.

She'd thrown the earbobs back at him, too, being either more highly principled or less intelligent than Marina. She had also kept him waiting for two hours, so it was too late to set out for Wiltshire that day.

8

He still had plenty of time to reach the Hall by Christmas Eve. That was the latest Bevin could be, for every year his sister cajoled the countess into letting her open the gifts that night after church, instead of waiting till the next morning. The dowager never held out much resistance to Allissa's wheedling, since she was equally impatient to rip into her own pile of packages.

When Montravan confidently figured his travel time, though, he had not taken into account the damage to his hand. The blasted thing couldn't be trusted to tool the ribbons of his curricle's spirited matched bays, and going on horseback the whole way holding the reins in his awkward left hand sounded cold and painful. Besides, Finster was full of dire warnings about splintered knucklebones grinding away at each other and the muscles around them until the fingers never moved again. Worse, according to Finster, a fragment of the broken bone could work itself loose and travel with the blood flow until it pierced his lungs.

So the prodigal son was going to return home in style: the coach and team, with driver and postilions and outriders, and the painted crest on the door with all those rubbishing lions and hawks.

But Bevin also forgot that Vincent was no longer around to make all the travel arrangements. Therefore blood cattle weren't waiting at the changes, just the usual posthouse breakdowns. The tolls had not been paid in advance, nor had suitable accommodations been booked. With so many other travelers abroad at the holiday season, oftentimes Bevin was lucky to get a bed at all, without having to share with Finster. The sheets were unaired; the food was deplorable and served in the public areas, since the private rooms had been reserved ages ago. Lord Montravan was not that much of a snob that he minded breaking his bread with sheep drovers; he did object to the dogs, though.

The trip was taking so long—and Bevin's patience was wearing so thin—that he decided to hire a horse for the last stages, bone slivers be damned. If he didn't get to Montravan Hall in time, he might as well be dead anyway.

The nags for hire at that last inn were an unprepossessing lot at best, but Bevin was considered a notable judge of horseflesh, so he picked the likeliest steed, a rangy black gelding with an intelligent look. The horse was so intelligent, he had definite ideas on where he wished to spend Christmas Eve. He waited a mile past that inn to express these sentiments, and Bevin was not turning back. The contest of wills over who chose which road left Bevin's left hand numb and the seat of his breeches caked with mud. He never let loose of the reins, consummate horseman that he was, and finally convinced the hard-mouthed brute to give the stables at Montravan a look-see.

Then the gelding cast a shoe, out of spite, Bevin was sure. The nearest village was a mere five miles down the road, according to the driver of a passing high-perch phaeton who not only didn't slow to give the directions, but also managed to splash a more liberal amount of mud on the earl's caped coat. The five miles afoot were cold, hungry, and at least *seven*, Bevin swore.

And the blacksmith was away at his daughter's in Skellington, two miles east.

There were no horses to be let in the little village, although the tavern proprietor thought old Jed Turner might lend his ass, now that farm chores were slacking off. Instead a boy was dispatched to fetch the blacksmith home with the promise of a generous reward. Bevin hadn't figured on handing over the ready every time he stopped either, since Vincent had always seen to all charges in advance. At this rate the earl would soon be forced to sleep in empty barns and eat winter-dry berries as cold and hard as that dastard's heart.

He sipped at his ale in the tavern for the time it took for Duncan the smith to get back, making each tankard last as long as possible, then had to stand the man a round to warm his innards. Bevin thought Duncan would warm up faster by heating the forge, but he refrained from pointing that out to a man who dwarfed Johnny Coulton in height and Prinny in girth. Duncan was, moreover, Bevin's only way of getting that black bone rattler back on the road, so he ordered another glass.

Johnny Coulton moved quickly for a big man. Duncan moved slowly, even for a big man. He walked slowly, readied his fires slowly, and took forever to shape one blasted horseshoe. And all the time he wanted to talk, about his daughter, about the state of the nation, about his craft. He even insisted, while the iron was heating, on the earl's trying his hand at the job. Bevin reluctantly bent a nail into a circle, just to show the smith that all noblemen weren't effete wastrels. Then he wiped the sweat off his brow with his throbbing hand.

The black didn't cooperate, naturally. They had to send to the tavern for two more men to hold the brute, which of course necessitated Montravan's standing them a round, too. By the time Bevin was back in the saddle, the gelding was well rested indeed. With a short memory for everything but his own barn, the black was more unruly than ever. By the time his lordship had the beast headed in the right direction, darkness had started falling. So had the snow.

It was Christmas Eve, and it was snowing. He wasn't coming. Most likely he had changed his plans and decided to spend Christmas with his new in-laws. More likely he couldn't bear to be parted from his bride-to-be, Petra thought irritably. That was entirely understandable, she told herself, not understanding in the least how he could leave Montravan Hall at sixes and sevens without him.

There was no head of the household to bring in the Yule log, no lord of the manor to greet the villagers who came trudging through the snow to carol for their benefactor. There was no Earl of Montravan to sit in the front pew at church, and no neighborhood nabob to pledge a new roof for the school. There was no dutiful son to soothe the dowager's nerves, and no loving brother to tease Allissa out of the sullens. And there was no smile for Petra.

Then his carriage arrived with Finster and the baggage. The countess swore Bevin was lying dead in a ditch somewhere and called for her hartshorn and vinaigrette.

"Don't be goosish, Mama," Allissa said helpfully. "Bevin is never so cow-handed as that. Be sure he's decided to spend his last nights of unfettered bachelorhood in the arms of some tavern doxy."

"What do you know of doxies, missy?" her mother demanded.

"I know a man's mistress gets nicer presents

than his family." Allissa had been eyeing the stack of packages neatly gathered on a piecrust table in the drawing room all week. The devious little minx might just have opened her presents and resealed them, Petra considered, except that Allissa was still on tenterhooks, working herself into a frenzy of excitement and despair when she had to wait.

The dowager was also sadly out of curl. The snow might keep her guests away, Cook's lovely goose might be overcooked if that rattlepate son of hers didn't get here in time, and the package Squire Merton placed on the piecrust table was much too large to be the ring Lady Montravan had hoped for. Besides, her companion had *two* presents from the dowager's own son, while Lady Montravan had only one. True, one of Petra's gifts appeared to be a book—from the size, shape, feel, and nonrattle of the package—but Lady Montravan was known to enjoy a good novel, too. Petra was a good enough girl in her way, the dowager admitted, but it was outside of enough that her firstborn was not only taking a bride to supplant his mother in his affections, but was also showing preference for a charity case.

So Lady Montravan had been more querulous than ever, demanding more and more of Petra's time, right on top of all the holiday preparations . . . and an outbreak of measles in the village. Petra had done what she could, working with the earl's steward to make sure there was enough firewood to go around and spending hours in the kitchens herself to ensure the afflicted families had proper nourishment without overburdening Montravan's already busy cooking staff. She tried to find time to visit the homes of the stricken families, singing carols to the restless, feverish children, cutting paper stars to win a weak, spotted smile.

If only it were as easy to put Allissa in better

spirits. The girl was anxious about meeting the new sister-in-law who was going to be responsible for Allissa's own presentation. She was in a fidge over attending her first New Year's ball, and she was near hysterics over that dratted inappropriate tiara. The present from Bevin *could* be the headpiece. The box was big enough, Allissa remarked at least twice a day. Petra decided Bevin should be drawn and quartered for sending those packages so early and putting them all through this adolescent agony.

Petra distrusted Allissa's hectic, glassy-eyed look and tried to get the younger girl to rest.

"Oh, do stop treating me like a child, Petra," Allissa snapped. "I am not the one snoring away or yawning over my sewing."

No, Squire Merton was the one having a catnap near the fire, and Petra was the one who was yawning, from being up since dawn. But Petra had had the measles, and no one, typically, could recall if Allissa had. That was something else Petra had to worry about.

A small hint to the dowager that perhaps the roads were getting slippery was enough to cancel the trip to church. Lady Montravan was delighted not to move from her sofa into the cold night, so she declared that they would do better to await Bevin here, or word of his demise.

They took turns reading the Nativity from the Bible, listening to the clock tick and the squire snore.

"Please, Mama," Allissa begged for the nth time, "can we please open the presents? Bevin is obviously not coming, and I *am* growing a trifle weary." She peeped at Petra through lowered eyelashes in an effort to enlist the other's sympathy. "You know I'll never get to sleep tonight with so much anticipation fluttering my nerves, and I do so want to be in looks tomorrow. You always say a woman needs her rest to be her best. Why, if I am too fatigued," she added slyly, "I just might grow ill or something." Petra tried not to stare at the slight blotch on Allissa's cheek. If she didn't notice it, perhaps the spot would vanish. Perhaps it was merely a blemish, and if the chit did indeed get to her bed, it would be gone by morning.

"I am sure Lord Montravan would not want us to be disappointed," she said. "Maybe we could open the other gifts first, since Finster is certain his lordship will arrive momentarily."

Lady Montravan was convinced. If that lobcock Willoughby Merton hadn't come through with a ring, she'd have to rearrange tomorrow's dinner seating. Sir Fortescue was invited, as well as old Redford from the Grange. Redford had one foot in the grave, but . . .

She jabbed the squire awake with the tip of her lorgnette. "We're opening the presents now, Willoughby, since we'll likely be out searching for Montravan all night." As if she or Allissa would go riding out with lanterns. Or sit up past the unwrappings.

"What's that? Montravan's lost? Downy fellow like that, I'd wager a monkey he's found a snug nest for the night." The squire's wink let them all know he didn't believe it would be any hot brick keeping Bevin warm that evening. Petra's heart sank lower. Everyone knew the man was a rake, so why should it bother her now, when it was Miss Harleigh's problem? She sighed, drawing the dowager's attention.

"We may as well start with Petra's gifts," Lady Montravan decreed. No surprises there, and no one could accuse her of hurrying the proceedings out of vulgar curiosity or greed.

They all opened their handkerchiefs to the usual

polite, unexcited mouthings. They all tossed Petra's hours of effort aside to reach for the next offering.

Allissa and Lady Montravan exchanged their gifts then, each receiving an elaborate new ensemble for the New Year's ball: gown, gloves, shoes and shawl. Cost had been of no concern, since they put the charges on Bevin's account.

"Oh, thank you, Mama," Allissa enthused, holding up the gown of spangled satin in the exact color blue as her eyes. "It's just what I wanted. However did you guess?" she asked for the squire's benefit, since he was the only one not along for the shopping and fittings.

Lady Montravan had to hold up her own new lavender sarcenet, with turban to match, complimenting Lissa on her exquisite taste. Then it was Petra's turn to open Lady Montravan's present. Petra was actually surprised to see the exquisite dress length of gold velvet, until she noted the slight water stain near the edge. The color would bring out the gold in her brown hair, Petra knew, and might even give some life to her brown eyes and honeyed complexion. Of course, there was hardly time to make up a gown by the New Year's ball, which Lady Montravan *might* have taken into consideration, but Petra expressed her honest delight enthusiastically enough to gratify the dowager's self-esteem as a gentlewoman of genuine generosity.

Allissa gave Petra a matching stole, which coincidentally also matched a stole Petra knew the chit had two of. No matter, Petra vowed, she'd be as finely gowned as any lady at the ball, even if she had to stay awake for the next six nights to do it. Why, she might even outshine Lady Belinda Harleigh. And the barnyard animals might speak at Christmas Eve. At least she wouldn't be ashamed at the ball, appearing as the poor hanger-on in made-over dresses.

Squire Merton adored his embroidered pillow. "Can't think of a more thoughtful gift, m'dear." He even had a tear in his eye as he kissed the dowager's pudgy fingers. She puffed out her chest until he got up, corsets creaking, to go buss Petra heartily on the cheek. "And I bet I know whom to thank for the effort. Why, it's Skipjack to the life. Just think, he'll be on my sofa forever."

Just think, Petra thought, she'd be in Lady Montravan's black books forever, too. It was a good thing she had already decided to leave after the new year.

While he was up, the squire fetched his own gifts to the ladies. Petra and Allissa each received a pair of York tan riding gloves, which Petra truly needed and appreciated, thanking the squire for his consideration. Allissa made barely polite responses, then waved a glove to tease Pug into a game.

Lady Montravan opened the box from her portly gallant and lifted out a fox tippet, complete with glass eyes. While the squire related every detail of the poor creature's gory demise, Lady Montravan was turning it this way and that, searching the box and tissue for the ring. "How nice," she said, tossing the object of at least seven hunts aside, knocking over a glass of restorative sherry. She mopped at the spill with Petra's handkerchief, then threw the soiled lace-edged linen to the floor.

"We might as well open Montravan's presents," she grumbled. "He's not coming."

"Don't you think we ought to wait for his lordship?" Petra suggested.

"No, I do not, miss, and I still make some of the decisions around here. I am worn out with the tension of worry and must seek my bed soon. If that rakeshame is so inconsiderate as to be late, then he cannot expect me to ruin my health. Allissa, bring the gifts. I'll start."

No one dared contradict the countess in such a mood, not even Allissa, who merely whined at her mother to hurry; she'd go next.

Lady Montravan unwrapped a magnificent ruby brooch. "Oh, the dear boy," she cooed, holding the pin to the lavender gown to judge the effect. Then she reached for the enclosed card just as a commotion was heard in the hall.

" 'Greetings of the season,' " Lady Montravan started reading when a disheveled, dirty earl tore into the room.

"Mama, don't!" he shouted. Too late.

" 'Looking forward to seeing you with your esteemed parents,' " she continued, puzzled. Then she shrieked. "He wants me dead! It's not enough that he's sending me to that dreary dower house; now he wants me in the vault with my ancestors! My heart! My heavens!" And she swooned dead away, there on the sofa.

9

"There's been a dreadful mistake," Lord Montravan tried to say into the ensuing chaos, but no one paid him any attention after Petra's first tentative smile. The butler was shouting for her ladyship's maid and the housekeeper, while Petra was scrambling under the sofa for the smelling salts. Squire Merton poured out another glass of restorative—and swallowed it down. Then he started coughing and bellowing for something decent a fellow could drink at a time of crisis. Footmen were sent running in all directions, and Allissa was gulping back sobs of frustration, saying that she'd never get her tiara at this rate and if her older brother was in such a hateful mood.

"That was despicable," she raged at him. "You know how Mama's nerves are so easily overset. And at Christmas, and your coming late! How could you write such a thing?"

"I didn't, brat, so stubble it," he began, looking on helplessly as a maid started burning feathers under Lady Montravan's nose.

Allissa snatched the card off the table and thrust it at Bevin. "It's your handwriting, isn't it?"

Petra glanced up from her place at the side of the reviving, moaning countess. Those were indeed Bevin's heavy, slanting strokes on the holly-bordered card.

"Yes, but the messages—" he began again, his

words lost anew to Lady Montravan's groans and clutchings of her heart.

Her mama being alert and her usual stridently complaining self, Allissa now felt free to gather up the box with her name on it while no one was watching. Petra glanced over, frowning, just as the younger girl ripped the wrappings apart. The earl had bought Allissa a tiara after all, but Petra was relieved to see the circlet was of delicate gold, with no ornate tracery and no diamonds. The coronet would look sweet with flowers woven through it, entirely in keeping with a young miss's debut.

"It's for babies!" the young miss wailed when she saw there were no diamonds. Then she reached for the enclosure at the bottom of the box.

"No!" Bevin shouted, leaving off patting his mother's hand and reassuring her of his continued devotion and affection, that the message was meant for Lady Belinda, who would not, after all, be . . . He jumped up and tried to seize the card, but Allissa danced out of his grasp. He couldn't very well wrestle with her over it, so, heart sinking, he watched as his spoiled sister's face grew redder and redder, just as it used to before she threw herself on the floor in a tantrum. Someone should have saved them all the trouble by drowning her then, he thought, when she began to scream.

" 'Happy hunting'! How dare you, Bevin Mont-ford! As if I'm going to the Marriage Mart just to snare the most eligible parti! Is that all you think of me, that no man will ask for me, but I have to go . . . go *hunting* for a husband? Just because you fell into the parson's mousetrap, you think all women are sneaky and devious, don't you? You are mean and nasty, Bevin Montford! Nasty, nasty, nasty, and you always have been, making me have those horrid governesses, and making me wait to go to London."

Allissa was sobbing in earnest now, totally beyond reason or control.

Petra left Lady Montravan's side to take Allissa into her arms. The girl felt warm, likely from her overheated emotional storm, Petra hoped.

Bevin was raking his fingers through his already mussed hair. "I didn't write that to you, Lissa, I swear. I wrote that for Squire Merton. Now where the devil has he gone off to?"

The squire had unobtrusively unwrapped his own gift, thinking to make a courteous thank you and a genteel early departure, seeing the dustup at Montravan Hall. The riding crop was a handsome one, but the earl's note gave Merton pause: *Greetings of the season, from a son who knows his duty.* Montravan was assuring his mother that he would fulfill his responsibilities to his name, that he was bringing home a fitting bride for her approval. However, Merton shook his head over the earl's meaning. Could the lad be thinking he'd been dallying too long with the dowager? Blast, could Montravan be aware of those intimate encounters in the conservatory? That dutiful son bit could mean Montravan might call a fellow out for not coming up to scratch. The earl was certainly hot-to-hand enough, and more than skilled enough to have Merton's knees knocking together. The squire decided to see about a new hunter—in Ireland. Tonight. He crept out the side door while Bevin was raging about riding the devil's own horse through a blizzard just to get to this madhouse.

Petra scowled at him, so he subsided, content to fill a glass with the brandy the butler had brought for Merton. She tried again to soothe the girl in her arms: "Allissa, dear, do try to calm yourself. I am sure there is an explanation. You are only upsetting your mother and making yourself ill."

"And likely giving Merton a disgust of us,"

Montravan added, aggravated that his mother's likeliest suitor had shabbed off. "So cut line. You're only blue-deviled that you didn't get the diamonds you wanted. Why, a seventeen-year-old schoolgirl with spots could only look nohow in diamonds and—"

"Spots?" Allissa screamed. Lady Montravan echoed with a hysterical "Spots?" and fainted again.

"Damnation!" swore Lord Montravan, and "Welcome home, my lord," said Petra.

Later, after the physician had gone and both invalids were well dosed with laudanum and in the competent hands of their maids, Petra sought out Lord Montravan in the drawing room. Bevin had had a bath and a snack in his room and was immaculately dressed in dove gray pantaloons and black coat, his hair still damp from its recent washing. Petra still wore her second-best gown, somewhat rumpled from her exertions, and her hair was coming undone, but she intended merely to stay a moment. She couldn't think it was altogether proper for her to be alone with such a handsome, virile man, even if he was her employer. Her reputation might suffer; her already tortured feelings certainly would.

"The physician thinks that the dowager is merely overset," she reported. "A good night's rest should restore her to normal."

Bevin muttered something about that being bad enough, which Petra ignored. She went on: "He feels that Allissa's case should be a mild one if she is kept quiet, which will not be easy, once she realizes she'll miss her first real ball."

Bevin nodded. "There will be others. I'm sure if I promise her an early visit to London, she'll be more resigned. And there must be some gaudy, trumpery bit of something in the village I can buy to win her back to humor, since she was not so fond of her present."

"The presents!" Petra recalled. "You never had yours." She quickly moved to the piecrust table and brought three packages back to where Bevin stood staring into the fire.

"I can wait, my dear. I daresay I have all the patience in this family."

But he looked as if he needed some cheering right now, Petra thought, noting how the flickering flames showed the lines of weariness on his face. "But the countess will not rise till just before church, and then the vicar and local families will arrive for nuncheon."

"Very well," he said, indicating she should take a seat, so he might sit and open the gifts. Her handkerchiefs were duly appreciated, one placed carefully in his pocket. And the robe and slippers were exclaimed over to such an extent that Petra was soon blushing. Bevin got up and poured out a glass of Madeira for each of them, then raised his in a toast. "You are the best thing that ever happened to this family, Petra. I do not know what we have done to deserve you, but I thank heaven you've taken us in hand."

Embarrassed, Petra sipped her drink. "I have done nothing, my lord."

"Nothing?" He held up the robe with its intricate work. "You call this nothing? Or the way you were such a pillar of strength through that bumblebroth tonight? You've even forgiven me for ruining Christmas by making sure I have my gifts."

Petra did not pretend to misunderstand. "However did you come to make such a mull of things, my lord? That is not like you in the least."

"Not like Vincent, you mean." He sank back into the chair opposite hers with a heartfelt sigh. "I

71

swear I know what hell is like. I feel as if I've been visiting there for the last three days."

He proceeded to tell her about the gossip in the clubs and about confronting his secretary. Then he described the horror of the mixed-up notes, with his "lady friend" receiving Petra's note of appreciation and Lady Belinda receiving Marina's congé.

"I realize this is all horribly improper, my discussing such things with you, but I knew you, at least, wouldn't fly into a pelter."

Instead Petra was giggling uncontrollably, especially when she realized Miss Harleigh would not be coming, that there would be no engagement. Her heart was so lightened, she practically danced across the room to return with the last parcel from the table, the one addressed to Miss Petra Sinclaire.

"I didn't get to open my gift, my lord," she said merrily, mischievously.

"Oh, Lord! Let me take the card out at least!" he begged. "And you might as well be calling me Bevin as you were used to, after witnessing my fall from grace."

"Not at all, my lord. You have not tarnished your image in my eyes, merely restored yourself to the ranks of us poor humans. The last time I saw you take a misstep was when you were conjugating Latin verbs with my father." She peeled away the tissue around the hair combs and exclaimed over their loveliness. "Oh, they are just the thing to go with my new dress, my lord." Then she unwrapped the book and raised shining eyes to his. "Except how can I finish sewing my gown when I'll be wanting to read this?"

"I'll read it out loud while you stitch," he offered unexpectedly, surprising himself as well as Petra.

"That's quite the kindest thing of all," she said with a catch in her voice, imagining nights such as this, by the fire. No, she dare not dream.

"Then be kind in return," Bevin was saying into her reverie, "and give me back the card."

She grinned, showing sudden dimples he'd never noticed, and shook her head, freeing even more soft brown curls to rest against her glowing cheeks. "Minx," he muttered appreciatively, racking his brain to think what message was left unaccounted for. It must be the one for Bibi, meant to go with the earbobs. What was the blasted message? He groaned.

Petra read the card, then lowered her head, her shoulders shaking. Rising, Bevin rushed to kneel by her side. "Please don't cry, my dear! You know I didn't mean it for you, whatever it says!" She kept on making whimpery sounds. "It cannot be that bad, Petra."

"Bad? It's wonderful!" When she raised her head, he could see tears glistening on her lashes. "I can figure out about the hair combs, but I am not sure about this," and she held up the book before going off into whoops of laughter. " 'Th-thinking of you in m-my arms,' " she tried to read through her giggles, " 'w-wearing just these.' "

Soon the usually somber earl was laughing so hard, his sides hurt, and he had to wipe his own eyes with one of the fine new handkerchiefs. Then he tenderly wiped Petra's cheeks with the same cloth.

"I've been a fool," he said, staying next to her, taking her hand in his.

"You certainly have," she agreed, "putting all your faith in that bounder."

"No, I mean about so many other things. My friend Johnny tried to tell me, and I never really understood. I was looking for a suitable bride, when I should have been looking for a woman who suited me."

"Lady Belinda?"

Bevin waved that away. "I hardly knew her, beyond her social standing. I know now that I should have sought a woman who can laugh with me, understand my failings, and share my concerns."

"Yes, I think that's important for a happy marriage."

"I never realized I already had all those things in my grasp. That is, I did realize, but I never understood I could have it all. I'm not doing this well, am I?"

"I'm not quite sure what it is you *are* doing, my lord."

"Bevin." He got up to pace, while she nearly shredded the handkerchief she'd labored over so long. "I had time on the long ride here to think, and all I thought of was how much I wanted to see you, be with you. Do you think you might ever consider . . . ? That is, after you've had a proper Season, and a chance to look over the crop of bachelors, and a proper courtship—"

"Never."

He kept his back to her. "That's it, then. I'm sorry, Petra, if I have embarrassed you. I never meant—"

"No, I mean I will never wait that long."

In two long strides he was next to her again, with his arms on her shoulders. "Do you mean that, sweetheart, do you really mean you might come to love me?"

"Silly, I've loved you forever."

The kiss that followed left them both shaken. Petra never knew a kiss could do such amazing things to one's insides—and outsides and upside-down sides—and Bevin never knew how desire could be so incredibly intensified by affection. It was the earl who found the willpower to set Petra away from him, at least a handbreadth. When he found his voice, he gasped, "I can see there is going to be nothing proper about this courtship after all."

"My lo—Bevin, I need to know, will you do *that* with other women? I mean, I know about your *chéries amours*, but I don't think I could bear it, after . . ."

Bevin stroked the back of his hand along her cheek. "After that kiss I don't think I'll ever want to look at another woman. I cannot hide my past from you, but I do mean to be a faithful husband. Do you know, when I thought about Belinda and Vincent, I realized I didn't truly care, except for my pride, of course, and the idea of having to worry about the paternity of my children. That's when I realized I wouldn't be happy with that kind of society marriage, where both spouses go their own way. I want a wife who will love me enough to mind if I stray."

"I'll mind! Why, I'll . . . I'll darken your daylights if you look at another woman."

"And if you so much as smile at another man, I'll call him out!"

So they sealed that accord with another kiss, which ended at the rug in front of the hearth, perilously close to the fire.

"Blast, I depended on you to be level-headed," Bevin complained, lifting her in his arms back to the sofa. Petra only grinned, so he kissed the tip of her nose. "This is no way for a gentleman to behave, and us not even formally engaged. Luckily I can remedy that." He reached into his pocket for a small box. "It's the family betrothal ring, from the vault. I was hoping, you see. I can have one made that will be more to your taste, but will you wear this for me, for now?"

"Not for now, forever."

As Bevin slipped it onto her finger, he murmured, "Merry Christmas, my love," but instead of the kiss he expected in return, Petra jumped up and ran from the room.

"I'll be right back," she said.

Bevin took the moment to straighten his clothing and vow to keep his passions under control—and pray for an early wedding. Petra was an innocent, a lady—and back within the circle of his arms before he could think of how many cold baths he'd have to take.

"I wanted to give you a special Christmas gift," she whispered, "to mark the occasion."

"But you've given me so much, two handkerchiefs and your love. What more could a man need or want?"

Petra smiled at his teasing and held out her hand. "Here, it's my father's watch. I want you to have it."

He took the gold watch on its chain and raised her hand to his lips. "I know how much this must mean to you, and I shall cherish it always as the second-finest Christmas gift I've ever received."

"After the embroidered robe?"

"After your love, my precious peagoose. But wait, I have another gift for you, too."

"But the ring and the book and the combs . . . It's so much."

"The ring is an heirloom, the book is in every bookseller's, and you must know Vincent selected the combs. I want to give you something all your own." Bevin was searching through his pockets, damning his valet for being so meticulous. At last his fingers touched the object he was seeking, and he drew out a small black circle, a horseshoe nail twisted into a ring, rust showing in spots, uneven welding in others. He proudly placed this ring on her finger, right above the diamond-and-emerald Montravan betrothal ring. "This one I made myself. Greetings of the season, sweetheart."

And every season.

HOME FOR CHRISTMAS

by
Jennie Gallant

1

A light dusting of snow covered the ground. Minute ice crystals hung in the air, sparkling like diamonds as the sun struck them. Elizabeth ignored the beauty around her; her mind had already raced ahead to London. In the usual way she would have enjoyed this week preceding Christmas at Bushmill Manor—the gathering of holly and fir boughs to festoon the saloon, the neighbors' visits, and mulled wine—but as the carriage lumbered down the road, she wished her uncle would whip the team to a faster pace. She could not get away fast enough to suit her. She felt as if she were escaping from prison.

In a very real way an unwanted marriage was a prison for a lady. And what a jailer Baron Rathborne would make! It was not just his age that repelled her. Although the baron was old enough to be her papa, he was still called handsome. He was tall and lean, with muscles taut from riding. His face was as thin and sharp as a Saracen's blade, with steely gray eyes that caused a chill to shiver up her spine. He looked at her as if she were a filly he was eager to break. She could almost hear the whip snap when he spoke.

"I am not at all sure this is a wise move, Beth," her uncle said, as the slow team plodded on. "Rathborne would have made you a fine husband. He is well-to-grass. He did not insist on payment of the note, you must know. He would have been within his rights, for it was what they call a demand note. I fear it was precipitate of you to have paid it off in full with your dowry. Of course, Bushmill will be yours when I am gone, so you are not actually out-of-pocket in taking a mortgage on it. I would never take a sou of your money for my own use. But you know that."

"Of course, Uncle," she agreed. Her uncle, John Reddish, was incapable of dishonesty and assumed others were as good as he. He was a creature of yesteryear. He still wore his white hair pulled back in a tail, and a black grogram overcoat that was rusty with age. He was happiest at home at Bushmill Manor, where he had been born seventy years before and had spent his life, running his estate with more generosity than wisdom. Over the years it had been necessary to borrow heavily to cover expenses. A year before he had consolidated various small debts into one large one. His friend Sir Hughe Wortley had obliged him in the matter.

"I cannot understand how Rathborne ended up with my note," he continued, "for it was Sir Hughe who lent me the money. I daresay Sir Hughe found himself short and did not like to dun me for payment. He knew I could not pay him a lump sum. It was kind of Rathborne to take my note."

Kindness had nothing to do with it, as far as Elizabeth was concerned. Rathborne had bought the note—or won it at cards—for the purpose of forcing her to marry him. He knew her uncle could not pay it off without selling Bushmill. And he knew she would not let her uncle sell his ancestral home. Reddish had given Rathborne his permission to propose to her, but her uncle had not been present at the proposal.

"It would cause me grievous pain to have to demand payment of this note," he had said, flipping the document in his fingers and smiling in his hateful, menacing way. "Of course, if you were to marry me, there would be no question of demanding payment in full. Your uncle could continue on at Bushmill until his death. I daresay we would not have long to wait."

He spoke of her uncle's death as something to be desired. Uncle John was the only father she had ever known. "I am honored at your offer, sir, but I am afraid I cannot accept," she had said.

His cold fingers jerked her head up and squeezed her chin. "Playing hard to get, are we? I like a filly with spirit."

She wrenched her head away and glared at him. "I am not playing, milord. I do not wish to marry you."

He uttered a low, mirthless laugh. "We shall see about that, my pet. I'll have you yet. By God, I will."

Elizabeth could take no more. She turned on her heel and ran from the room. Uncle John could not comprehend her refusing Rathborne, but he was too softhearted to force her to accept.

"Poor Rathborne," he had said, shaking his head. "This will hit him hard. I know the pangs of lost love, my dear. How I miss my Mary, after all these years. But then you do not care for him, so that is that. I hope it is not young Butterworth you have in your eye? I know your Aunt Martha feared he might come up to scratch last spring, but as he did not, you must forget him. No doubt some other lady has been taken in by his title and accepted him by now. What is his title, by the by?"

"He is the Earl of Wyckholme, Uncle."

"That's it. I was at Harrow with his uncle. The Butterworths were all oilers. More butter than worth, we used to say of his uncle. A little joke. Unkind, perhaps, but still I am happy you did not accept young Butterworth."

"He did not offer," she said calmly. But the disappointment of his not offering had not gone away. To hear her uncle say he had probably chosen someone else could still wrench her heart.

Her uncle spoke of other things. "We shall remain only a few days at your aunt's house while the lawyers attend to our business matters. With luck we shall be home for Christmas. I shall have a regular payment scheme drawn up, so that you can sue me if I do not pay on the dot. Heh, heh."

Elizabeth assured him she was not worried in the least.

"With Christmas coming on, there will be a rout or two you might want to take in," Reddish continued. "A pity your aunt will not be there. Her daughter is expecting a child any day now. It was kind of Martha to let us use the house anyhow."

Elizabeth knew her uncle did not care for parties, but he had packed his ancient silk stockings and knee breeches to do the pretty. She fell into a reverie of daydreaming. She did not really think Wyckholme had become engaged, or she would have read it in the journals or heard of it from her friends. She had made a wide circle of friends during her first Season the spring before. She wondered vaguely why Wyckholme had not offered for her. He had certainly appeared to be interested. But then he had a reputation with the ladies. It seemed the year before he had been on the verge of offering for a certain Lady Alice Swanson, and she had not managed to bring him up to scratch either.

Perhaps Uncle was right, and Wyckholme was more butter than worth. He could certainly dump the butter boat on a lady—did it in the most offhand way, yet with devastating effect. "I dreamed of you last night," he had said once, when they were out driving. "You dainty, gauzy blondes belong in dreams. I always fear I have imagined you, that

I shall awaken one day and find you are gone. You are too beautiful for the real world."

Upon hearing that she was a dainty, gauzy blonde, Elizabeth had begun arranging her toilette accordingly, with flowing chiffon shawls and dainty accessories. She had softened her coiffure to loose waves that seemed suitable for a dream girl.

"I don't mind that you cannot waltz," he had said on another occasion, before she was given permission to waltz by the patronesses of Almack's. "I shall just sit here and swim about in those big blue lakes you call eyes. If you notice me drowning, you will save me, Miss Parrish. A kiss should do it."

"I never heard of a kiss saving a drowning man."

"The chaperons keep it a deep, dark secret from the youngsters, or the gents would all be throwing themselves into ponds and punch bowls." Wyckholme always talked a deal of nonsense.

Though it was still late afternoon, night had fallen when the carriage arrived at Aunt Martha's house on Belgrave Square. Its occupants, fatigued from the trip, wanted nothing but dinner and an early night's repose. Before retiring, however, Elizabeth took time to write a notice to the journals that Mr. John Reddish of Bushmill Manor in Surrey and his niece, Miss Parrish, were in London for a short visit to Mrs. Mannering on Belgrave Square. If anyone wanted to see her, he—that is to say Wyckholme—would know she was here. She sent the notice off with a footman that same evening, to ensure its being in the journals the next day.

The morning brought no visitors, but only a letter from Mrs. Mannering with a dozen requests and suggestions as to the running of her house. There were rooms to be aired, dustcovers to be removed and put away, a good many items to be cleaned and others to be brought out of temporary storage, the coal man to be notified to bring a load of fuel. While Elizabeth was poring over the letter, the door knocker sounded. She rose in excitement. Wyckholme! He had come already! And it was snowing, too! That did not look like disinterest!

Sage, the butler, soon entered the room and handed her a small parcel. "This arrived for you by liveried footman, Miss Parrish," he said, impressed by this exalted means of communication. "He did not wait for a reply."

Elizabeth tore the parcel open eagerly, with no thought in her mind but that Wyckholme had sent her some small welcoming token and a note asking when he might call. She found herself holding a small tin box covered in fading blue velvet, and her heart hammered in excitement. It was too large for a ring box, yet its make certainly suggested that it contained jewelry. She lifted the hinged lid and found herself gazing at a sparkling diamond neck-lace. A gasp of pleasure wafted up to her throat as she held it aloft to catch the sun's rays.

Beneath the necklace rested a small sheet of folded paper. Her fingers trembled as she lifted it.

My dearest Elizabeth: Please accept the Rathborne necklace as a token of my esteem. I told you I did not give up easily! I shall be in London on Christmas Eve day to see if you have changed your mind yet. Your faithful servant, Rathborne.

She dropped the letter and necklace as if they were live coals. How dare he! Presumptuous devil! She gazed down at the necklace with a feeling of revulsion, yet it was a pretty thing. The large gems in front had a blush of pink, which no doubt made them even more valuable than white diamonds. The stones were arranged in a star formed by a large, brilliant cut diamond in the center, with pear-shaped diamonds making up the points.

She had heard of the Rathborne diamond necklace. It was said to be worth ten thousand pounds. Did he think to bribe her with jewelry? She stuffed the note and necklace into the box and went off in a fit of indignation to show them to her uncle.

"Look what Rathborne has done, Uncle!" she said, placing them on the desk before him. "This just arrived by special footman. Read his note."

"Ah, the Rathborne diamonds! Poor Rathborne." He glanced at the note. "What an excellent fellow he is. Would you not like to keep the necklace, my dear? I do not mean marry him because of the diamonds—they only pepper the stew."

"I don't want this. You must return it at once!"

"I should not like to entrust it to the mails. It would be best if we took it home with us when we go. You must write a note in the meanwhile, of course, to put the poor devil out of his misery. Not that a refusal will please him, but at least he will know his fate."

"Will you write it for me, Uncle?" she pleaded. She did not want to have anything to do with Rathborne.

"That might be best. Dear me. I hardly know what to do with such a valuable thing. I wonder if it would not be safer in a bank. Martha has no safe in the house."

"Yes, do get it out of here, please," Elizabeth urged. She did not even want to be under the same roof as any item belonging to Rathborne.

"Very well. We shall take a drive downtown this afternoon if the snow lets up. I shall see if I can find a few books of sermons to tide me over the winter at home while we are there. I know my old sermon books by heart. And perhaps I shall pick up something by Scott. He was recommended to me by the vicar, so he cannot be one of these modern writers. Take Byron, now. I would not want you reading such heathenish stuff, filling your head with corsairs and bandits. The vicar has no opinion of Byron."

Elizabeth spent her morning attending to her aunt's instructions. The snow had stopped, so immediately after lunch she bundled up in her warmest pelisse and bonnet for the drive downtown. They were just on their way out the door when they had a caller. As they were at the door when he arrived, her heart did not race in expectation that Wyckholme had come. It was only Mr. Grue, an old friend of her uncle's from Dorking, near Bushmill.

"I see you are just leaving, John," Grue said. "I shall come back later. I saw your notice in the journal that you were visiting Mrs. Mannering. Is there any special reason for it?"

"Come in, come in," Reddish said, returning to the hallway. "We can go out any time. What brings you to London?"

"My Maggie insists on coming for a fortnight every winter. She will be inviting you to dinner one of these evenings." He turned to Elizabeth. "Good day, Miss Parrish."

"How nice to see you," Elizabeth said, swallowing her disappointment. She knew her uncle's way when he was with his cronies. They would sit for hours over their teacups, talking about farming and politics, until it was too late to go out. "I shall ask Mrs. Horton to make tea, Uncle."

"Very kind of you, my dear. And perhaps some of her excellent gingerbread."

Elizabeth remained with their caller for half an hour to pour the tea and make polite conversation. After that time she went to her room to begin writing notes to some of her friends to arrange meetings. When she returned to the saloon much later, she saw her uncle was showing Mr. Grue the necklace. Uncle had obviously been telling Grue how it came to be here.

"Unfortunately Beth feels she cannot accept his offer," he was saying to Grue. "She will look long and hard before she receives a better one."

Grue gave Elizabeth a meaningful look that told her he had a more accurate notion of Rathborne's character. "As to that, John, you would not want to force her. I daresay Miss Parrish knows what she is about. There are plenty of fish in the sea."

"There is no question of forcing her. We were just on our way to the bank to store the necklace safely away when you arrived. We will deliver it to Rathborne when we return."

Grue lifted the necklace and held it to the window. A frown seized his craggy features. "Do you have a loupe, John?" he asked.

"Eh? What do you mean?"

"I do believe these stones are not diamonds. They are strass glass. I have an eye for gemstones, from my days in India, you know. I am quite sure—"

Elizabeth stared at him in alarm. "There is a magnifying glass in the study," she said, and ran off to get it.

While Grue applied it to the necklace, Mr. Reddish found an explanation for the ersatz gems. "Rathborne is too clever to entrust genuine diamonds on the road, where a highwayman might steal them. He has had this copy made up to give Beth a notion of what she is missing. What a deal of trouble he has gone to!"

"Are you sure they are fakes?" Elizabeth asked. The note had stated "the Rathborne necklace" in no uncertain terms. It occurred to her that Rathborne might not be as rich as everyone thought. He was a known gambler. Perhaps he had had to sell his jewelry.

"I would bet a monkey this large stone at least is a fake," Grue said, still peering at it through the glass. "Why, it is not even pink! I detect a sliver of colored silver paper peeking out over the edge of the mounting. That suggests to me that he has had a copy made up in a hurry."

"Let us take it down to Rundell and Bridges and have them look it over," Mr. Reddish suggested. "If it is only a copy, there is no need to go to the expense of hiring a bank box."

"An excellent idea," Grue agreed.

Reddish went for his hat and coat, and Grue exchanged a worried look with Elizabeth. "I wonder what Rathborne is up to," he said. "You were wise to steer clear of him. He is as cunning a rogue as you'd meet in a day's march. I smell some trickery here."

"Uncle will not hear a word against him."

"Your uncle is too trusting for his own good. But we shall get to the bottom of this, never fear."

The two gentlemen left immediately. Elizabeth felt upset at what Mr. Grue had intimated. Was Rathborne attempting some trick to force her into marriage? Did he plan to say he had sent her the original necklace and that she or her uncle had made this switch to strass glass? He would demand payment for the original, which would mean selling Bushmill.

She paced the floor, unable to settle back down to writing her letters. In her mind the menacing face of Baron Rathborne loomed, and that mischievous proposal. "I'll have you yet. By God, I will."

"By God, you will not!" she said grimly.

It was an hour later that her uncle and Grue returned. Her uncle had an ugly welt over his left eye, and his coat was muddy.

"Uncle! What on earth happened?" she demanded.

"A glass of brandy, if you have one," Grue said, and assisted Mr. Reddish to the sofa while Elizabeth poured a glass of wine, as her aunt did not keep brandy in the house.

Mr. Reddish was beyond speech. It was for Grue to tell the tale. "We were held up by a pair of masked footmen just as we alighted from the carriage to enter Rundell and Bridges," he explained. "They snatched the jewelry box, belted your uncle over the head with the butt of a pistol, and took off on horseback. We raised a great hue and cry when your uncle recovered, but there was no hope of catching them. I blame myself for letting John set out at footpad hour. I should have known better if he did not. Thank God the necklace was only a copy. If it had been the original . . ."

Icy fingers clutched at Elizabeth's heart. "Rathborne did this," she said. "He sent those ruffians to snatch the necklace, so we could not prove it was a copy. He will hold us to ransom to pay for it. He knows my uncle's sense of honor would insist on repaying every penny."

"Or something of equal value," Grue said, with a knowing look. "It is certainly an effort to force you to have him."

Mr. Reddish shook his head. "I will not believe such a thing of Rathborne," he said. "He is a gentleman."

As they spoke, a peremptory knock sounded at the door. Elizabeth felt in her bones it would be Rathborne, come to claim her. She shrank behind Mr. Grue. Sage entered and announced, "Lord Wyckholme, for Miss Parrish."

Elizabeth felt such a rush of relief that her knees buckled, and Mr. Grue had to sustain her. He looked to the doorway and saw a handsome young gentleman rigged out in the highest kick of fashion. Crow black hair crowned a well-shaped head. The eyes were nearly as dark. They looked like black diamonds in his rather pale face. His features were regular, but it was his lively expression that lent him a certain air of diablerie. He was dressed in an exquisitely cut evening jacket. His physique was on the lean side, which added to his elegance. But he looked by no means ill nourished. It was the lean, muscled body of an athlete, with broad shoulders.

He looked across the room to Elizabeth's fainting form and smiled. "I hoped you would be happy to see me, but I must say I did not expect to knock you off your feet, Miss Parrish."

At first glance Elizabeth saw only the same whimsical Wyckholme who had courted her so delightfully last spring. But as she gazed at him longer, she saw the genuine pleasure glowing in his eyes. Surely there was an eagerness there, or was he only ill at ease at her violent reaction?

He turned to Reddish, still resting on the sofa, and chattered nervously, "Good evening, sir. Or good afternoon, whichever the case may be. Let us say happy twilight hour and be done with it. Bumped into a door, did you, sir? Shame on you." Then he glanced at Mr. Grue. "I don't believe I have the pleasure of your friend's acquaintance, Miss Parrish. No matter. Any friend of yours is a friend of mine." He strode forward and gave Grue's hand a shake. "Wyckholme," he said.

"Grue," Mr. Grue responded, as Elizabeth seemed to be speechless.

"Grew?" Wyckholme said. "Who, me? I don't believe so. My clothes still fit at least. I have not grown too big for my breeches." He looked down to check his trousers.

Elizabeth found tongue then. "Oh, do stop being such a ninny, Wyckholme," she said. "My uncle has been robbed and beaten, and now I shall have to marry that hateful Baron Rathborne." On this speech she burst into tears.

Wyckholme looked warily about at the elderly gentlemen before offering her his shoulder. "Perhaps I have chosen an inopportune moment to call?" he said, with the pained look of a trapped animal.

2

"Oh, it is you, Butterworth," Mr. Reddish said. "As you can see, we are all at sixes and sevens. It might be best if you returned another time."

Mr. Grue thought a noble friend an excellent thing to have at this time. Young Wyckholme was awake on all suits. He might even be helpful in getting to the bottom of Rathborne's scheme.

"Don't mind Mr. Reddish," he said with a smile. "If you like a good story, milord, do sit down."

"I love a good story, but if it is the one about the bishop and the opera dancer, I have already—" Elizabeth directed a killing stare at him.

"We have just had an extraordinary experience," Mr. Grue continued, ignoring the interruption.

Wyckholme's dark eyes glowed with interest. He cast a questioning glance at Reddish before allowing himself to be seated and accepting a glass of wine. Grue briefly outlined the situation.

In Elizabeth's view Grue did not place enough emphasis on Rathborne's intention to force her into marrying him. "He sent that necklace with the intention of stealing it back. He knows Uncle cannot repay him. He thinks I will feel duty-bound to marry him," she explained.

Wyckholme listened, then spoke. "But if he planned to steal it back, why send a fake necklace? He is protecting himself twice. A fellow don't usually use a gun and a sword at the same time."

"Rathborne did not know I would be here," Grue explained. "Neither Reddish nor Miss Parrish realized it was a fake, but I have some experience with gemstones."

"That being the case," Wyckholme said, "he would hardly be expecting Mr. Reddish to dash the thing off to the jeweler for examination. That is where you were set upon by footpads?"

"Yes, I see your point," Grue said, frowning.

"It was demmed foolish of you—" Wyckholme intercepted a glowering look from Reddish and changed his wording. "That is to say, it was unwise of you to have set out carrying jewelry at footpad hour without at least the protection of a pistol. The footpads do loiter about the jewelry shops. The pickings there are more valuable than elsewhere. The banks, the jewelry stores, and the gentlemen's clubs at closing time, when the winners' pockets are jingling, are considered choice spots for footpads. They each have their own locales. Interlopers are discouraged from poaching."

"Is it possible to discover which ruffians operate outside of Rundell and Bridges?" Grue asked. "Perhaps we should call in Bow Street."

"Bow Street?" Wyckholme lifted his head and laughed. "Then you are not interested in solving the case this century? Bow Street will do you no good. They must work within the purlieus of the law. It will be more efficacious to venture beyond that narrow pale in this case. I happen to know which footpads have the Rundell and Bridges concession."

Reddish narrowed his eyes. "And how would an honest man come by such information as that, Butterworth?"

"By keeping his eyes open, sir, a practice I highly recommend. I make it a point to be on terms with the fraternity of thieves. It is cheaper to give them a pourboire from time to time than to be robbed when you happen to be carrying a full purse. A couple of fellows called Tinker and Boxer have the concession at Rundell and Bridges. The odd thing is, they never wear masks. Could you describe the shape and size of your attackers, Mr. Reddish?"

"The one that hit me was a great, hulking brute. T'other was short and slight."

"Then it was not Tinker and Boxer. Tinker is a regular ladder, about six feet and a half, very slender build. Boxer is built like a badger, low to the ground, heavyset. They do not ride either. They've no need of horses. They can both run like the wind."

"I wager it was Rathborne's henchmen," Elizabeth said. "He might have had them watching the house, to follow Uncle when he went out."

"If it had been Rathborne's intention to snaffle the necklace back, he would have had his men slip into the house at night while you were all asleep," Wyckholme said. "He'd have no reason to suppose Mr. Reddish was strolling about town with it in his pocket." He cast a suspicious look at Grue.

Grue just smiled. "You are thinking I might have been working with Rathborne, that I encouraged Reddish to take the thing for authentication, knowing the robbers were lurking about the jewelry store."

"Ridiculous!" Reddish scoffed. "I have known Edward Grue forever. If insulting my friends is your notion of help, Butterworth, I suggest you stick to simpering at the ladies and leave this matter to wiser heads."

Wyckholme replied blandly, but Elizabeth sensed the rising anger in his tone. "Oh, I do assure you, Mr. Reddish, I seldom simper. Leer, perhaps."

"Now do be calm, John," Grue said. "I am the one who suggested that I was involved. As the matter has arisen, I should tell you I am not on terms of intimacy with Rathborne. I dislike the man quite cordially. He got the better of me in a business deal, by means no gentleman would have used. I am the last person he would ask for help in a matter of this sort."

"That is true," Elizabeth said.

Reddish shook his head. "You are all being very hard on the baron. I have known him forever and have never received anything but the utmost kindness from him. Why, just last week he sent me a dandy green goose and has promised me another for Christmas. I wager it was common thieves who robbed me. I only hope you are right in thinking the stones were paste, Grue."

"There is one way to find out," Wyckholme said. He had the undivided attention of all his listeners. "I shall take a run over to Stop Hole Abbey and speak to the lock. Fingers Molloy runs the fencing operation there."

Grue smiled in satisfaction. He translated Wyckholme's plan to a confused Mr. Reddish. "Lord Wyckholme is offering to speak to the man who buys stolen goods."

Reddish roared like a lion. "I do not want you consorting with known criminals on my behalf, Butterworth. You will end up with a bullet in your back. What you do for your own pleasure is your concern. Your knowledge of their jargon tells me you are no stranger to the thieving fraternity, but I pray you will not undertake any dangerous enterprise for me."

"Actually I was doing it for Miss Parrish," Wyckholme replied blandly, "and to satisfy my own curiosity. I shall have a word with Tinker and Boxer while I am about it." He rose languidly from his chair. "Will you be at home later this evening, Mr. Reddish?"

"We will hardly be out frolicking with this hanging over our heads" was his ungracious reply.

Wyckholme's nostrils pinched, but he maintained an outward show of civility. "Then I shall return anon. I have a card game arranged at my club for elevenish. Charming meeting you, Mr. Grue." He bowed. "Nice to see you again, Mr. Reddish. And Miss Parrish." His eyes gazed softly at Elizabeth. "Don't worry, my dear," he said.

"What time will you come back?" she asked.

He cocked his head to one side and thought a moment while murmuring to himself. "Dinner with the countess at eight, a ride—no drive—to Stop Hole Abbey, half an hour for questioning and bribing, return to Belgrave Square. Say, ten-thirty."

"You will be careful," she said.

"Fear not. I have a guardian angel. His name is Gabriel, no relation to the archangel of the same name. He is my groom-cum-bodyguard—a bruiser I am training at Jackson's Boxing Parlor. Weighs fifteen stone. A punishing left. I also have a pistol. Until later, adieu." He made an exquisite bow and left.

"Caper-merchant!" Reddish scowled. "Canting jargon and criminals. Just what you might expect of a Butterworth."

"Just the fellow you require at this time, John," Grue said. "What do you have against him? I found him amusing."

"The very image of his uncle. An oiler. He used to oil around my Mary."

Grue put his head back and laughed. "You can hardly blame young Wyckholme for that. He was not even a gleam in his papa's eye when all that happened. Let him lend a hand. I daresay he will prove more efficacious than Bow Street. They are woefully short-staffed, you must know. And now I must be running along."

Elizabeth accompanied their guest to the door. "I like your Wyckholme," he said to her. "He will make you a better husband than Rathborne."

"Oh, indeed we are not engaged, Mr. Grue," she said, with a flush of embarrassed pleasure.

"I hardly think he is putting himself to so much trouble for your ungrateful uncle. John treats him abominably. We shall be in touch about having dinner. Good night."

Elizabeth went off to see about dinner. She and her uncle dined alone. While her uncle spoke of the lost diamonds and Rathborne, Elizabeth's thoughts wandered to Wyckholme. His calling so soon after their arrival indicated he still had some feelings for her. If only Uncle would not be so rude to him. After dinner they went to the saloon to await his return.

Wyckholme arrived promptly at ten-thirty, bearing no trace of physical hardship. Every hair was in place, his kid slippers unmarred by so much as a splatter of mud. After making his bows, he took up a seat by the grate and opened his budget.

"The Rathborne necklace has not turned up at the Abbey. Of course, it is early days yet. It may appear in a day or two. I have arranged to be notified at once if it does. It was not Tinker and Boxer who assaulted you outside the jewelry store, Mr. Reddish. They have taken the week off to try their skills at Bath. Lord Egremont is taking a large party there for Christmas."

"Very kind of you, I'm sure, Butterworth. Don't let us keep you. No doubt you have a dozen balls and drums where you are being missed."

"You are entirely welcome, Mr. Reddish, but as I mentioned earlier, I have only a deck of cards awaiting me. I have time for a glass of wine," he said, rather pointedly.

Elizabeth was quick to fill him a glass. He leaned

back comfortably and began nattering. "My mind keeps harping on the sword and pistol," he said. "Why would Rathborne send fake diamonds if he meant to steal them? Why not send the originals? You are quite convinced Grue is as innocent as he says?"

"I trust Mr. Grue implicitly," Reddish said, with a thundercloud of a look.

"But then you also trust Rathborne, if I am not mistaken?"

"He is horrid!" Elizabeth said.

"So he is," Wyckholme agreed. "In certain quarters he is called the Rat—behind his back, of course. One does not wish to incite his wrath. He has three notches in his pistol."

"You mean he has killed three men!" Elizabeth gasped. "Did you know that, Uncle?"

"I don't believe a word of it. If he did anything of the sort, he was forced into it. A duel to protect his honor."

"Honor can be restored by a less fatal wound," Wyckholme said. "A shot in the shoulder will suffice. One killing might be excused on the grounds of accident, a poor aim. Two begins to look like carelessness. When I hear of a man having killed three times, I suspect not his aim but his temper."

"You must watch out for him when he comes to town," Elizabeth said. "If he learns you are helping us, he might make you number four."

"That had occurred to me," Wyckholme replied. "He is planning to come to London, then, is he? Your notice in the journal mentioned you were remaining only a few days. I had hoped—er, thought he might be remaining in Surrey."

"His note said he would arrive on Christmas Eve day."

"Too proud to come haring after you immediately,

yet too lovelorn to wait until your return," Wyckholme suggested, with a teasing look.

"It shows a proper regard for Beth's feelings," Reddish said. "He is not trying to rush her by darting to her door the instant she arrives."

"Like some eager, unlicked cubs," Wyckholme said, smiling at Elizabeth to tell her he meant himself. "But then age cools the fires of passion. He would be but a lukewarm lover."

This was exactly the sort of talk that gave Reddish a disgust of Wyckholme. Just so had his demmed uncle dangled after his Mary. "I will thank you to keep a civil tongue in your head, sir!" he exclaimed. "There will be no passion or lovers in this house."

"One can only wonder the baron bothers to come at all." He drew out his watch and glanced at it. "Time for my game. I shall keep an eye on developments and return, sans passion, and, alas, sans love. Adieu." He bowed to Reddish, lifted an inquiring eyebrow to Elizabeth, and went out.

"I shall see you to the door," she said, following him. "You must not mind Uncle," she apologized. "He is so terribly distraught over losing the necklace."

"I enjoy his little lectures. He keeps them brief, just as I like." His casual smile faded, to be replaced by genuine concern. He seized Elizabeth's fingers and said, "About Rathborne, Miss Parrish. Would you actually be forced to accept the bounder if we cannot sort this business out?"

"He threatened to demand payment on a note of Uncle's. He contrived to buy the note from Sir Hughe Wortley. I had to give my dowry to buy it back. And now if Uncle feels he has to pay for the necklace besides, he will be forced to sell Bushmill. It would kill him, Wyckholme. Bushmill is his life. I would have very little choice in the matter." She looked at him with fear darkening her lovely blue eyes.

His hand moved to her waist. "Poor Elizabeth. We cannot allow that to happen. If you are to marry a scoundrel, he ought at least to be amusing. I have a wide range of jokes—dance fairly well, sing a little."

She looked at him, wondering just how much of this was mere whimsy and how much he meant. "I wish you would not make a joke of it," she said, twitching away from his arms.

"I am not joking, my dear. One can be serious without being sober. The necklace's not showing up at Stop Hole Abbey suggests Rathborne arranged for the theft himself. An ordinary thief would certainly have taken it there. Yet how did he know your uncle would be at the jewelry shop?"

"It is as we said: Rathborne had Uncle followed when he left the house."

"No, the word among the coves is that a pair of interlopers were loitering about Rundell and Bridges for an hour before they snaffled the necklace. The coves keep an eye on such matters. In fact, the lads were warned off twice by friends of Tinker and Boxer. The thieves were waiting, which suggests they knew your uncle would be arriving. Grue must be involved, despite his protestations."

"That is out of the question. Grue and Rathborne have been at daggers drawn for years."

"Then the thieves were not waiting for anyone in particular. They were lurking about on spec. Rathborne had nothing to do with pinching the necklace. Its theft at this time was merely coincidence extending her long arm. I keep wondering about those four days Rathborne mentioned as the time he would come to claim you. If it were I, I would not have waited so long."

"You do not have the reputation of rushing into

marriage," she said, to remind him of his lack of offering last spring.

"These things depend on circumstances—like having a guardian's permission, for instance. Rathborne obviously had your uncle's wholehearted approval. What I meant was that four days is about the time it would take to have a copy made."

Elizabeth was reluctant to drop the subject of marriage and eagerness but tried to turn her thoughts to the business at hand. "But he already had the copy made. He sent it to me."

"So he did. But if his plan was to say you or your uncle had substituted fake stones, then *you* would have required time to have copies made, if you follow me."

"Oh, how devious! He thinks of everything. I will end up married to the wretch; I feel it in my bones. He makes my flesh crawl, Wyckholme." A shudder seized her, as if to demonstrate her feelings.

"There is one sure way to thwart him. He cannot marry a married lady. We could dart to Gretna Green for a hasty marriage over the anvil. Or if that is a little too outré for you, I could visit a bishop and get a special license."

She looked at him suspiciously. "Would you really do that, Wyckholme?"

Before he replied, Reddish's gruff voice called from the saloon, "What is keeping you, Beth?"

She gave a *tsk* of annoyance. "I am coming, Uncle."

Wyckholme's lips clenched. He reached out and opened the door, then closed it with a loudish bang. "That is the sound he has been waiting for," he said.

Elizabeth pressed her fingers to her lips to suppress a giggle. "You are up to all the rigs, Wyckholme."

"If that is a compliment, I thank you. If it is a dig

that I am no better than I should be, then I am deeply offended. Now about the necklace. A pity Tinker and Boxer hadn't snaffled the thing. Then I could recover it and see who had made the copy. There are fellows at the Abbey who would know at a glance whose work it was. I could bribe the name out of them."

Elizabeth noticed how smoothly Wyckholme had redirected the course of the conversation. There was no more talk of Gretna Green or a special marriage license. "Is there no way we could recover it?" she asked. "What would the thieves have done with it?"

"Amateurs would probably not even realize it was a fake. They might try to peddle it on the street or to a jewelry shop. I can check the shops, but if they sold it to some provincial, the thing might be on its way to Land's End or Scotland by now."

Elizabeth sighed. "It was very kind of you to try to help, in any case."

"Why, you sound as though I have already failed, Miss Parrish. I shall take care of it, one way or the other."

She peered closely at him. "What do you mean?"

"I would prefer not to add to the igloo that is building between your uncle and myself by being overly rash. Why does he dislike me so? I have never done him any harm. It seems very odd, as he usually likes everyone else—even Rathborne."

"He knew your uncle at Harrow," she said.

"Ah, Uncle Harold. Yes, I see. To know him was to loathe him. I speak only of gentlemen, by the by. The ladies thought old Harry quite the thing."

"Yes, I fancy that was exactly the trouble."

"He married a duke's daughter. And an earl's. And a very well-to-do merchant's as well, I believe. Sequentially, you understand. He was not a bigamist, but only rather hard on wives. Do you know, I think I mentioned Harry to your uncle when I—"

Reddish's voice thundered from the saloon. "Is he gone yet, Beth?"

A bold grin seized Wyckholme's lips. "As well hang for a sheep as a lamb. This is what he thinks we are up to—we might as well do it."

He crushed her roughly against him and tightened his arms until her breath stopped. His lips found hers and pressed a hot kiss on them. Elizabeth knew perfectly well her duty was to be outraged, but she could not seem to summon the proper emotion. Other feelings overcame her in a tide of warm rapture as she experienced the wonder of her first kiss. It was even better than she had imagined.

The embrace was a wildly beautiful thing, intoxicating her senses with delight. He kissed her until she felt she must be glowing all over, like a gaslight on a dark night.

Then he suddenly released her. "Shame on you, Miss Parrish. I am not that sort of gentleman," he scolded, but his voice was unsteady. He uttered a light, inane laugh and slipped out the door. She huddled against the cold night air as he waved his fingers and disappeared into the darkness.

"Beth, what is the holdup?" her uncle called.

"I am coming, Uncle," she said, and went in a daze back to the saloon. She had to avert her face, for she knew it could not possibly be the same face she had taken into the hallway with her. She had changed in some deeply meaningful way. She felt she was now a real woman. "He is gone," she said.

"Good riddance. I trust he will not be returning to pester us with his nonsense."

"He will be calling tomorrow, Uncle," she announced, with womanly authority.

"Don't encourage the fellow, or you will end up with an offer."

Elizabeth swallowed her smile. "Would you like some warm milk before bed?"

"I am tempted to put a drop of wine in it. I know I shall not sleep tonight."

"I shall ask Sage to bring us both a posset. I feel a little restive myself."

She hardly gave a thought to Rathborne's skulduggery. It was thoughts of Wyckholme that kept her most pleasantly awake.

3

Mr. Grue returned to Belgrave Square the next afternoon and was there when Wyckholme arrived, which was all that enabled Elizabeth to escape the house.

"Beth is pretty busy," Reddish said when Wyckholme invited her out. "Her aunt has left a list of instructions as long as your arm. You are not forgetting the silver, Beth."

Grue laughed the pretext away. "I am sure Mrs. Mannering does not expect Miss Parrish to do the polishing herself. Let her go, John. It is a lovely day. The snow has melted. You ought to get out and enjoy the sun, too."

"It gives me a headache," Reddish said, but he at least had the grace to know he was behaving badly. "Run along then, Beth, but do not be late to dinner," he said gruffly.

Elizabeth was not tardy to snatch her bonnet and mantle and leave. "Where are we going?" she asked her companion.

"To Hyde Park, to see what we can discover about the necklace."

"To Hyde Park, in the dead of winter? No one will be there."

"He had better be! I have been to the jewelry shops." He reached in his pocket and held up the necklace. It sparkled in the sunlight, but it did not sparkle with the prismatic brilliance of real diamonds.

"You found it!" she exclaimed. "How . . . where did you get it?"

"At Aylmer's jewelry shop on Poland Street. The fellow who sold it to Aylmer was surprised to hear it was made of paste. He was asking a thousand pounds for it. He was given twenty-five. The jeweler pried out a few stones to show him the foil backing. That convinced him he had stolen a worthless bauble."

"Do you know who the man was, the one who sold it?"

"A fellow called John Smith," Wyckholme replied, with a derisive shrug. "It is usually a John Smith or a William Jones or some such generic fellow who sells stolen goods. He inherited it from his aunt. Inheriting is the usual method of acquiring hot goods. This particular Mr. Smith was a great, hulking brute, or words to that effect. The build coincided with your uncle's attacker. We will have no luck pursuing him, nor does it matter. We have the necklace."

"But it is only paste."

"Fingers Molloy will tell us who made this paste copy. He is meeting us at Hyde Park."

He assisted Elizabeth into his crested carriage with the nobleman's lozenge on the door, arranged a fur rug over her knees and hot bricks at her feet, and headed to the park.

"I daresay your uncle would not approve of my taking you to mingle with thieves. It might be best if you omit this incident from our outing when you are giving an account of it, as you will no doubt be asked to do, since you are out with the abominable Butterworth. Hyde Park in itself can hardly be construed as mischievous, even in winter."

"No indeed, but anyone with a name like Fingers

could. I hesitate to inquire how he came by such a nickname."

"I would certainly hesitate to tell you. You are much too young and innocent." Without two seconds' hesitation he added, "The name Fingers comes from his early days as a pickpocket. Best daddles in the business. He'd have your watch out of your pocket and off its chain while you were blinking. He's moved on to better things now."

"Very edifying, Wyckholme. I shan't tell Uncle a thing. It is kind of you to give up so much of your time to help me."

"Indeed it is, and you may be sure I am the sort of bounder who will expect payment in full."

"What do you mean?" she asked hopefully. That "in full" sounded interesting.

"Why, I shall expect you to call me Landon, as my friends do. Even that can hardly repay me in full for my generosity. No, I demand more than that. I must also be allowed to call you Elizabeth when we are beyond your uncle's hearing. I am not reckless enough to attempt it under his roof, even if I am Harold Butterworth's nephew."

"Is that all the payment you demand?" she asked with a moue. "Your assistance comes very cheap, Wyckholme."

"What wicked dissipation were you hoping for, Elizabeth?" he asked, sliding a glance in her direction. "You feared I might demand a lock of your hair? A tryst by moonlight? What racy notions you provincial lasses harbor under your demure round bonnets. You will seduce me yet."

"This is not a round bonnet!"

"Mea culpa. It is the coincidence of its having a round shape that misled me. But then it has a feather, which removes the odium of being a *plain* round bonnet at least."

"It is a poke bonnet!" she insisted. "Only a very low poke bonnet."

"The highest kick of fashion in Dorking, no doubt. I wonder what Rathborne sees in such a low poke bonnet. I would have thought he would favor a higher poke as being more fashionable."

"What he sees in it is me."

"We were wandering amid metaphors, my dear. Or was it metonymy, or even synecdoche? One of those horrid literary jungles, in any case. What I meant was why he chose such an innocent dove as your sweet self. I would have thought a highflier more to the wicked baron's taste."

"He called me a filly," she said, eyes flashing. "He likes a filly with spirit, so that he may have the pleasure of taming it."

"Surely you mean *her*, as we are speaking of fillies," Wyckholme said, but he did not use his customary bantering tone. He clenched his hands into fists, and his jaw squared in anger. "The old roué. Your uncle was mistaken to think he lacks passion. He has a passion for cruelty."

"I shan't marry him," she said in a quavering voice. "He cannot make me. I would rather scrub floors." She looked hopefully to see if Wyckholme had a special license to show her.

He unclenched one hand and moved it toward her, but only to squeeze her fingers. "No, no. You are a lady. Governessing is the proper punishment for ladies who are so unwise as to be penniless," he said, with a rueful smile.

They soon entered the park. The carriage stopped at the barrier, where the groom opened the door. Wyckholme alighted and assisted Elizabeth from the carriage. They walked along a path into the park. The ground was clear of snow, but soft piles of it sat like cotton batting on the shaded boughs of fir trees, lending a wintry touch.

"Fingers is to meet us by that stand of elms," he said, pointing into the near distance, where a solitary man in a fustian coat and misshapen hat was leaning against one of the trees.

The man came forward, looking all around, as if he feared a Bow Street Runner was lying in wait for him. "You got the sparklers?" he said out of the side of his mouth.

Wyckholme produced the necklace. The man stuck a loupe in his eye and examined it, stone by stone, for two minutes. Then he handed it back. "Catchpole," he said.

"You're certain?" Wyckholme asked.

"Sure as God made me ugly phiz. I'd know his work in the dark. Wasting his time on glass, is Catchpole. He can cut a facet as well as a Dutchman."

"Where would I find him?"

"Got a set of rooms in Long Acre, hasn't he? On Angel Court. Has a sign in his window and all. Can't miss him. He'll ride rusty for a stranger, though. Best tell him Fingers sent you. He'll whittle the scrap."

"I am obliged, Fingers."

Wyckholme dropped a golden coin into Fingers's palm, and Fingers disappeared behind the tree.

Wyckholme said to Elizabeth, "I shall take you home and go to visit Catchpole."

"Could I not go with you?" she asked. "We have been out for only fifteen minutes. Naturally I will not mention to Uncle that we visited Long Acre."

"I trust you will not," he said, and accompanied her back to his carriage.

The drive east along Piccadilly was pleasant. They passed many tonnish carriages, where heads turned to see whom Wyckholme was escorting. Past Charing Cross Road, the neighborhood deteriorated sharply. Wyckholme had a little difficulty discovering Angel Court, but once they were there, Catchpole's rooms were easily found. In the window of a squat and squalid old stone house was a sign advertising jewelry repairs and replacements: F. CATCHPOLE, PROP.

It was the sort of neighborhood where a carriage left with only a groom was in imminent danger of losing its team, and perhaps even its wheels and seats. The marauders came in gangs. Even as they looked about the street, a group of ragamuffins were regarding it speculatively. Wyckholme reached under the seat and drew out a pistol. He lifted it and aimed it at the young fellows.

"Wyckholme!" Elizabeth exclaimed. "Good God! You cannot shoot them for just looking!"

"This is merely to let them know what will happen if they attempt to take it for a ride." The gang took off, and Wyckholme handed the pistol to his groom before entering the house.

F. Catchpole sat at a deal table with assorted disassembled pieces of jewelry before him. His grizzled head was bent over a magnifying glass clamped to the table to allow him to use both hands on the work under the glass. He looked up and regarded them with a suspicious eye.

"What is it then?" he asked in a rough voice.

Wyckholme placed the paste necklace on the table, dropped a golden boy beside it, and said, "Fingers said you could tell me about this."

"I could," Catchpole replied, "but the fancy man I made it for gave me three of them for making it," he said, nodding at the coin, "and another two for keeping me clapper closed."

Wyckholme dropped two more coins on the counter. He put his hand over them and said, "I know who had it made. I only want to know where and when you made it for Rathborne."

"So you know that much!" A dirt-grimed but

shapely hand reached out and drew the three coins forward, along with the necklace. He stuck the necklace under his glass and nodded. "I could have done better, but he was in a rush. And working away from me shop—I don't care for that. I did the job at Rathborne Hall last week, in his lordship's own study, with a scapegallows of a fellow hanging over me shoulder the whole time, for fear I snaffled a few stones or smashed his safe. 'Twas an honest job, I figured. I saw no need for such secrecy. Rathborne owns the original. Hardly plan to steal it from hisself, eh?"

"He gave it to me pretending it was made of real diamonds!" Elizabeth exclaimed.

Catchpole shook his head. "I call that shoddy. A Smithfield bargain, I warrant."

"Just so," Wyckholme said. "About that safe, Catchpole. The original necklace was returned to it after you finished your working sessions?"

"Quick as winking. The safe could be opened by the right set of digits—and I don't mean numbers," he added, with a wicked grin, flexing his fingers. "Mind you, it'd take a proper wild rogue for the job. Rathborne had a bruiser sleeping in the study whilst I was staying there."

"I doubt he takes that precaution now that you have left," Wyckholme suggested.

Catchpole was not slow to grasp his meaning. "I don't fancy prigging anything from Rathborne. He'd suspect me straight off. An ugly customer."

"So he is. Thank you, Catchpole. I think we agree that you and I have never met?"

"You didn't give your name," Catchpole pointed out.

"An oversight on my part. Mr. Jones," he said, and shook Catchpole's hand. "I am obliged to you, Catchpole."

They returned to the carriage, which stood unmolested, waiting for them.

Elizabeth congratulated him and said, "We know now that Rathborne had this copy made up especially to con me, but how does that help us, Landon?"

He looked pleased that she had used his Christian name. "We have merely confirmed that fact, as we already knew it, or practically knew it. What we have learned is where Rathborne keeps the original."

"It would be impossible to break into his house and safe."

"Very little is impossible. It would be difficult for such law-abiding citizens as you and me. What we require is a topnotch ruffler. No ordinary prigger will do for this job."

Elizabeth looked at him blankly, as if he had cropped out into Greek. Wyckholme explained. "The canting crew—that's the criminal element—is divided into twenty-three discrete orders, from rufflers to kinching coes. Rufflers are the top lads."

"What are kinching coes?" she asked.

"Children who beg and steal to keep alive, poor blighters. What we require is the best ruffler in London, viz, Dandy Dawson."

She regarded him suspiciously. "How does it come you know these people, Wyckholme?"

"I have always found that a broad acquaintance is not only mentally stimulating but also useful. I am on terms of familiarity with archbishops and brewers, with the canting crew and dairymaids. Have you observed we are working our way from A to Z?"

"I wager you don't know any Z's."

"Oh, ye of little faith! I number more than one zany among my acquaintances. Also modistes and the prime minister. Well, his wife, at least."

"I cannot imagine what you would want with an archbishop," she said.

He turned to her and smiled blandly. "Or the prime minister's wife, come to that. She is no beauty. As to an archbishop, one never knows. . . . That special license we mentioned might be convenient one day."

Elizabeth refused to leap on the hint. "I see you are prepared for any contingency life might throw in your path."

"Nearly any contingency. I do find your uncle difficult to conciliate. Polishing the silver—that was truly scraping the bottom of the barrel for an excuse to keep you from driving out with me."

"Yes. Do you know where to find this Dandy Dawson?" Elizabeth asked, as they sped back toward the fashionable part of London. "I doubt he resides in the west end of town."

"He has a set of rooms there, also in the east and north and south ends of town. He changes his various rooms frequently, which makes things a little difficult."

"Why does he do that? Good gracious! It could take days to find him by visiting all his rooms. Why does he have so many establishments?"

"There are times when he does not want to be found. Unless he is hiding out, and I have not heard of any big job he's pulled recently, I expect he will be at Jackson's Boxing Parlor this afternoon."

"Let us go—"

"No, my pet. Don't bother rolling your gorgeous eyes at me. I have entertained you enough for one outing. You will have to make do with a forger and a ruffler. There are some places that even I will not take a lady to. Jackson's is one of them."

"Is it your plan to ask Dawson to steal the necklace from Rathborne Hall?" she asked a little later.

"Precisely. You show great promise as an accom-

113

plice. You can add one and one and get two. Dawson could get into the royal mint, if he had a mind to, but he is always careful. He'll want a rough plan of the house, with the location of the study, where the safe is."

"I can tell you that. I have been there half a dozen times. It is on the west side of the hall, about halfway down the house. The main saloon occupies thirty or forty feet—it is a majestic chamber, all done in crimson and gilt. Then there is a little sort of ladies' parlor with two Adam fireplaces. It is very nicely got up in shades of blue and white. He had it redone, probably for me. Then the study, with oak paneling and carvings by Grinling Gibbons."

"We can do without the descriptions," he said curtly. "I plan to rob the place, not buy it. One begins to wonder that you turn your nose up at such elegance. What is on the other side of the study?"

"The library. With French doors. To the outside, I mean."

"Excellent! Rathborne's reputation for a nervous trigger finger is such that Dawson will not want to do the job until Rathborne has left."

"He comes to London in four days' time."

"Yesterday it was four days' time. Now it is three. And he will be traveling for part of one day. I wager he will arrive in London the day before he calls, to visit a proper city barber. I shall ask Dawson to leave tomorrow and watch for Rathborne's departure."

"But what if Rathborne brings the real diamonds to London with him?"

"London is the last place he'd bring them. He wants folks, mostly Bow Street, to believe he sent the real diamonds to you. He won't want them in his apartment. One never knows. If you or your uncle had suspected they were fakes, you might insist on having his house searched. He would not risk putting them in a bank either. One of the clerks might recall his visit. No, I fancy they will be resting comfortably in the safe in that oak-lined study with carvings by Grinling Gibbons."

The carriage drove up to Mrs. Mannering's house on Belgrave Square and stopped. "What shall I do if Dawson does not get the necklace, Landon?" she asked in a small voice.

"You do not trust me, my dear!" he said, more shocked than offended.

"Indeed I do! But just in case you do not find Dawson, for really he seems a very mobile ruffler, or for some reason he cannot carry out the scheme, or he decides to keep the necklace for himself, or sell it back to Rathborne, or in case the diamonds are not there, or—"

Wyckholme regarded her with an expression composed of surprise and disapproval. "What a lot of 'or's! You are a regular quinquereme. Nothing will go wrong. I shall find Dawson, and he will find the necklace. The reason he is the top ruffler is that he is completely trustworthy. He would not pull any stunt on the man buying his services. And he would certainly not risk his reputation for a piddling necklace."

"It is worth ten thousand pounds! Surely that would be a great temptation for a common thief."

"Dawson is not a common thief!" he said reprovingly. "Besides, he is a friend. I once let him hide out at Wyntan Priory when the law was after him. And an excellent guest he was, too. He paid the servants such lavish tips, they are still after me to have him back. He happened to be innocent, on that one occasion. Fear not, Dawson owes me a favor."

"He will still expect to be paid a great deal of money, I daresay?" she asked uncertainly. "You know I have lent Uncle my money. I could hawk Mama's pearls or perhaps go to the loan merchants."

Wyckholme's lips moved unsteadily. "That is always one possibility, of course, but I rather think we shall save that for a last resort. I shall be privileged to be your banker, ma'am. And I do not charge cent percent. Only fifty."

She looked at him sharply. "That was a joke, Elizabeth. You may feel free to smile. Smiles, you must know, are a lady's usual payment for favors granted."

"Well, I shall certainly pay you in cash if you have to expend any money on my behalf."

"In that case I shall start keeping an account book. Let me see, now. Thirty pounds for purchase of the paste necklace."

"You said twenty-five!"

"No, no. I said the merchant on Poland Street paid twenty-five. Naturally he had to make a profit. Thirty pounds. Three golden boys to Catchpole, one to Fingers Molloy. Whether or not Dawson demands payment, I must cover his expenses. That is a trip to Rathborne Hall."

Elizabeth cleared her throat. "Would you mind if I paid you on an installment plan, Wyckholme?"

"We are very formal suddenly. How would that work, Miss Parrish? One smile a day?"

"Oh, you are too ridiculous." She laughed. "Of course I shall pay you more than smiles."

"Rash words! I shall hold you to that, Elizabeth. I expect a good deal more than smiles, I promise you," he said, with a look she could not quite trust. "And now I shall not let you kiss me good-bye, for I see your uncle is peering through the curtains like a provincial quiz."

"When shall I hear from you? About Dawson and so on."

"That depends on how soon I find him."

"You will keep in touch."

"Indeed I shall. You have no idea how I look forward to your touch." On this flirtatious remark, delivered with the noble mien of a judge and the hot eyes of a rake, he reached out and just touched her cheek, then handed her down and escorted her to the doorway, where he squeezed her fingers and said, "I enjoyed our stroll about Hyde Park."

"I shan't forget, though I feel horrid lying to Uncle."

"Lying? I would hardly call it lying. More of an omission. He is not likely to ask if you went to Long Acre, is he? No, of course not. The man has no imagination. It is at most a prevarication. A little white prevarication. You'll get used to it. Just so you do not lie to me. I believe we can put it under the heading of honor among thieves."

"I do feel like a criminal," she said.

"You'll get used to that as well. Adieu."

He pressed her fingers and left, smiling rakishly.

4

"I trust we will not be seeing young Butterworth this evening?" Reddish asked Elizabeth when she went into the saloon. "Mrs. Grue has asked us to dinner."

Given the difficult nature of his task, Elizabeth did not expect to see Wyckholme before the next day. She was happy enough to have the diversion of dining out. The Grues were privy to all their troubles. Rathborne and the necklace made up the evening's conversation.

"Such a wretched visit you are having." Mrs. Grue tsked. "We must go out for an evening while you are here. Edward has hired a box at Drury Lane. Come with us tomorrow, do."

"I cannot feel like gallivanting with all this on my mind," Reddish replied. "Take Beth out. I am sorry to see her deprived of any socializing while we are here."

"Not totally deprived," Grue said roguishly. "Lord Wyckholme has been to call a few times." He and his wife exchanged a knowing look at this prime piece of fortune.

It was settled, not wholly to Elizabeth's satisfaction, that she would accompany the Grues to Drury Lane the next evening. Her reluctance was due to a hope that Wyckholme might invite her out. By the evening, however, she was happy to have something to do, for she had still not heard from him.

Even if he was having difficulty finding Dawson, she had thought he would keep her informed. By the time the Grues arrived, she was on thorns. Why did he not call? Had he grown tired of helping her? She knew his reputation was uncertain. Were it not for his title, he would have been called a here-and-thereian.

A play was enough of a novelty for Elizabeth that it proved a welcome distraction. She enjoyed the outing as much as her perturbed mind allowed. At the intermission she went to promenade the corridors with the Grues to ogle the rest of the audience and be ogled in turn. Some acquaintances from last spring's Season recognized her and suggested future engagements. Her visit was of such short duration and her immediate present so troubled that nothing definite was arranged. The warning bell for the recommencement of the play sounded, and the audience began to filter back to the boxes.

Elizabeth glanced along the corridor and saw Wyckholme. He was looking directly at her. Her first instinctive surge of joy was soon overlaid with annoyance. He might have invited her to accompany him! When he caught her eye, he gave one worried look and quickly turned away to speak to his companion, a pretty young lady. He did not even nod. She might as well have been a stranger. Her annoyance congealed to anger.

"Why, there is young Wyckholme!" Grue exclaimed, thinking Elizabeth would be thrilled. He called to Wyckholme and began hastening the ladies toward him.

"Good evening, sir. Miss Parrish," Wyckholme said stiffly, and immediately walked off. He did not even wait to be presented to Mrs. Grue. Elizabeth's cheeks flamed with humiliation.

Grue said in confusion, "I daresay Wyckholme had arranged this outing with his friends before he knew you were in town, Miss Parrish. It was gauche of me to go bothering him."

"She is not nearly so pretty as you, Elizabeth," Mrs. Grue said supportively, peering at the lady with Wyckholme.

It hardly needs saying that the latter part of the drama onstage was virtually ignored by Elizabeth. She had recognized the spoiled beauty with Wyckholme as Lady Violet Coltrane, the daughter of a marquess. Elizabeth did not recognize the other two couples who made up the party, but they looked fashionable. Why had Wyckholme been so cold to her? If he had made the arrangement for this outing before her arrival, he might have told her, written a note if he could not call. He knew how worried she was. That he was out enjoying himself while she was in the worst pickle of her life was not only humiliating, it was downright dangerous. For if Wyckholme was not going to rescue her, she had to get busy and rescue herself.

She broached the subject with her uncle as soon as she returned from the play. "What are we going to do about Rathborne, Uncle?" she asked.

"If worse comes to worst, you will just have to marry him, Beth. I know he is not the man you would have chosen, but love will come in time. He is an excellent parti. You will be Lady Rathborne, and living so close to Bushmill. Why, I will not be losing a niece; I will be gaining a nevvie."

"I will not marry him," she said grimly.

"I daresay we worry for nothing. Very likely the necklace Rathborne sent you was a copy, and we will all enjoy a good laugh when he hears how we have been worrying. It would be an excellent thing if you would have him. It would keep the likes of Butterworth away. I cannot care for the simpering fellow. Only one more day and Rathborne will be here. We shall all return home to celebrate Christmas in the country."

One more day. It was this troublesome phrase that Elizabeth took to bed with her. She thought wistfully of the Christmas festivities she was missing at home. They had made no effort to decorate Aunt Martha's house for the season. The rooms were not laden with the aroma of cinnamon and plum pudding. No carolers would stop at the door to sing to them.

But that was the least of her worries. She tried to think of a plan to rescue herself but had little success. She knew that F. Catchpole had made the copy of the necklace for Rathborne, but would he go on the stand and say so in court, knowing what an ugly customer Rathborne was? Even if he did, would the court believe Rathborne had sent her the copy if he swore he had sent the original? If she got the copy from Wyckholme, that would prove at least that Rathborne did not have it. How could he account for not having it? Would the fact that it was in her possession not prove her innocence? Or would it only further indict her? Rathborne could say she had had a second copy made, since he had waited four days to come to London. The court would want to know how she came to be acquainted with F. Catchpole. In her estimation Wyckholme had sunk so low that she could not count on his admitting any part in her doings. These wisps of worry chased each other around her brain until dawn, when she finally fell into a troubled sleep.

Everything seemed worse in the dark, alone. The morning brought a more reasonable outlook. For one thing the leaden sky promised snow, which might prevent Rathborne from coming to London. She remained at home in the morning, hoping for a call from Wyckholme. When he did not come, she sent a note off to his house asking him to call that afternoon. She declined a shopping trip with Mrs. Grue to be at home when he came. And still he did not come. Several hours later she received a brief note from him.

Dear Elizabeth: Fear not, D. has been found and dispatched to his destination. I expect to hear from him soon. It is best, for obvious reasons, that we not meet. I shall call when I recover the item. Your servant, W.

She puzzled over this vague document, wondering at his elliptical way of writing. D. was obviously Dawson. "His destination" was Rathborne Hall. "The item" could only be the necklace—but why did he not say so? It soon darted into her head that Lady Violet had sat by his side as he wrote the note. He did not want her to know what he was doing.

Elizabeth was relieved to hear that Dawson was on his way to Rathborne Hall, but she puzzled long over that curious "It is best, for obvious reasons, that we not meet." What were these reasons, so obvious to him and so obscure to her, that they not meet? Was it a reference to her uncle's intransigence? They could have arranged to meet outside the house, in a shop on Bond Street, for instance. To fool Uncle would require only one more lie, and Wyckholme did not jibe at that. Indeed, he had urged her to lie to her uncle. That was surely the mark of a dissolute man.

Was he betrothed to Lady Violet? It was odd that no one, including him, had mentioned it. Such a prime piece of gossip would have been related by one of the friends she had met last night at the play. He had not hesitated to drive out with her the day before yesterday. He could hardly hope to keep such a public outing as that from Lady Violet. Yet he had all but cut her last night, when he was with the lady.

"I shall call when I recover the item," he wrote confidently. Not "if I recover" it, but "when." Was that a lie to appease her? She dashed off another note to Wyckholme, not bothering with any evasions, but calling a necklace a necklace.

"If you cannot come, please send the paste copy of the necklace today. I shall repay you the thirty pounds." She felt she must have something to return to Rathborne when he called on the morrow, even if it was only a set of paste stones.

The reply, delivered within the hour, was enough to make her blood run cold.

Dear Elizabeth: I don't have the item you request. Sorry. But you must not worry. I am handling everything, as I <u>promised</u>. Sincerely, Landon.

He had underscored the "promised," but what she kept reading and rereading was the troublesome sentence, "I don't have the item you request." What had he done with it? It was her only hope of salvation. She had quite settled that she would have Bow Street drag F. Catchpole into court to testify that he had made that copy for Rathborne. Without the evidence she hadn't a leg to stand on. It was very little consolation that her "servant, W." had become hers "sincerely, Landon."

She realized, as she fretted in solitude (her uncle was out arranging the mortgage business that afternoon), that Wyckholme's whole attitude to this affair had been much too cavalier to denote any serious intention. It was merely a game for him. He consorted with known felons of every degree. Why had she trusted her fate to such a worthless fribble? She had done it in the hope that he would have pity on a damsel in distress and fall in love with her. That was the top and bottom of it. As if Wyckholme would be caught by such a simple trick. He could not even spare half an hour of his day to come in person but only dashed off those heartless notes. She loathed him, and herself for trusting him.

The sky grew darker as the day progressed, but the snow held off. Before she went to bed that night, she had one more trouble placed in her dish. The footman smuggled a note into her hands with a whisper that it was "private," by which she understood the sender had requested that her uncle not know about it. This sounded like the work of Wyckholme, and her heart raced in excitement. In her joy she even found a reason for Wyckholme's not coming and for his strangely vague notes. He had stayed away to avoid antagonizing her uncle, and he had written vaguely lest the notes fall into her uncle's hands.

This note, obviously, was of a completely different character. Her hopes soon painted it in the rosy hues of a billet-doux. She took it to her bedroom and opened it with trembling fingers. The handwriting was not Wyckholme's. She glanced to the ending to see who had written it and saw "Ed. Grue." Her eyes raced back to the beginning.

"Dear Miss Parrish: Please forgive my writing to you in this clandestine manner, but I thought you might not wish to distress your uncle. You can break the news to him more gently. I met Ld. Wyckholme on New Bond Street this afternoon with the same party that had accompanied him to Drury Lane. One of the gentlemen was a Mr. Tom Gripply. Gripply, as you are aware, is Rathborne's family name. I inquired of the young gentleman if he was related to Rathborne. He admitted he is a nephew. This may mean nothing, but I am concerned that Ld. Wyckholme is so close to him. My fear, of course, is that Wyckholme is in league with Rathborne. I am sorry to trouble you further at this time. It may all mean nothing, but I thought it proper to advise you. You will know better than I how the situation stands between you and Wyckholme. If there is anything I can do, you have only to ask. Your sincere friend, Ed. Grue."

Elizabeth read the letter and sank onto her bed. Wyckholme was not only not helping her, he was in league with the hateful Rathborne. Now she understood why he had written in that obscure way. He did not want to commit to paper anything she could produce in court. Dandy Dawson was not on his way to Rathborne Hall to steal the diamonds. It was all a ruse to keep her from doing anything to help herself. She did not even have a set of paste stones to give Rathborne when he called.

Rathborne would say he sent the original necklace, valued at ten thousand pounds. Her uncle would insist on paying him for it. Uncle would have to sell Bushmill Manor. Her dowry would be gone, and if she did not marry Rathborne, she and Uncle would be cast into the streets.

A glance at her watch told her it was now ten o'clock. It was pitch-black outside. She had no idea what she could do to save herself. And tomorrow. Rathborne would come. She felt she should warn her uncle that matters had just become even more complicated. But what was the point? There was nothing he could do. There was no point in both of them lying awake, worrying.

In the morning the snow had finally begun to fall. It came in large, soft flakes that floated past the window and starred the dry grass. Elizabeth made a fresh toilette. She chose her most unattractive gown and dressed her hair in a spinster's bun in an effort to look ugly enough to turn Rathborne from his vile scheme. Her face was pale, and there were purple smudges under her eyes from a lack of sleep. Her nerves were stretched taut as piano wires. Almost worse than having to marry Rathborne was the realization of Wyckholme's treachery.

Her uncle cast a frowning look at Elizabeth when he joined her at the breakfast table. "You might fix yourself up a little before Rathborne arrives, Beth," he suggested. "You look as if you were attending a wake, not an engagement. Have you given any more thought to having Rathborne?"

"I suppose I must," she said, and drew a deep sigh.

"Good! I am glad to hear you have come to your senses. Now you must not worry about the necklace. I have been thinking it over, and I am certain Rathborne would never send real diamonds by a footman. He will bring the original with him, never fear."

Elizabeth just nodded. It seemed the ultimate irony that after being forced into marrying Rathborne, she would never wear the necklace that was the cause of it all. How could he present it to her after their marriage when he was claiming it had been stolen? There was only one minute of her future marriage she anticipated with any pleasure, and that was finding the necklace, wherever Rathborne had hidden it, and flinging it in his face. Or perhaps she would really steal it and run away. He could not report it stolen again.

"Ah, good! I see you are smiling now," her uncle said happily. "I knew you would come to your senses. Why do you not peruse Martha's fashion magazines while I attend to business? Rathborne will want to deck you out in style."

The whole day yawned before her. She did not expect to see Rathborne before afternoon, as he had to drive from Surrey, weather permitting. She went to her bedroom to try to plan some means of escape. She kept her door open to hear the knocker if anyone called that morning. Her thoughts kept returning to Wyckholme and his part in this dastardly affair. At eleven o'clock the rattle of the door knocker roused her from her sad reveries. She thought it might be Mr. Grue and wanted to thank him. She ran into the hall and peered over the banister.

The arrogant voice from the hall was Lord Rathborne's, and her blood chilled in her veins. She heard the stamping of feet to knock off the snow. Mr. Reddish heard the knocker and went rushing forth to welcome his caller.

"Lord Rathborne! Come in, come in. Beth is eager to see you. The poor girl is going into a decline with waiting."

"Indeed!" was Rathborne's sneering reply. "Had I known of her eagerness, I would have been here sooner. My blood mare, Jezebel, was foaling, and I could not leave the Hall. She had a fine colt yesterday."

He had delayed coming to claim his prize because of a horse! "Pity it wasn't a filly," Elizabeth muttered. "You would have enjoyed breaking her."

Her uncle led Rathborne into the saloon. Elizabeth knew she would have to face her tormentor soon, but she put it off as long as she could. When the door knocker sounded again, she raced once more to the banister. It was Mr. Grue who was shown in. He was accompanied by Wyckholme. Elizabeth's glum forebodings were overcome by curiosity. What charade had Wyckholme and Rathborne cooked up between them? She ran downstairs just as Wyckholme was brushing the snow off his shoulders and handing the butler his curled beaver and cane.

Wyckholme looked to the staircase and gazed at her, with a mischievous smile curving his lips. Then he walked forward to meet her and handed her a small packet. "The necklace," he said. "Just in the nick of time. Your suitor is eager. I did not expect him until afternoon."

They followed Mr. Grue into the saloon. Rathborne rose and bowed formally to Elizabeth. His cold eyes raked her from head to toe, displaying no pleasure but a sort of grim satisfaction. That look said it amused him that Elizabeth had rigged herself out in this guise to spite him.

"Charming, as usual," he said. "Your uncle has just given me the joyful news, my dear."

"I am afraid my uncle is mistaken, Lord Rathborne," she replied. "I have changed my mind—a lady's privilege. Of course, I must return your generous gift." She handed him the packet Wyckholme had given her and watched closely, like everyone else in the room, while he opened it.

Rathborne's face was white. His nostrils pinched in fury as he lifted out the necklace. "What is this?" he exclaimed. "This is not the necklace I sent you. It is paste."

Elizabeth's eyes flew to Wyckholme, who smiled and winked.

Mr. Reddish cleared his throat and said, "It is the necklace you sent to Beth, milord. We did think it was paste. That is to say, Mr. Grue here is quite an expert on gems—"

"I sent the Rathborne necklace. What trick is this?" Rathborne demanded. "I shall call Bow Street at once."

"Take another look, milord," Wyckholme suggested. "You have scarcely glanced at it, and the light here is dim. Take it to the window. I think you will find it is the original."

Rathborne directed a blighting stare at Wyckholme but strode to the window and examined the necklace more closely. He was too cagey to display his astonishment at what he held in his hands. It was his necklace! How the devil had Miss Parrish got hold of it? He turned a cold, questioning eye to Wyckholme.

"So it is," he said. Then he turned to Reddish. "My apologies, sir. In the agitation of the moment, with your niece's refusal ringing in my ears, I must have lost my head." Then he turned to Elizabeth with a scathing look and continued. "I usually recognize a diamond of the first water when I see it, but occasionally even I am mistaken."

"Your confusion is perfectly understandable," Wyckholme said. "You saw what you expected to see, milord."

Mr. Reddish was not at all happy with this unexpected outcome. "But you said you would have him, Beth. I have already told Lord Rathborne. This is deuced awkward, I must say. What reason can you have for changing your mind?"

"I am afraid that is my fault," Wyckholme said. "As Elizabeth had definitely rejected Lord Rathborne's offer, I offered for her myself, and she accepted. Sorry, Rathborne. Blame it on the hot blood of youth." His eyes just flickered over Rathborne's silver temples.

"My congratulations, sir," Rathborne said, with a civil bow. "I am sure you two youngsters will deal famously. I begin to see I did not fully appreciate Miss Parrish's . . . nature. We shall have a drink later, Wyckholme, and you will tell me all about it. I am curious to learn how you got the better of me."

It was at the necklace that he glanced, not his lost bride.

"It will be my pleasure, Rathborne. Shall we say Brookes's Club, at about four this afternoon?"

"I shall be there. Good day, Mr. Reddish. Elizabeth. And may I take this opportunity to wish you all a Merry Christmas." He bowed to the group and left.

Mr. Reddish was far from happy with this new turn of events. He said to Beth, "Why the deuce did you tell me you would have Rathborne if you had already accepted Butterworth?"

"That is my fault," Wyckholme said. "A lover's spat, but all is well now."

"How did you manage to recover the necklace, Beth?" was her uncle's next question.

"Wyckholme . . . found it," she said, looking to him for elucidation.

"And it was the original all along," Reddish said, rubbing his ear in confusion. "You were mistaken about that, Edward. I am a little surprised that Rathborne sent it by footman, but then he would not want to give Beth a set of paste stones."

Mr. Grue was beginning to suspect just where Wyckholme had "found" the original and was very curious to hear the whole story. "Rathborne did not send the original, John," he said. "How did you get hold of it, Wyckholme?"

Wyckholme's face underwent a quick change of expressions, from confusion to guilt to rapid recovery in an uneasy smile. "I borrowed it?" he said, in an unnaturally high voice, almost making the assertion a question.

"It was at Rathborne Hall, was it not?" Grue persisted.

"Well, yes. It was."

"And Rathborne was there himself until this morning."

"No, actually he left yesterday afternoon. I ... er ... borrowed the necklace from his butler. Explained the situation here, left the copy in its place, knowing how sorry Rathborne would be to have caused a moment's concern over the misunderstanding."

"That copy in his safe will be a surprise when Rathborne returns to Surrey," Grue murmured, chewing back a smile.

"That was well done of you, Butterworth," Reddish said reluctantly. "You were stealing Rathborne's fiancée behind his back, but like a gentleman you gave him every opportunity to fight for Beth, fair and square—which is more than your uncle ever did. It was kind of you to bring the necklace to London for him. Of course, Rathborne sent the copy in error. No one but an expert could tell the difference. I do feel sorry for poor Rathborne. This will be a great disappointment for him."

"He has Jezebel's new colt to console him," Elizabeth said.

"He would have preferred a filly, no doubt," Wyckholme said, with a smile at Elizabeth.

"I daresay you young lovebirds would like to be alone," Reddish said. "No harm in it now that they are engaged—without Wyckholme's having asked my permission, I might add."

"Thank you, Uncle," Elizabeth said, and gave him a hug.

He whispered in her ear. "You need not have the fellow, Beth. It made a good excuse to turn Rathborne off without hurting his feelings unduly, but we shan't announce the wedding yet. No doubt young Butterworth will do something to put himself beyond the pale of polite society before long if we are a little patient. That will be our chance to turn him off."

Mr. Grue got a hand on his arm and led him to

131

the study. Reddish's complaints trailed behind him as they went. "Pretty forward of Butterworth to go speaking to Rathborne's butler behind his back. And how does it come he had the copy? He did not tell us that. I wager he hired those ruffians who stole it. I have every confidence Beth will turn him off e'er long."

Wyckholme took Elizabeth's hand and led her to the sofa. "It is nice to be appreciated. Do you share this intention of turning me off?"

"Only if you did not mean that offer?" she said, her tone making it a question.

"Saving Rathborne's feelings was not my top priority. I doubt he has any."

"In that case I shall dart down to the journals this very day to put in notices of our engagement. Will Lady Violet be angry with me?"

"I trust not. Engaged ladies are seldom angry. Lady Violet is engaged to my younger brother, who is on his way home from the Peninsula. I daresay you know Gripply is Rathborne's nephew?"

"Yes, Mr. Grue told me."

"When I learned Gripply was seeing Lady Violet's friend, I arranged a few outings to see if he knew anything about his uncle's doings. It was from Gripply I learned that Rathborne was expected in London last night."

All this came as a great relief to Elizabeth, but she still had a few questions. "Why did you not call, and why did you write those strange notes, Landon?"

"For the same reason I barely nodded to you at the play. I was uncertain whether Gripply was working with his uncle. If it was the case, then I did not want him to suspect my involvement in the matter. The reason for my strange notes was that Gripply might have intercepted them. He is Rathborne's nephew, after all. I could not reveal that Dawson was on his way to nab the sparklers. I thought I explained—"

"You said, 'for obvious reasons.' The reason was far from being obvious to me."

"Now you understand, and I am ready for you to throw yourself on my bosom and offer me anything I wish in the way of a reward, like a well-reared young heroine." He took her hand and gently massaged her fingers.

She glanced at him from the corner of her eyes. "I cannot imagine what you mean, Landon."

"This younger generation is sadly lacking in imagination. To say nothing of toilette. Why the deuce have your got your nice hair scraped back like a washerwoman's, Liz?"

"I wanted to give Rathborne a disgust of me."

"I rather think that gown you are wearing would have been sufficient. No need to overdo it. I shall expect my lily to be fully gilded when I take her to a party this evening."

"Are we going to a party? How lovely! Where is it?"

"Chez moi. I believe in doing our engagement up in the highest style, as I have waited so long to claim you. I tried to ask your uncle's permission at the end of the Season. He called me a here-and-thereian. I mean to say! There are over half a million words in the English language. Did he have to choose such a mediocre one? I daresay it was my innocent mention of Uncle Harry's having known him at Harrow that did the mischief."

"Your Uncle Harry tried to steal Mary from him. Mary was his wife, though not at that time. About that party . . ."

"A small family party. We shall feast on champagne and other wicked aphrodisiacs, and when you have got me foxed, you may embrace me ardently beneath the mistletoe."

"If the snow lets up, we shall leave for Bushmill Manor in the morning to celebrate Christmas at home. But are you quite sure you want to marry me, Landon? I mean, you have not even kissed me since we became engaged," she said, adopting a moue.

"My dear, I take leave to tell you, you are a baggage. You have no sense of propriety. What a delightful surprise."

On this ambiguous compliment he pulled her into his arms for a long kiss that fulfilled all her daydreams, and he added a few touches she had not even dreamed of. When she lifted her head and glanced out the window, she saw the snow was still falling, no doubt making the country roads impassable.

"It looks as if we might not make it home to Bushmill for Christmas," she said.

"No matter, we will be home in London instead. Home is where the heart is. And as I have sunk into maudlin sentiment, let me add, no place is home without you, my dear baggage."

"What a lovely Christmas present," she said, and kissed him again.

LOVE
À LA CARTE

by
Joan Smith

1

"The wretch! The odious wretch!" Miss Leigh exclaimed, from behind the pages of the latest journal.

"Another article by Monsieur Bongoût?" her chaperon inquired. Lady Violet Ashden, spinster daughter of the late Lord Exmoor and Miss Leigh's chaperon, set aside her embroidery. "It is really too bad of Bongoût. What had he to say of La Maison Dessus this time?" she asked eagerly.

"He has made it his winter's sport to ruin me." Miss Leigh adjusted the offending journal to read aloud the food critic's latest attack on her dining establishment.

"He says, 'It is a little-known fact that in France in the seventeenth century, Louis the Thirteenth prepared his own food, not because he enjoyed cooking, but because he feared being poisoned. I would recommend that anyone foolhardy enough to dine chez La Maison Dessus do likewise—for the same reason. Last evening I tempted fate and dined once more at The House Above, to see if it was really as bad as former visits indicated. My column will be brief today, for I am still recovering from an attack of acute indigestion. Briefly, then, the fowl was foul, the *biftek* burned, the vegetables varnished, and the dessert a disaster.' Ignoramus! The carrots were not varnished!" Miss Leigh snorted. "They were glazed. Has the great Monsieur Bongoût never tasted glazed carrots before? And he calls himself a connoisseur of haute cuisine."

"They do taste varnished, though, the way Pierre does them," Lady Violet said. "They should be only lightly sautéed in butter with a little sugar, after boiling. He uses too much sugar and burns it so that it looks like varnish. And tastes like it."

"I know," Miss Leigh said. Setting aside the journal, she propped her head on her hands to consider her disastrous state.

Every penny of her ten-thousand dowry had gone into La Maison Dessus, so-called because it was situated above a set of offices. She had thought the location, near Drury Lane, would draw the theatergoers. She had refashioned the dreary rooms into a charming dining room, with fine mahogany tables and chairs, the best china and cutlery (though not sterling silver), expensive carpets and wall hangings, and had a standing order for fresh flowers every second day. The kitchen was equally expensive, featuring a roasting range with spits and a copper hood to direct the fumes to the chimney flue, a cast-iron oven, a Bodley range for boiling water and vegetables, and a great many other aids to haute cuisine.

Miss Leigh was not so foolish as to have expended her time and money without having an excellent chef lined up. Indeed, it was chef Pierre Picard who had put these lavish ideas into her head. She had dined sumptuously on his cuisine for two weeks while visiting her aunt, Mrs. Thatcher, at Bath. Mrs. Thatcher was a well-known gourmet, famous for her dinners even before she had discovered Pierre.

Cybele, Miss Leigh, had been visiting her aunt to recover from the trauma of her papa's death. Mrs. Thatcher had mentioned that if she were younger, she would take Pierre to London and set him up in a stylish dining establishment to make her fortune.

"You would be surprised how much money there is in it," she had told Cybele. "The trend began in France after the revolution, when the patrons of the great chefs lost their heads. After the trouble was over, the chefs had no one to hire them, so they opened their own kitchens and became famous in their own right. Pierre worked in one of them, which is where he learned his skills."

"But would it be proper for a lady to run a dining room?" Cybele had asked.

"I see no harm in it. A dining room is not a gaming hell, after all. It could be done anonymously. Naturally you could not call it Miss Leigh's Table, or anything of that sort. I am sure there is a fortune in it, but alas I am too old. I must be near the baths. It might be a project to lift you out of the doldrums, Cybele. You continue looking very peaked, and your papa has been dead for ten months now. It is time you went up to London."

The idea had seemed too outré at first, but as Cybele thought about it, it began to seem less strange. Ladies were writing books on cookery. Why not go the next step and open a dining room? Her aunt, Lady Violet Ashden, had invited her to London. Violet thought the dining room a fine idea, though she seemed to think of it as a sort of joke on society rather than a business enterprise. She was a merry soul who could find amusement in anything. Her old gray eyes sparkled, her gray hair bounced when she laughed, and her bulging stomach bounced in time with it.

"It would be vastly amusing," she said several times. "And we could dine out without expense when we go to the theater."

Pierre Picard had been consulted. He had rushed off to London and found the location, above the of-

fices near Drury Lane. It was Pierre who had over-
seen the fitting up of the kitchen, but Cybele and
Lady Violet had arranged the actual dining area.

Cybele had felt such a thrill when she entered the
dining room on its opening night. It was in autumn,
at the beginning of the Little Season, when the the-
aters had just reopened. Everything looked exactly
as she had planned. Crystal sparkled in the flickering lamplight; perfume from the expensive hothouse
flowers filled the air; the ton came and uttered ap-
preciative sounds. The wine, chosen by Pierre, was
excellent. Then the dinner had arrived, and Cybele
realized she was faced with disaster. Pierre was a
wretched cook! How was it possible?

Beef, which should have been pink and juicy, was
dark, dry, and stringy. Roast pork, which should
have been white and tender, was as red as a rose
beneath its charred exterior. Sauces were lumpy or
runny or a gelatinous mass. The desserts were
equally disastrous. The whipped cream was runny
and reeking of an excess of vanilla; cakes were dry
and hard. And Monsieur Bongoût was there to
write it all down—and bruit her shame to the far-
thest corners of the city.

"It must be the new stoves," Cybele announced.

Pierre was called to Half Moon Street to give an
account of his performance. He sat slumped in a
chair, his dark head bowed and his swarthy face
pale.

"I sorry, misses. Was no good. I cannot do it. Is
too much food. Is too many peoples."

"But you have plenty of help in the kitchen,"
Cybele reminded him. Every one of them was eating up her money.

Pierre shrugged his narrow shoulders in Gallic
confusion. "Is no good. They not cooks. They dis-
robe the vege . . . *pommes de terre*. I need my Nan-
see."

"Then get it, whatever it is," Cybele exclaimed.

"She no come. She stay with Madame Thatcher at Bath. She is broke my heart. She say she will no more marry with me."

"*She?* Good God! You mean Nancy Otis, Mrs. Thatcher's housekeeper?"

"But yes. My Nan-see. She always helping me at Bath. She is making the sauces and fixing the stoves. Is no good without Nan-see."

"I shall write to Mrs. Thatcher this very night," Cybele said, though she was by no means sure her aunt would part with this treasure. Nancy had been with her for ten years.

"Is no good," Pierre said wearily. "We have the grand fights. She not wanting me to come to London. I am thinking I will be the grand success, like Papa, Lucky Pierre. Then she comes. But no, I am on-lucky Pierre, me."

Nancy had been appealed to and blankly refused to leave Bath. If Pierre wanted to marry her, he must return to Bath. New assistants had been hired, new, simpler dishes tried, but to no avail. And all the time the money continued flowing out of Cybele's bank account. Monsieur Bongoût seemed to take a fiendish delight in reporting the debacle in his column.

As fall drew to a close and winter yawned before her, Cybele became desperate. The former crowds had dwindled to a trickle, but Monsieur Bongoût kept returning. What would she do if she lost her whole investment? She would be virtually penniless. She would have to go home to Seven Oaks and become her elder brother's pensioner, or become the permanent companion of one of her aging aunts. Neither future appealed to her in the least. It was all Monsieur Bongoût's fault, or half of it, at least, and she didn't even know who he was, for of course he did not write under his own name.

"If I could find out who this Bongoût is, I would try to bribe him to write a good review," she said to her aunt.

"There is no point trying to bribe Sinden," Lady Violet replied.

Cybele stared in astonishment. "Sinden? *Lord* Sinden? What makes you think *he* is Monsieur Bongoût?"

"He must be Monsieur Bongoût. Sinden is full of pranks. I adore him. Did you not notice he was at the restaurant on the five evenings before Bongoût's column appeared? No one else has been there five times, except us. And I must say, Cybele, I do not think my poor digestion can take another attack."

"Sinden?" Cybele said again, in disbelief. She had taken the notion that Lord Sinden continued going to La Maison Dessus only because she was so frequently there. She thought he had a tendre for her, although he showed it in a very odd way, with satirical comments. And all the time he was out to destroy her! "Surely he cannot be Bongoût."

"He has a very nice palate," Lady Violet said, smiling in memory of the tasty meals she had enjoyed at his table. "His was the first English table to introduce a turkey stuffed with truffles in the French style. A little rich for my taste, but interesting. And his chef, Drouin, is every bit as good as Carème. Mind you, I think Carème does a better *pièce montée* for the conclusion of the banquet. I have heard that Sinden goes into the kitchen himself when he does not have company, but I daresay it is all a canard. I cannot see Sinden in a kitchen."

Cybele sat, fuming. How had she thought that hateful Lord Sinden liked her? He didn't like anyone. His chiseled face wore a perpetual sneer, and she sneered right back at him, which appeared to be his notion of flirtation, as she was one of the few ladies he honored with a dance at the balls.

"How dare he be so thin when he is nothing else but a glutton, with his truffle-stuffed turkey," she said. "I am quite sure Bongoût is the little fat man who has been at the dining room half a dozen times."

"No, dear, that is Harry Beecham. He is a minor actor at Drury Lane. He goes for the convenience of the location, and of course, the wine. You must have noticed—two bottles a night. He hardly touches the food."

"He is an actor! And here I have been smiling my head off at him, trying to put him in a good humor so he will write well of us."

"You had best direct your smiles at Lord Sinden instead," Lady Violet suggested archly.

Cybele just shook her head. "No, I do not care for him in the least. He is much too clever and satirical for me."

"He is an excellent parti," her aunt said. "There seems to be something in him the ladies like. He is very much sought after. I have thought, from time to time, he had some interest in you. You know that way he has of looking out of the corner of his eye. It is only your lack of encouragement that catches his interest, very likely," she said, with no awareness of giving offense.

Cybele did not think herself a beauty, but she was not so utterly plain that she had never piqued a gentleman's interest before. She was a little taller and leaner than fashion decreed that year. In fact, at home, where no verbal holds were barred, the word "ladder" was commonly used to describe her. Ladders could wear their gowns with a certain flair, however, and Cybele was decidedly elegant. When she had reached one and twenty last year without accepting an offer, she began pulling her chestnut hair into a Grecian knot. This simple style was flattering to her classical features.

"If Sinden is at Lady Fulham's rout party this evening, Cybele, you should be nice to him," Lady Violet suggested.

"I can hardly ask him to give the dining room a good review. He would know that I own it."

"I doubt it would ever cross his mind. He would not suspect a lady of such a thing. There is no denying it is a little strange."

"Then what would be the point of being nice to him?"

"Well, my dear, when the dining room is forced to close, you will be looking about for a husband," Lady Violet said, with a coy smile.

"The dining room will not close!"

"Oh, my dear, you take it too seriously." Her aunt laughed. "It was great fun while it lasted. I admire your courage in flouting society, but now it is time to be getting on with the serious business of nabbing a husband. Of course, Sinden might be looking for some lady with a bit of a fortune," she added, and actually allowed a frown to crease her brow. "Not that he needs it, but you know how these toplofty gentlemen are."

"I won't let it close," Cybele said firmly, and went to the study to examine her accounts.

A close perusal of the long column of figures told her she could hold on until the end of January. She would advertise for a new chef—again. This procedure was carried out at regular intervals. Three new chefs had been hired and released. They were brought in as assistants to Pierre, but the cuisine only became worse, if that was possible. The good chefs preferred the relative sinecure of working in a noble household, where their duties were less strenuous. She would write once more to Nancy

Otis as well. Perhaps if she wrote of Pierre's unhappiness, of his pining for her, she would come.

And if she did not, disaster was staring Cybele in the face. Aunt Violet was right. It was time to begin thinking about life after La Maison Dessus, and after the loss of her fortune. What gentleman would have a dowerless bride without even any claim to real beauty? Certainly not an out-and-outer like Lord Sinden. But she would scan the partis at Lady Fulham's rout this evening for a widower or elderly bachelor who was not too nice in his requirements.

She sat on at the desk, shoulders slumped in despondency, thinking of her future—and the past. She had had such glorious visions of her dining room being the talk of London. Once it was a culinary star, she thought she might acknowledge who was the genius behind it. Society would not be severe on a lady undertaking a successful business venture. And when the fortune began to roll in, she would buy a mansion on Berkeley Square, and a handsome coach, beautiful gowns. It was all folly and vanity. She had wanted to set the Town on its ear.

She had been a fool to think she could make a fortune on a dining room. Her brother, Lawrence, knew nothing of the scheme. When she reached her twenty-first birthday, her dowry had come under her own control. Lawrence would want to know what had become of it if she came home penniless. For the rest of her life, she would have to listen to his lectures and complaints. It was unthinkable. She must begin to line up a potential husband, in case La Maison Dessus failed.

To this end she took particular pains with her toilette for Lady Fulham's rout that evening. She abandoned her Grecian knot and had her aunt Violet's woman dress her hair in a more festive style, with curls over her ears, held back by pearl combs. In lieu of her usual plain silk shawl, she borrowed a livelier one in a flowered pattern to brighten up her bronze gown and wore a set of peridots at her throat to add to her color. All these enhancements ill-suited her severe face and manner. Her gray eyes refused to smile; they mocked.

Her small court of beaux were not slow in coming forward to greet her upon her arrival at the rout party. Sir Leonard Falkaner, a baronet, complimented her on her new hairstyle when he stood up with her for the opening minuet. He was a gouty bachelor of forty-five years. He would do her no good; he was dangling after her dowry. Mr. Dorman, her second partner, was a more likely candidate for marriage. His late wife had left him a profitable dairy farm in Sussex, and three daughters, the eldest just two years younger than Cybele. Mr. Dorman also admired her new hairdo.

During the second set Cybele became aware of Lord Sinden, lurking just inside the doorway. He did not deign to ask any of the unaccompanied ladies to stand up with him. He often just stood, looking through his quizzing glass at the girls with a pained expression on his face, as if they were a particularly ungainly herd of cattle at an auction. Suspecting now that he was the hated Monsieur Bongoût, Cybele found her eyes turning to look at him. He looked bored and disdainful, as usual. She doubted that he was admiring the new hairdo.

Nor was he. It was Cybele's classical restraint that had first brought her to Lord Sinden's attention. Her aloof charms stood out amid the fulsome blondes, with their simpering smiles. He was indeed intrigued by her lack of attention to himself as well. He sensed that here was a woman cut in his own mold, a little out of the ordinary. She did not fawn or flatter. She merely tolerated the attentions of those who sought her out. He had recently begun to feel, however, that she might have recognized a soul mate by now and thawed a little toward him.

Well, it seemed she was thawing, all right, but her smiles were directed at old Tom Dorman. Sinden's pique mounted as he watched her dance. Had she changed her style to please Tom? Surely she was not going to settle for a widower old enough to be her papa? He would give her the next dance and quiz her a little.

When the set ended, he pocketed his quizzing glass, detached himself from the wall, and drifted toward her, a sardonic smile firmly fixed on his thin lips.

"Miss Leigh," he said, with a small bow.

"Lord Sinden," she replied, with an even smaller curtsy.

"May I have the honor of the next dance?"

Now why the devil was she glaring at him like that? She looked as if she wanted to scratch his eyes out. Some delightful mystery lurked here. His lips curved minutely, and his eyebrows arched in a question.

"Cat got your tongue, Miss Leigh?" He turned to Dorman. "Tom, you don't mind? Or am I intruding at a moment of high drama? You will tell me if Miss Leigh has just done you the honor of accepting an offer. It would be too farouche of me to intrude on your bliss if that is the case."

"Indeed, she has not, the minx." Dorman laughed.

Cybele swallowed her spleen and said, "I will be happy to stand up with you, Lord Sinden, if you are quite sure the wall can hold itself up without your support."

His eyebrows rose a notch higher. "If we feel

them begin to tremble, we shall both rush forth and add our frail bodies to buttress them."

He put a peremptory hand on her elbow and led her away. "I was sure your new toilette heralded a softening in your disposition, but I see I am mistaken," he said. "You look a perfect quiz, Miss Leigh."

"Why thank you, milord. You are too kind."

"I have a comb in my pocket if you would like to tidy yourself up. I believe we have time before the waltzes begin."

"As every other gentleman I have spoken to particularly complimented me on my new hairdo, I shall refuse your kind offer, but I do thank you for noticing."

He bowed.

"I am surprised your keen interest in food leaves you time to also be an expert on ladies' toilettes," she snipped, and immediately regretted it. She did not want him to know she knew his other identity.

"Ah, you have heard of my little luncheon banquet. The pâté de Strasbourg truffe en brioche was a small success, if I do say so myself."

"I am sure you are too modest, milord. Everyone is singing its praises."

He looked at her askance. "I assure you, *everyone* was not at my table."

"The pâté's fame has spread. Like the emperor's coat, it is much praised without having actually been seen, or, in this case, tasted."

His austere face softened in a smile. "Now that is more like it! I am happy to see your tongue has not suffered the same fate as your toilette and become common."

He handed her a small black comb and led her from the ballroom. "Regarding the pâté, it was a visual delight as well, actually, but your analogy is not quite accurate. Unlike the emperor's coat, the pâté did exist, once upon a time."

2

"Put the comb back in your pocket," Cybele said when they reached the edge of the room. "It would look odd for me to change my hairdo in midrout."

Sinden's lazy eyes flickered over her chestnut hair. His glance did not linger, nor was there disdain in it, but just the merest soupçon of amusement. Yet like a small dash of bitters in a drink, it flavored the whole. "You are concerned about looking odd, are you?" he asked. His look suggested she looked downright bizarre, yet half a dozen ladies in the room wore a similar coiffure.

Although Cybele felt the sting of his scorn, she replied coolly, "Only that others should find my behavior strange."

"Other than whom?"

"Other than you," she said bluntly. Her intention was to show her utter disregard for his opinion.

The mischievous Sinden chose to interpret it as a compliment. "I am flattered, Miss Leigh," he said, with a bow. "I had not realized you held me in such high esteem that my finding you odd does not concern you. We are too close to allow a few freakish starts to destroy our friendship. I take that as a compliment."

"Take it any way you like."

He returned the offending comb to his pocket. "Now that you and I are bosom bows," he said, inclining his head toward hers, "I shall venture to mention the shawl." A reckless smile flashed in his dark eyes.

"You don't approve of it either?"

"Not on you—and not with that gown. Lilies are best left ungilded. You have a duty to society, ma'am. Who will show the ladies the path to good taste if *you* abandon the cause? You are the only lady in London with a true sense of style. The others are merely fashionable."

Cybele did not like Sinden, but she respected his judgment and was insensibly flattered at the compliment.

"Perhaps it is a trifle much," she allowed, looking down at the gaudily flowered silk.

"No, a good deal too much. What causes this aberration in your usually superb taste? You are too young for panic to have set in."

"We all have a bad day occasionally."

"Those are the days, or evenings, when one should stay home with a good book."

"Or at least avoid the few who are perhaps overly nice in their demands." She fully expected a response to that "overly nice."

Sinden said, "Have you decided to accept Dorman?"

The abruptness of his question startled her. She soon figured out what he was getting at. "Say what you mean, Lord Sinden; namely, am I rigging myself out like a deb in an effort to get an offer from him. You already know he has not offered."

"I beg to differ. Until your rash outburst, I knew only that you had not accepted. And that is not an answer to my real question. Why have you given way to this provincial style?"

"I seem to remember someone saying impertinent questions should be ignored. Who was it, I wonder?" Her kindling glance identified Sinden himself as the someone. "Shall we have a glass of punch?" she added, to show that the subject of toilette was finished.

"Certainly not. Lady Fulham has no notion of making punch. She uses too much pounded sugar. The wine is equally heinous. I would not offend your palate by offering it to you."

"You will not con me with Petruchio's tricks. I am no Kate."

"Yet you play the shrew surprisingly well. We shall have orgeat."

"I do not care for orgeat."

"Nor do I, but at least it is an honest drink."

They went to the refreshment parlor, where Cybele insisted on a glass of the overly sweet punch and Sinden sipped unhappily at a glass of orgeat.

"You need not look as if you were Sophocles accepting the glass of hemlock," she scolded. "You will offend Lady Fulham's feelings."

"She offends mine with this sort of refreshment."

"You are absurd! This is all an act. Why, you are as bad as Monsieur Bongoût, with his ridiculous railings against that new French restaurant." She knew Sinden's pride was his weak point. A blow at it was as good a weapon as any.

"The place is an abomination."

"I thought the *pommes au roi* were rather good."

"Overdone. I trust the *roi* refers to Louis. Even our old King George is not mad enough to take *that* dish as a compliment. I admire Bongoût. It is every Englishman's duty to rail at the second rate. If we do not complain, we will soon be given the third rate. Someone must uphold the nation's gastronomic standards."

"Lo, how the mighty have fallen. When Nelson exhorted every Englishman to do his duty, it was a matter of life and death. You should be ashamed to invoke his words in such a paltry cause as a piece of overdone meat."

"A man's meat is hardly a paltry thing. What is more important to us than food?"

"Charity should be more important. I daresay it never occurred to Monsieur Bongoût that he is ruining the life of that poor French émigré who runs La Maison Dessus. What will become of him when Bongoût has driven off all his customers?"

"I suggest he open a tanning factory. He has a flair for creating leather."

"Ruining a man is hardly a matter for sarcasm, Lord Sinden," she snapped.

Sinden could not fail to notice her angry reaction to his charges. He remembered seeing Miss Leigh at the dining room on a few occasions. She was obviously a friend of the owner's. He decided to probe the matter more deeply.

"I hardly think the chef is his own banker. Fear not that he will be ruined. Some gentleman with more money than taste is behind him. My hope is to goad the owner into hiring a decent chef. The location is ideal, and the room itself is in tolerably good taste. You don't happen to know who owns the place?"

Tolerably good taste! The place had cost a fortune! "I haven't heard," she said vaguely. Her eyes strayed off to the doorway as she spoke, an indication that she was not telling the truth.

"Let me know if you do. I would like a word with the owner."

"Why? Do you know a better chef for hire? Is that it?" she asked eagerly.

His suspicions rose higher. Was Dorman the fellow behind La Maison? His pockets were well inlaid, and he set a wretched table at home. Sinden had attended one of his suppers. Miss Leigh's defense of the restaurant annoyed Sinden. He would have scorned the idea that he was jealous, yet he was developing an otherwise inexplicable dislike of Dorman.

He set aside his empty glass, took Cybele's, and said, "Let us not discuss business. We are here to dance. The waltzes are nearly finished. Come."

She had little choice but to accompany him back to the ballroom. Sinden waltzed as well as he did everything else. He was a famous whip, an outstanding speaker in the Upper House, a dandy of the first water, and was known to have a way with the ladies. They enjoyed one waltz without mentioning the prickly subjects of food or La Maison Dessus again.

When the dance was over, he said, "There is a new play opening at Covent Garden tomorrow night. Will you and your aunt come with me?"

Although they usually had one dance together at the balls and routs, this was the first time Sinden had formally asked Cybele out. It indicated a growing seriousness in his attentions. If she must marry, Sinden would be a great catch. Yet she felt in her bones he would never offer for a penniless lady, nor would she be content with such a demanding husband.

He noticed her hesitation and was surprised. "Are you otherwise engaged?" he asked.

"Nothing important. I . . . yes, I expect Auntie will be happy to attend. She enjoys a comedy."

Surprise rose to indignation. Sinden was not accustomed to having his invitations accepted so diffidently. "It was not primarily Lady Violet's company I was seeking."

"Oh, I will be happy to attend as well, milord. Thank you. I look forward to it."

"With something less than eagerness, I think?"

She gave a teasing smile that showed the enchanting dimples at the corners of her lips. "You must blame it on my astonishment, Lord Sinden.

153

Here I thought you disliked my new style, but I see it has affected you, too. You never asked me out before."

"Return to your old style—for me." He lifted her hand and placed a kiss on the air an inch above it. "I asked you *despite* the new style, not because of it. And now I see Lord DeVere is legging it toward us. I doubt it is my company he wants for the country dance."

"It is pretty well known that Lord Sinden does not condescend to perform the country dance. I, being a good deal less toplofty, enjoy it."

"I shall return to my wall. It will be missing me. À *demain*."

Lord DeVere carried her off, and Sinden did just as he had said. He returned to stand by the wall, ignoring half a dozen unpartnered ladies. When he was joined by a few other unattached gentlemen, he compounded the offense by carrying them off to Brookes's Club for a game of cards.

Lady Violet was delighted with her niece's conquest. "If you play your cards right, you might very well get an offer from him," she exclaimed, as they discussed the outing over breakfast the next morning.

"I do not particularly want one."

"Excellent!" Lady Violet smiled. "The very way to nab him. Sinden will never be caught by chasing. The less you like him, the higher your chances of becoming Lady Sinden."

"I am only going to try to talk him into sense about reporting on the restaurant. I gave him a few hints last night. With repetition he might come to realize the unfairness of what he is doing."

"You will never convince Sinden that bad food is good, my girl. He is famous for his taste. Did you write to Nancy Otis?"

"Yes, I laid it on with a trowel, told her Pierre is going into a decline without her. My Aunt will be furious with me if I succeed in luring Nancy away. Let us hope we can find a new chef before Christmas."

"Is there something special on at Christmas?" Lady Violet inquired.

"No, but there is usually a rash of parties at Christmas. Bachelors, in particular, often entertain at a public dining room. If we could provide them a good meal, it would help us reestablish La Maison to favor."

"Ah, I thought perhaps you were planning some gala party at La Maison yourself."

The idea appealed to Cybele. A gala party, with the height of the ton invited to La Maison, might be just the shot in the arm it needed. But first she must hire a good chef. It would seem odd for a lady to have a dinner party at a public dining room, however. She must find some ruse to account for it.

The excuse came to her at the play that evening. Lord Sinden had invited five guests to fill his box. Lady Violet's escort was Mr. Jerome, an aging Whig politician whose special area of expertise was America. Lord and Lady Monmart were newlywed friends and coevals of Sinden's. As might be expected of an out-and-outer like Sinden, the evening was carried out in high style. A box on the grand tier, wine served at the intermission, and a supper at the Clarendon to follow. The evening was enjoyable.

Cybele could not like to knuckle under completely to his request for her old style. She reverted to the Grecian knot but wore a paisley shawl. He did not seem to notice the shawl, but he smiled complacently to see the old coiffure.

"Enchanting, Miss Leigh," he said when he called for her.

"And so comfortable," she replied coolly. "It obviates the need for doing the hair up in papers."

"Simpler styles are always the best."

She glanced at his intricate cravat. "You should tell your valet so, Lord Sinden."

His long, elegant fingers made an involuntary move to his cravat. He looked momentarily uncertain. Was it possible that Lord Sinden was unsure of himself? What a revelation!

"Are you familiar with the play we shall be seeing?" he asked. *Twelfth Night.*"

"I studied it at Miss Gwynne's Seminary. I thought it rather silly, but then Shakespeare is always better seen than read."

Lady Violet rushed in to thank Sinden for the outing. She thought Cybele was overdoing the role of hard to get. One of them must be obliging.

The main pleasure of the evening for Cybele was just being out amid the ton. She enjoyed checking her friends to see who was there and with whom, how they were behaving, and what they were wearing. Once or twice Sinden reached out his hand and redirected her opera glasses to the stage. He did not rebuke her in words but just lifted his eyebrows in an admonitory way. Cybele gave a bold smile and returned the glasses to what she wished to see. She did not observe Sinden's little smile of satisfaction at her waywardness.

When the play was over, he said resignedly, "Shakespeare is not for everyone. Now I understand your lack of enthusiasm for this outing. Next time I shall find a nice, weepy melodrama for you. I hope the remainder of the evening will be more to your liking."

Lady Monmart said, "Where are we going for dinner, Sinden? Not that horrid new French place, I hope?" Cybele looked daggers at the woman.

"Certainly not. One mistake an evening is more

than enough. I have booked a table at the Clarendon. We shall meet you there."

Sinden drove the remainder of the party to the hotel. The dining room there was not more elegant than La Maison Dessus, but it was more fully occupied. Several parties without reservations were turned away. Cybele hoped some of them would go to La Maison, but the alternatives being mentioned were the Pulteney and Reddishes Hotel.

They dined on quails *en papillote*. "Do you know," Sinden said, "I was actually served a *stewed* quail at La Maison Dessus last week. It was the name of the dish that fooled me. *Caille Meunière*, it was called. I suspected no worse than a bed of onions, but it had been *stewed*. Any chef worthy of the name knows quails cannot be allowed near water. It robs them of their delicate flavor. It is like boiling lettuce."

"I prefer it roasted myself," Lord Monmart said, "but this crust is so light. Quite delicious."

"You would think that French chef at La Maison would have a way with pastry at least," Sinden continued. "But if I had to choose the dining room's worst aspect, I think it would be the leather crusts. Have you heard who is behind La Maison *Désastre*, Monmart?"

Cybele's gorge rose higher at every slur on her establishment. La Maison *Désastre*! And both the Monmarts had laughed loudly at the witticism. It would certainly appear in Bongoût's next column.

"I heard 'twas Albany," Monmart replied.

"I heard that as well, but it ain't true," Sinden said. "I asked him. I was sure Bongoût would smoke out the owner before now with his attacks on the place. I own I am curious. The only one who has rushed to its defense is Miss Leigh," he said, smiling at her. "She feels Bongoût is overly harsh toward it."

"I just feel sorry for a new business that is having trouble establishing itself," Cybele said.

"Feel sorry for the poor innocents who are being duped of the price of their dinners," Monmart advised her. "And a good, stiff price they charge at the place, too."

"Food is very dear," Lady Monmart said. "It costs the same whether it is well prepared or badly."

"Now there is a housewife speaking," Lord Monmart said proudly. The Monmarts were still aglow with the bliss of married life.

The conversation finally moved on to other subjects. The Monmarts mentioned they were going to Devon for Christmas. They were leaving on the twentieth.

"For we must attend Lady Castlereagh's Christmas party on the nineteenth," Lady Monmart said. "Kind of her to have a little do for those who must remain in town for one reason or another. It is sad to be away from home for Christmas."

"Oh, I don't know," Lady Violet said. "There is the Christmas concert at Drury Lane on the twenty-third. The new Italian tenor, Signor Borimini, will be performing. They sing all the old traditional hymns and carols, and there are usually half a dozen dinner parties after."

Cybele listened and began to make a plan to rescue her dining room. She and her aunt Violet were remaining in town for Christmas. They would be attending the concert. . . . She would invite a largish party to La Maison Dessus after. The convenience of the location was a good enough excuse to hold the affair away from home, especially when the weather might be inclement. But first, of course, she must make some arrangement for a new chef.

There were a few more odious comparisons to the desserts at her dining room when the chantilly was

158

served. Other than that the evening was a success. Sinden had certainly exerted himself to show her a good time. She saw that he was not so haughty among his own friends as in a larger company. He seemed eager to please her, in his own rather high-handed way.

When he took her home, he asked if she would drive out with him one afternoon. Perhaps they would visit the new winter exhibition at Somerset House.

"That would be lovely, Lord Sinden. I look forward to it."

No date was set, but she had no doubt she would hear from him again soon.

Over the next days she began to canvass her friends to discover who would be in town over Christmas and who was attending the Christmas concert at Drury Lane. Her aunt was informed of the plan and entered into it with great merriment. "I shall invite Lady Hertford. She will bring along Prinny—depend upon it."

"If only she would!" Cybele exclaimed, trembling with excitement. A recommendation from the Prince Regent would be as good as a royal patent.

Unfortunately Lady Hertford declined, but she suggested a few of the royal princesses might be interested. They were not encouraged to go much into society, but such an innocent diversion as a concert might be allowed. In the end Princess Elizabeth, the highflier of the royal nest, accepted. It was rumored she even had a parti in her eye, the Hereditary Prince of Hesse-Homburg, familiarly known as Humbug.

Cybele was fully occupied, but not so busy that she failed to notice Sinden was in no hurry to call. When three days had passed without seeing him, she began to feel fretful. She assured herself she did not care in the least that he had not come, yet it was strange. Had he discovered her secret? Did he think it farouche of a lady to be involved in business?

Lord Sinden's absence had a more innocent explanation. He had driven home to Hazelton House in Sussex to make arrangements for his own Christmas party. It was his custom to invite a dozen congenial friends for a week's revels to celebrate the season.

The next Cybele heard of him was another scathing attack on La Maison Dessus in the *Herald*. As she feared, he had now officially dubbed her dining room La Maison Désastre. She was having no luck in finding a new chef; Nancy had declined the invitation in no uncertain terms—and Cybele had invited twenty-four guests to dine at La Maison Désastre on the twenty-third of December.

On top of it all Sinden had not left town, as Lady Violet thought. He must have been here last night, or how had this column got into the paper today? Yet he had not called on her. As if all this were not bad enough, an even worse suspicion began scratching at her mind. Had he suspected she was the owner of La Maison Dessus all along? Was that why he had invited her out, to test her? And having confirmed it, he was now going to ruin her?

Horrible man! Her first impression of him had been correct. He was an arrogant, mean, hateful creature, and if he did come to call, she would give him a piece of her mind.

3

On the fourth day after attending the play, Lord Sinden called on Cybele and was met with the marble-hard face of deep displeasure. He would not have been surprised if she had refused to drive out with him. The name Tom Dorman immediately flashed into his head. In the end she accepted, but only to get him away from Lady Violet for a private battle.

"I would have called sooner, but I have been out of town," he said, when they were comfortably ensconced in his chaise, with a fur rug to warm their laps and heated bricks to keep the chill from their toes.

"How nice for you."

"Nice for you as well, I hope."

"I did enjoy your absence," she agreed.

"That was not exactly my meaning, Miss Leigh. I was at Hazelton House, arranging a Christmas fete. I hope you and your aunt will do me the honor to be at the party."

He waited for her exclamation of delight. An invitation to Hazelton House was a prize above pearls. Duchesses had hinted in vain.

"We are remaining in London over the holiday," she replied, without so much as a blink of regret.

The only evidence of Sinden's astonishment was a slight pause while he assured himself she had misunderstood him. "I am inviting you to Hazelton for Christmas," he said.

"I am not hard-of-hearing, milord. We have decided to remain in London."

"But surely you would rather get out of town."

"On the contrary, I enjoy Christmas in the city. In fact, I am having a party myself."

"Perhaps you could postpone it."

"That would be impossible. The arrangements have been made for some time."

Yet *he* had received no invitation to this party. The thing went from bad to worse. "I see." He waited, but still no invitation was extended, even at this late date. "A grand ball, is it?"

"No, simply a dinner after the concert at Drury Lane—at La Maison Désastre," she added, staring at him like a lizard about to snap out its tongue to catch a fly. "Naturally we would not subject one of your refined taste to such a dinner."

"You might at least have given me the option of refusing."

"It had not occurred to me it would give anyone pleasure to refuse. If that is the case, then I extend you an invitation now, milord."

"Thank you, Miss Leigh. I accept," he said angrily.

"*What?* But you have already arranged your own Christmas party." Instead of gratification, she appeared displeased.

"I shall unarrange it," he growled. "You were the first person I was inviting. If *you* cannot come, I shall have it another time. For New Year's, say. Or have you other plans for that as well? A tea party, perhaps?" he said, to show his low opinion of her Christmas dinner.

"I believe Lady Violet has accepted an invitation elsewhere for New Year's," she lied.

"I shall speak to your aunt and discover when it

will be possible for you to find time in your busy schedule to come to Hazelton House."

"It is exactly as my aunt said," she said crossly. "You want me to go only because I refuse. If I had leapt at the offer like the other ladies, you would never ask me out again."

Sinden was thrown into confusion. He had met ladies sly enough to pretend to have some grudge against him, to incite him to interest. But those cunning creatures were not likely to advertise their schemes. Nor would they announce them with such obvious ill humor. In his confusion he forgot his haughty role and asked bluntly, "What the devil is eating you, Cybele?"

"I did not ask you to use my first name, milord. We are hardly on such terms of intimacy as that."

"You will not divert me by that ruse. Why have you taken me in aversion? What have I done?"

"Nothing. You are just being your usual hateful self."

"Well, upon my word, I think you are hard on me. I thought you would be pleased that I was arranging a party in your honor."

"Well, I am not pleased! You should have asked me first."

"That was presumptuous of me," he said, though he did not believe it. He felt quite sure she had made her little plan in pique, to show him a lesson. "I apologize."

"You are putting me in the wrong when I had no idea why you did not call after you said you would."

"I should have let you know what I was about. I wanted it to be a surprise." He began to see that her anger was really at herself, for having to miss his Christmas fete. This was a perfectly acceptable reason for annoyance. "But why the devil are you having your party chez La Maison Désastre? Do you plan to invite your worst enemies?"

"I am not so vindictive. I am having it there because I feel sorry for Pierre," she said. She had to say something.

"You are personally acquainted with the chef?"

"Yes," she said, then had to account for this unlikely acquaintance. "He was seeing my aunt Thatcher's housekeeper in Bath. He is trying to make his fortune so that Nancy will marry him and come to London. She does not want to leave Bath, but I feel certain she would if Pierre had a great success."

"So it is an affair of the heart," he said, smiling. "You should have told me."

"Would you write a better review, now that you know?"

"I? Where did you get the idea that I have anything to do with those reviews?"

"Cut line, Sinden. I know perfectly well you are Monsieur Bongoût. Why else do you keep going back to dine on white leather?"

"It is true, I am Bongoût, but I wish you will keep it a secret. If the hoteliers knew my identity, they would see that I am served their best. The idea is to see what they serve to the general public. Have your aunts put their money into this venture?" he asked.

"No."

"Mr. Dorman, perhaps?"

She looked surprised. "No. Why would you think that?"

He tried to look unconcerned. "Just an idea. Well, my conscience does not permit me to write a good review, but I shall desist from writing more bad ones. And in a way I thank you. It was a penance to keep returning to La Maison. I felt I owed it to the place to try all its offerings. One never knows, the chef might have a way with oysters, or lobster, or *something*. There must be *some* reason he was put in charge of such an expensive place. He never indicated who was his banker?"

"No," she said. Naturally Pierre had never found it necessary to tell her she was his banker. They both knew it very well.

"I wish you will ask him," he said. "The rumor persists that Albany is behind it. He denies it vehemently, but then he would never admit to a failure. I should not like to be too hard on Albany. He is a friend."

Cybele began to perceive that Sinden had a real flesh-and-blood heart beneath his cynical exterior. She thought she might appeal to his mercy. "I believe someone of modest fortune has put all his money into the place," she said vaguely.

"If he has, he is a fool. I would advise him to find himself a new chef. It cannot be difficult to find one better than Pierre."

"I daresay it is more difficult than you think. The nobles' houses snap up all the good ones."

Sinden reached out and took her gloved hand in his. "Enough about that. Now that we have straightened out that little misunderstanding, let us discuss Christmas, Cybele. May I call you Cybele?"

She shrugged her permission as if it gave her no pleasure, but she did feel a little thrill to see her fingers resting intimately in Sinden's and to hear her name on his lips. It was also a coup of major proportions that he had planned his Christmas party with her in mind and was willing to change it to suit her.

"May I escort you this evening?" he asked.

"That must depend on where you are going, Lord Sinden. We have accepted an invitation to Lady John Teale's rout party. I daresay half a dozen duchesses have beckoned you thither."

"Only two. I shall go to Lady John's rout instead. I would be pleased if you would call me Sinden, by the by. I mention it as you are too stubborn—which we shall call nice—to do so without an express invitation."

He was rewarded with a fleeting glimpse of the dimples. For Sinden, asking to use a lady's first name was as good as a commitment to offer for her. He had expected a more extravagant show of joy when he finally committed himself to a lady, but overall he was content. He liked that Cybele had an unsuspected streak of romance beneath her chilly exterior. It was romantic, and kind, of her to subject herself to dinners at La Maison on a fairly regular basis to foster the love affair of her aunt's housekeeper.

That evening he meant to stand up with Cybele twice. That would give society a hint of his intentions and get rid of such hangers-on as Tom Dorman. He had the carriage driven to New Bond Street to allow them to descend and walk along, looking in shop windows. The cold turned their cheeks red; their breath formed small clouds that hung on the still air. A fine snow had begun to fall. It seemed to sway in the air, like a lace curtain caught in a breeze. The lights from shop windows turned the powder of snow on their heads and shoulders to diamonds. When Cybele admired a little statuette of a shepherd in a toy-store window, saying it reminded her of home, he insisted on buying it for her.

She accepted it shyly, with a self-conscious look that told him she had some notion of his feelings. They returned to the waiting carriage, glad to escape the chilly air.

"I hope you do not think I was hinting, Sinden," she said, setting the parcel aside.

He arranged the fur rug over her lap in a proprietary manner. "I know you better than that. We bosom bows do not go in for hints and roundabouts in our talk. We say what we mean. It is one of the

things that first attracted me to you, Cybele."
Again she smiled shyly. "Are you not curious to
know what was the other thing?"

"I suppose I am."

He reached across to her banquette and just
touched his finger to the side of her lips. "Those enchanting dimples," he said softly. "I like the way
you resist flaunting them. Most ladies with dimples
wear out their faces with grinning. You allow only
a discreet glimpse of yours." His fingers lowered to
her chin and gave it a familiar little squeeze.

Cybele hardly knew what to make of this new
side of Sinden. She had driven out with the express
intention of giving him a good bear garden jaw, and
here she sat, smiling like a moonling because he
liked her dimples. She found, over the next days,
that Sinden improved upon closer acquaintance.
His sneers decreased, to be replaced by smiles and
quiet compliments, without ever exceeding the
bounds of good taste.

Lady Violet allowed her charge to stand up twice
with him at Lady John Teale's rout that evening,
giving rise to speculation that Sinden must look
sharp or he would be caught in parson's mousetrap.
The next afternoon Sinden took Cybele to call on
his aunt, the aging Countess of Early, who served
them orgeat and macaroons in a chilly drawing
room of august proportions, with a grate that de-
fied the rules of science and gave forth a great deal
of smoke without fire or heat. After a deal of quizzing and squinting and head nodding, the countess
expressed mild approval of Cybele. "A pretty creature, and well behaved," was the verdict whispered
in Sinden's ear when she contrived a moment alone
with him at parting.

Sinden offered an indirect apology, or at least an
explanation, for the call en route home. "Aunt Aure-
lia is the doyenne and real head of my family. I am

allowed the title; she wields the power. We must all pay our respects to her. These stilted calls are necessary only once per season, however. And a good thing it is, too, or we'd be kippered by that smoking grate."

When Cybele complained to her aunt of the boring outing that evening, she learned the reason for it.

"You must know old Lady Early is a nabob, with no children to leave her fortune to. Sinden would not like to displease her in his choice of bride. Why, it is as good as a wedding call, Cybele. I did not know it was Lady Early you were to visit. I was sure it would be the Ebbings."

Cybele assumed that Sinden, although rich, was still interested in enlarging his fortune. It was not likely he would knowingly offer for a dowerless lady, and it was becoming increasingly clear both that he meant to offer for her and that she was going to lose her investment. No new chef was found, and Nancy remained adamant on not removing to London.

Pride forbade Cybele from admitting her folly to Sinden. Yet to accept an offer from him under false pretenses was worse. She saw only one way out of the dilemma: she must turn him off before it came to an offer. The next time he invited her out, she would refuse. She would also refuse to stand up with him at the next rout or ball. That would give him the idea she no longer cared for him. A few hints had told her he was jealous of Tom Dorman. Perhaps she would let him think she favored Tom.

That evening when she met Sinden at a small rout party, she declined his offer to stand up for the cotillion.

"Ah, someone has beaten me to it. I was held up by a caller just as I was about to leave home. The next set then. And do save me the waltzes, Cybele."

"I am afraid that is impossible, Sinden," she said, with such a woebegone expression that he felt she must be ill.

"I hope your card is not all filled up so soon!" he said, chagrined.

"Oh, no, though I have promised Mr. Dorman the country dance," she said, to bring Dorman into the equation.

The orchestra members began tuning up their instruments. Sinden went to hold up the wall, from which vantage point he watched to see which partner was usurping his place. To his considerable astonishment Cybele did not dance at all. Why had she refused him? Within an instant he leapt to the conclusion she was unwell. He immediately rushed off to the card room to inform Lady Violet.

"You are enjoying your game," he said. "I shall take Cybele home."

"That is kind of you, Sinden." She smiled. She was certain Cybele would receive her offer that very night—until she remembered Sinden had not asked for permission, and he was not the sort to omit the proprieties. Perhaps he had written to Cybele's brother.

Sinden hastened back to Cybele. "I shall take you home," he said. "I can see you are not feeling at all the thing. You are pale as paper."

"I cannot go home. I just got here," she said weakly. "And Aunt Violet—"

"I have spoken to your aunt. She should not have brought you out when you are obviously under the weather."

"But my card is half-full."

"I shall speak to our hostess and let her inform Dor—the other gentlemen. Come now, Cybele. We don't want you ill for your own Christmas party. It is probably only a touch of flu. A day in bed will put you back in form. I should not have made you walk in the snow the other afternoon."

He felt guilty to see that two feverish spots of red were forming on her pale cheeks, and her eyes had the glazed look of an invalid's. Sinden was angry with Lady Violet, and with himself for having taken Cybele for that walk in the snow, but mostly he was concerned for her health. When he felt the trembling in her fingers as she placed them on his arm to leave the rout, and when she gazed up at him with her great, sad eyes, a surge of love and protectiveness swelled up in him.

In the carriage he insisted on wrapping the fur rug around her shoulders, with his own rug over her lap. He carefully tucked it around her ankles, but she was still silent and shivering.

"I shall warm you," he said, and moved to her banquette to put his arms around her.

She placed her head on his shoulder with a weary sigh, reluctant to interrupt these few intimate moments with a confession. Yet Sinden was being so thoughtful that it seemed a good moment to tell him all. He could not rip up at an invalid. And really he had good reason to. She had let him publicly court her. Society was fully expecting an announcement of their betrothal. Everyone would assume he had jilted her, for it was inconceivable that any lady in her right mind would refuse him. She knew in her bones that Sinden would hate to be labeled a jilt. He always behaved with the utmost propriety vis-à-vis the ladies.

All these sad thoughts whirled through her mind as they drove through the quiet streets, with the black, bare trees stretching their arms to the silver sky and the snow twinkling in the street all around. She really must tell him tonight, as soon as they reached home. This was the last time they would be together on good terms.

"I have enjoyed your company these few days, Sinden," she said on a wistful note.

His arms tightened around her. "They have been the happiest days of my life, my dear. Have you decided when you can come to visit me at Hazelton? Mama is eager to make your acquaintance."

"Oh, as to that, I do not think this is the time to discuss it." His mama! He really was serious!

"You are right. It is selfish of me to be badgering you at this time. We shall wait until you are feeling more the thing."

They subsided into a longish silence, with Sinden's arms holding her close until the carriage drew up in front of the house on Half Moon Street. Sinden began unwrapping the fur rugs.

"This is so warm and cozy, I hate to leave," she said, smiling sadly.

"If you were not feeling poorly, we could bundle up and go for a drive through the park. It's lovely in winter. I often go alone at night, after a party or a long session in the House. It is so still and serene, it puts life in perspective."

"Let us do it tonight," she said, to prolong these last few moments together.

"Don't tempt me, Cybele," he replied. His hands rested on her shoulders. "We shall do that and a good deal more when you are better. We shall go skating at Hazelton, and riding." She looked up at him, her eyes encouraging. "I think you know my feelings for you," he said in a husky voice.

His head hovered above hers, his dark eyes gleaming in the moonlight. A small smile curved his lips. How had she thought he was cynical and supercilious? As she watched, his head lowered, and she felt his lips touch hers. She could not tell whether it was his lips or her own that trembled so. Then the kiss firmed, and the trembling invaded her whole body. She closed her eyes, but the diamond sparkle of moonlight on snow only increased, like a shower of stars falling all around her. His arms drew her closely against his masculine warmth and strength. She wished she could stay there, safe and warm in his arms, forever.

When he released her, his face wore a dazed expression. "Cybele," he said, and just gazed at her, like a man in a trance. "I should not have taken that liberty. Now I hardly know whether it is worse to propose without speaking to Lady Violet first or to let you go without speaking."

"Oh, you must not propose! Indeed you must not. The kiss meant nothing."

"It meant a good deal to *me*!" he exclaimed, a little hurt. "I hope you are not in the habit of allowing gentlemen such familiarity."

She drew her bottom lip between her teeth, wondering how to explain her dilemma. "Of course I am not. It is horrid of you to suggest it. Anyone might lose her head once, with the moonlight and . . . and the fur rug," she added foolishly.

"Then I shall hold my offer until the proper moment. But I must—I shall say I love you."

"Oh, no! You must not. You really must not, dear Sinden."

"It is done. The die is cast."

"But I have not said I love you."

He just smiled softly. "Your lips said it. *À demain*, my dear." He placed a small kiss at the corner of her lips and assisted her from the carriage.

As far as Sinden was concerned, he was engaged. Imagine his astonishment the next afternoon to be told by Lady Violet that while she had not the least objection in the world to giving her permission, she was afraid Cybele had forbidden it.

He just looked at her, too astonished to speak for a moment. "But did she give no reason? Is there another man, someone at home. . . ." "The kiss meant nothing," she had said.

"No, no. She had no beaux at home." Tom Dorman was the next thought that popped into his head.

"There is no one else she prefers, Sinden. You may rest easy on that score. She is very fond of you."

"I am afraid I don't understand. Has she taken some foolish vow not to marry?"

"Good gracious, no. She goes to church on Sunday, but she is not a fanatic."

"There must be *some* reason!"

"It is for your own good," Lady Violet said mysteriously.

"Insanity in the family?" he ventured.

"Certainly not! At least not the inherited sort, though I fear the girl did go a bit far with—but never mind."

Sinden crossed his arms and settled into his chair with a permanent look. "I am not leaving until I hear the reason. I *know* Cybele loves me. I could not be mistaken about *that*."

Those crossed arms spoke of a long afternoon of quibbling. Since she knew Sinden would get it out of her eventually anyway, she decided to set his mind at ease. "It is her fortune, you see," she explained in a low voice. "It is gone."

"What did she do with it? Is it gambling debts?" he asked, with a frown of disapproval. Duty and desire warred in his breast. It would be foolish to marry a known gambler who would dissipate the Sinden fortune. Yet the loss of her fortune itself was not enough to quench his ardor.

"In a manner of speaking. She put every penny she owned into La Maison Dessus."

He stared in disbelief. "Good God! So that is why she is always railing at me to stop roasting it. I wonder she is still speaking to me. But why did you permit it, ma'am?"

"It was really her aunt Thatcher's idea. It seemed like a good investment at the time." She leaned forward conspiratorially. "The trouble is Pierre. He cooked sublime meals at Bath, Sinden. I shall never

forget his roast pork with prune sauce. It fairly
melted in the mouth. And the lobster! It was divine.
Such a jewel seemed wasted in the provinces. We
thought he could make Cybele rich, but once we got
him away from his Nancy, he fell apart. He wanted
her to come with him, and really we all thought she
would, for she had accepted his offer. But she is the
managing sort who likes to keep the upper hand.
She wants to bring Pierre to heel. It seems her special skills were necessary to his art. Either that or he
cannot forget her long enough to cook a proper dinner. We have written begging her to come, telling her
Pierre is suffering a perfect hell of lonesomeness
without her, but the obstinate creature refuses to
budge. And there is no point telling us to hire another chef, for we have tried that a dozen times."

Lady Violet was sorely discomposed when Sinden
put his head back and laughed aloud.

"It is no joking matter!" she said severely.

As far as Sinden was concerned, a bad chef was
not much more than a joke, when he had feared
Cybele was insane, or a hardened gambler, or in
love with someone else.

"Why the devil is she having this big Christmas
party when she knows the food is so appallingly
bad?"

"She hoped to induce Nancy to come, or to hire a
new chef and serve a good meal to the ton, but of
course it did not work. The poor girl is distracted
with worry. She cannot carry the expense of the
place past the end of January. Her fortune will be
gone—and to have to lose you on top of it. Well, it
is really the outside of enough."

Sinden just sat, smiling and thinking. "You have
mismanaged the matter, ma'am. Why should
Nancy come running when she knows Pierre is suffering without her? It is only a matter of time until
he returns to Bath, giving her the upper hand for

the remainder of their life together. Well begun is half-done, you know. What you must do is let Nancy think Pierre has found a replacement, both in the kitchen and . . . er . . . elsewhere."

"A new girlfriend, you mean?"

"Precisely. That will bring her running."

"But there is no time to arrange it before Cybele's Christmas party."

"We have two days until the party. Write to Nancy this instant, telling her how well the restaurant is doing, now that Pierre has found a new female assistant. Let us make her a Frenchwoman. A little aura of foreign glamour might help. Hint that he is very happy and no longer speaks of Nancy. In fact, tell her she may consider herself free to consider other offers for her hand. If she cares for him, that should do the trick. I shall have my footman deliver the letter and wait for a reply. He can take a carriage and bring Nancy back with him if she agrees."

"Do you think it will work?"

Sinden's eyebrows rose a fraction of an inch. "It has been my experience that jealousy is a very strong goad to action," he said cryptically.

He still felt some lingering annoyance that Cybele had not been truthful with him. She had tried to manage him by her evasions and deceit. He would take this opportunity to show her a lesson. "And, Lady Violet, there is no need to tell Cybele what we are about, or that I know she is the owner of La Maison Dessus."

"I shan't, for if your scheme fails—and it probably will—she will not want you to know of her folly. She must be allowed to keep her pride, for her heart will be broken."

"Well, perhaps cracked," he allowed, but he was sure that a betrothal would provide an excellent glue.

4

Cybele was pulled in two directions over the next days. It was of the utmost importance that she not give Lord Sinden an opportunity to propose, which made staying in bed a good idea. And indeed, she felt decidedly unwell to consider her future, penniless and alone. On the other hand, she had to consult with Pierre on her all-important dinner party. They agreed that if he simplified his offerings, even he might be able to present something edible, if not tasty.

On the first afternoon she spoke with Pierre in her office, but she was officially unavailable when Sinden paid both an afternoon and evening call. Upon learning that she was indisposed, he sent a pretty bouquet of flowers and a note adjuring her that she must by no means see anyone until she was thoroughly recovered. On the same page he assured her that until he had the pleasure of seeing her again, he would not be able to eat, sleep, or something else that was either "breathe" or "bathe." His erratic handwriting showed his state of perturbation.

By the second afternoon Cybele was so eager to see him that she went belowstairs, but she warned Lady Violet she must not leave them alone for an instant. Cybele wore her aunt's oldest woolen shawl to make herself look unattractive and sat by the grate to uphold her role of an invalid. Sinden did not appear to be suffering from a lack of either rest, food, or breathing (or bathing). He took no notice at all of the worn shawl, but he did display the proper admixture of concern for her well-being and pleasure at her presence. He had brought a box of fruits from the concession houses at Hazelton to tempt her into appetite. He peeled her an orange, and while she ate it, he spoke.

"Your aunt tells me you are disturbed about your Christmas party," he said, arranging a pillow for her back and another for her head. His warm fingers managed to brush her cheek as he arranged the latter. His secret smile told her it was no accident. "I suggest you let me handle those arrangements for you. I am considered a tolerable judge of cuisine. I shall speak to Pierre."

"Perhaps your chef could speak to him," she said hopefully. The unspoken request hovered in the air between them: *Let your Drouin lend a hand.*

"Unfortunately Drouin has long been in the habit of taking his annual holiday over the Christmas season. I usually go home to Hazelton, you see, so I have no need of him at that time. He leaves for Paris tomorrow, to bring himself up-to-date on the new gastronomic developments."

It had already occurred to Sinden that he might send his Drouin into the breach for the party, but Drouin had cut up stiff when he suggested it. There had been no word from Nancy. A note from his footman stated that she was "wavering." He wished his footman had been more explicit. Was she likely to waver toward London in time? If not, he saw nothing but financial disaster for Cybele.

"Pity," Cybele said, her shoulders sagging. "I have ordered Pierre to prepare a most simple meal. Roasted fowl, Westphalian ham, perhaps a turbot in white sauce."

"To paraphrase Samuel Johnson, that would be a

good enough dinner, but not one to invite folks to. For a special occasion they will be expecting a potage, perhaps *potage d'orge perlée à la Crécy*; a *relevé de poisson, truite au bleu à la Provençale*, or if turbot, at least with *sauce aux homards*, followed by a *noix de veau à la jardinière* and perhaps *poulets à la Reine. Escalopes de volaille aux truffes* would be interesting."

Cybele started at such a fancy menu. "That would be courting disaster! Better a simple meal well prepared—or at least edible—than an extravagant debacle." She wanted to throw herself on Sinden's mercy. If she told him she was the owner of La Maison, surely he would insist that Drouin stay in London and help Pierre. Yet she feared he would be angry at her deception.

"You are right, of course," Sinden said. "Leave it to me. I shall consult with Pierre and see what he is capable of. Your job is to regain your health and prepare your toilette. It will be drafty in the theater. Be sure you wear a warm shawl."

Cybele accepted these paternal orders in good part. "That is kind of you, Sinden, but I really feel I know better what Pierre is capable of."

"I shall take every precaution to see his efforts do not exceed his capabilities," he assured her.

"Let Sinden handle it, dear," Lady Violet suggested. "He knows food better than we do."

Cybele allowed herself to be talked into this scheme. At least she had no fear that Pierre would give her away. He had strict instructions never to reveal who was behind the dining room. When he visited Half Moon Street, he came to the back door in the disguise of a delivery man.

Cybele prayed for a snowstorm of such proportions that it would be impossible to get a carriage through the streets. The day of the concert and dinner arrived bright and sunny. It was one of those crisp winter days when the sky is a dazzling blue and the sun almost brighter than in summer, yet the air is cold. It had been arranged that Sinden would call for Cybele and her aunt to accompany them to the theater. The concert was to begin at four o'clock, the dinner at seven.

At three o'clock he paid Lady Violet a quick call. "Nancy has not come," he said.

"We are ruined," Lady Violet declared, turning pale. "Thank God we at least stuck to simple dishes. I shall send my own cook to lend a hand. She would have no notion what to do with all those truffles and aspics and gelinottes you spoke of t'other day, but she can roast a fowl at least."

"I had hoped to serve a really splendid meal, so that Monsieur Bongoût might give La Maison a good review." He peered to see if Lady Violet was aware of his secret.

"Cybele told me the other day," she said.

"I feel she might have shared *her* secret with *me*."

"She is ashamed of it."

"I must run along and speak to Pierre. Don't wait for me. I shall join you at the theater."

Cybele could see her aunt's agitation as soon as she came downstairs. "Has Sinden not arrived yet?" she asked.

"He wants us to go on without him," Lady Violet said. "He will meet us there."

This, added to Cybele's worries over the dinner, was enough to put her in a cross mood. As the time was running close, they soon left for the theater in Lady Violet's carriage. The second disappointment was that Princess Elizabeth had begged off at the last minute. Old Queen Charlotte had come down with the flu and required the assistance of all six of her daughters.

The concert was good, despite the lack of any

royal guest. The old carols brought back memories of happy Christmases at Seven Oaks, when the carolers used to sing outside the house and come in after for a warm drink. The house was decorated in holly and mistletoe, and the delicious aromas of Christmas pudding and sugar and spice permeated the air. Friends and relatives used to stop by to pay their respects and enjoy a glass of mulled wine.

She should have gone home for Christmas. Instead of that, she was sitting in a dim theater with a group of mere acquaintances, with the awful specter of her dinner looming before her. Why did Sinden not come? What could have delayed him?

"He will be at La Maison, trying to repair the disaster there," her aunt said.

When the concert was over, Cybele forced a stricken smile onto her face to greet her guests and lead them off to La Maison. For this special occasion the tables had been pushed together to form one long table the length of the room.

It seemed every one of her guests asked where Lord Sinden was. Cybele murmured vaguely that he had been detained. Once in the dining room, she was busy playing the hostess, directing all her guests to their proper seats. And still no sign of Sinden. When it was time to sit down, the seat beside her was empty.

"He is not coming," Cybele murmured to her aunt. "What can have happened to him?"

"He will be here," Lady Violet said firmly. "The fact is, Cybele, he knows the restaurant is yours. He had suspected it for some time and finally weaseled a confirmation out of me, so you may be sure he will come. He knows how important this dinner is to you."

Lady Maigret, sitting across from Cybele, wore a snide smile. "Even Lord Sinden's appreciation of your beauty was not sufficient to lure him to La

Maison Désastre. I daresay all the *good* dining rooms were booked up," she added forgivingly. "I don't mind what I eat. It is the company that makes the meal," she said, with a look at that empty chair.

Cybele picked up the menu, expecting to see the simple dishes she had recommended. Her eyes fell on such complicated offerings as *filets de volaille à la maréchale* and *les boudins à la Béchamel*. She didn't even know what they should look or taste like.

"He has ruined me," she said to her aunt in a dying voice.

It was all becoming horribly clear now. Sinden was angry at her not jumping at his offer, or implied offer. He was taking this petty revenge. He despised her for letting him become involved with a lady who owned a dining room. He thought it unacceptable for a lady to be involved in business. He knew her fortune was tied up in La Maison, and he had not come. She fully expected to see another savage attack on La Maison tomorrow when she opened the *Herald*, despite Sinden's not even being there to try the food.

Waiters appeared with the soup. The menu told her it was *potage d'orge perlée à la Crécy*, the potage Sinden had suggested and that she had rejected as too difficult for Pierre. It was a tasty bouillon with sherry or some wine, flavored with barley, onion, and spices. It was not only not a disaster, but her own taste buds confirmed what her guests said: "Delicious!" At least they were off to a good start. This was followed by other dishes. The turbot in lobster sauce was also good. The fish was neither overdone nor transparent from undercooking. Best of all, the sauce was free of any lumps but lumps of lobster. Some brandy, liqueur, or wine lent it an exotic taste.

"I must have this receipt for my chef!" Lady Gainford exclaimed.

Success followed success as assorted aspics, *volailles*, and gelinottes appeared. Wine flowed freely, lending an air of gaiety to the party. Talk and laughter filled the room. Several guests mentioned they must bring a party here soon.

"The place has obviously got a new chef," Lady Maigret said. "Someone ought to tell Monsieur Bongoût."

Lady Violet smiled and said to Cybele, "It seems Nancy has come to London after all." She could not say more, but this cryptic message was understood by Cybele.

After several courses and removes the meal closed with the traditional plum pudding, aflame in brandy. The footmen carried it to the table. Like everything else, it was delicious. Cybele knew she should be happy. By some miracle Nancy had come, and her investment had been saved. But Sinden had not come. In fact, he had tried to ruin her. The succulent plum pudding tasted like ashes.

Finally the dinner was over, and her guests began to leave. Cybele and Lady Violet remained behind to compliment Pierre and welcome Nancy to London. When the last guest had delivered the last thanks and compliments, they headed down the hallway to the kitchen. The homey sound of clashing pots and pans came from the end of the hallway to greet them. The servants were talking and laughing in the aftermath of a job well done.

Cybele pushed open the swinging door and looked at a scene of domestic confusion. Every counter and tabletop was covered with discarded dishes. Steam rose from the copper kettles, where water was boiling for the monumental washup to come. The maids were sharing leftover sweets while the footmen finished off the partially full bottles of wine. And in the middle of it all, with a white apron covering him from collarbone to ankles, stood Lord Sinden, trying the plum pudding. Every hair was in place. No spot or spatter marred the pristine expanse of apron.

"Perhaps just a soupçon more of nutmeg, Drouin," he said to the aproned man beside him. Then he turned and saw Cybele. He removed the apron and handed it to Drouin. "Drouin brought the plum pudding from my house," he told her. "There wasn't time to make it. A proper plum pudding requires aging."

Cybele looked, wiped her eyes, and looked again. She was obviously having a hallucination.

"You have come to offer your congratulations to the chefs," Sinden said, beckoning to Pierre Picard and Drouin. He placed an arm around the shoulder of each, and together they made a bow.

"Sinden! What on earth are *you* doing here?" she exclaimed.

"I performed in only a supervisory capacity. When I supervise Drouin at home, I usually make it to the table for dinner. As the kitchen was a new one for us, however, I felt my place was here. Any reasonably civilized person can make polite conversation at table. Fewer of us can properly season a ragout or time the removal of an aspic from the ice cupboard. One does not want it overly firm when it reaches the tables, yet not quite jiggling. I think it was a success?"

"But you said Drouin was going to Paris."

Sinden looked warily at his chef. "I convinced him otherwise," he replied. The grin that stretched Drouin's lips suggested a substantial bribe.

Pierre was also smiling. "My Nan-see—she comes!" he exclaimed, and in the euphoria of the moment, he forgot the proprieties and threw his arms around his employer.

"I was sure she was here already," Lady Violet said, looking around the room.

"But no. She comes after *Noël*, for to be married with me and help me with the cookings. Then La Maison Dessus will be the bestest dining room *de tout Londres*."

"Never underestimate the power of jealousy," Sinden said aside to Cybele. "We had only to drop Nancy the hint that Pierre had a new *amour* in his eye, and she suddenly felt an overwhelming desire to remove to London. Unfortunately your aunt Thatcher was having a Christmas party of her own and could not let her leave in time to be here to-night."

"You have all done very well, and I thank you," Cybele said, shaking hands with the two performing chefs. "Open some wine bottles for yourself and your assistants, Pierre." Then she turned to the supervisor. "And thank you, milord supervisor. You seasoned the sauces superbly."

"Monsieur Bongoût was satisfied," he said. "Need one say more?"

"I trust he will write a good review of La Maison, despite not being at the table."

"My absence will help to keep my identity secret, *n'est-ce-pas?* You've no idea the shifts people will go to in order to coax a good review out of me."

Drouin helped Sinden on with his jacket, and Sinden accompanied the ladies out to the door, where their carriage awaited. "May I join you soon at Half Moon Street?" he asked.

"We shall be waiting for you," Cybele said. "And thank you, Sinden. You have gone to a deal of trouble on my behalf."

"We could not let you lose your fortune. Folks would say you were marrying me only for my money—if you decided to marry me, that is to say." His eyebrows lifted in a question.

"Now they could say only that I am after a title," she replied, "if I decided to marry you."

"Cybele!"

"We shall be waiting for you. Don't be long." A trail of tinkling laughter hung behind her on the cold air as she went to the carriage.

After overhearing that bit of banter, Lady Violet realized her role was to remove herself from the saloon when Sinden called later that evening. She held herself in readiness for his call in the study. The meeting was brief. "Have I your permission, Lady Violet, or must I write to her brother?"

"I am acting in loco parentis. You have my permission, Sinden. Good luck."

He found Cybele sitting in front of the grate, gazing into the leaping flames, with a besotted smile on her pretty face.

"Thank you, dear Sinden," she said shyly, reaching out a hand to welcome him.

He took up a seat beside her and held her hand. "You should have told me, you know."

"I never said I did *not* own La Maison. I said my aunts had not invested. And when you asked me if Pierre had ever told me who was backing him— well, naturally he never told me, because I already knew."

He gave a scowl. "Have you been seeing a lawyer behind my back? You answered the letter of the questions, but not the spirit of them."

"I did not want you to feel sorry for me or to offer for me thinking I had a dowry when I had none. If I had let you offer, I was afraid you would feel obliged to marry me after you learned the whole truth."

"I do feel obliged to marry you, but your dowry or lack of one has nothing to do with it. Is that the only reason you would not hear my offer?"

"Yes," she said, with a smile that gave a fleeting

glimpse of her dimples, "for to tell the truth, I thought we should suit uncommonly well. Your satirical ways might put off other ladies, but I pay them no heed. I know it is only your gauche way of hiding that you feel uncertain. You are not like that with your friends." She waited for his reply to that taunting charge of gaucheness.

"You understand me uncomfortably well, madam. I wonder if I shall ever understand you. How could you think I would not help the woman I love if she had told me the truth?"

"I didn't know you loved me at first! You had a very odd way of showing it."

"That was before we were bosom bows. Now that we are on terms of some intimacy, it is time to put off my mask of satire. I love you, Cybele," he said simply. "Will you marry me?"

"I should be honored, Sinden. And you *will* give La Maison a good review? You see the extreme shifts we dining-room owners are put to in order to get a good review from Monsieur Bongoût!"

"Cybele!" He saw the laughter in her eyes and pulled her into his arms. "Wretch!" The word was smothered to silence as his lips found hers.

THE CHRISTMAS BALL

by
Leslie Lynn

1

Lady Athena Cummins drew aside the leather curtain that covered the carriage window, keeping out the chilly draft so that her youngest sister, Lady Persephone, might view the bustling streets of Burnham-on-Crouch. A sparkling layer of ice frosted every bare tree branch and etched designs upon the rooftops. Snow scrunched under the boots of three village children who dashed past, their laughter echoing in the cool, still air, with arms full of fir boughs to decorate their homes for Christmas.

Athena viewed the rapt expression on Persephone's face with an aching heart and forced a smile. "Do you feel chilled with the curtain open?"

"I am chilled to the bone!" Facing them, Minerva, their sixteen-year-old sister, pouted. "Do close the curtain. We do not want to be seen gaping like the veriest commoners. What can be keeping Mama?"

"She is searching for a feather the exact shade of puce to compliment your costume for the Christmas ball." Athena, whose back was to the driver, nudged the warming brick over to Persephone's slipper-shod feet. She worried constantly that the cold made her sister's legs weaker; and despite the fact that Persephone couldn't walk, she should have sturdier boots, no matter the cost.

"Persephone, would *you* like me to close the curtain?"

Persephone lifted a pinched little face from the

folds of a cashmere shawl Athena had found in the attic and presented to her for this outing. Her peaked cheeks held just a tinge of pink, but her enormous sherry brown eyes sparkled. "No. I do so enjoy watching everyone prepare for Christmas. It is so festive—"

"Oh, look, there are Squire Randolph and Gregory!" Minerva's squeal of delight interrupted. Athena had to crane her neck to see out of the window. "And fancy that! His lordship, Gregory's own lieutenant, is with them!"

Even out here in Essex the rumor mill had been busy for weeks with tales of Lord Andrew Finchley's visit to Willowwood for the squire's masked Christmas ball. Although she very properly pulled her head away from the window, Athena couldn't take her gaze from him as the trio strode by. His fine black riding boots shone to perfection, and a many-caped coat swung with his gait. She caught only a glimpse of a snowy cravat folded in such a brilliant fall, she felt sure half the young men in the county would be attempting it by morning. The biting wind swept his glossy black hair off his chiseled, arrogant face. Catching a glimpse of cold sapphire eyes, she suddenly believed every tale repeated of his rakish ways in London and the Peninsula.

For a moment the object of her attention appeared to glance straight at her, a faint smile playing at one corner of his mouth. Just as she had done at age five—when dear, sweet Papa brought home a new Mama for her—and had continued doing ever since, Athena tried to make herself invisible. She shrank back against the crimson squabs and tucked her chin into her woolen scarf.

Why would such an august personage travel to the wilds of Essex for a mere ball, particularly one as unusual as Squire Randolph's and just one week before Christmas?

"Ain't that the Cumminses' town carriage? Must pay our respects." Squire Randolph, having just returned from the local surgeon, had Gregory's arm supported in his own strong grasp.

Drew wasn't sure why he had agreed to come to this off-the-mail-route little town, but he had promised Gregory; and Gregory had saved his life, in a roundabout way. So here he was, having to do the pretty, when he could have been snug at home with any number of highfliers.

Gregory turned with as much animation as Drew had seen since the Pyrenees toward a stately black carriage, its wheels picked out in scarlet. His first impression was that the carriage contained two females, an insipid miss straight out of the schoolroom and a young girl whose lively expression and remarkable eyes showed promise of beauty.

Only after Gregory leaned down to speak into the window did Drew notice the third occupant. From the way she buried her face between her bonnet and her scarf, he could tell neither her age nor her appearance, just a pair of green eyes, begging to be ignored. If not for the quality of the fur edging her cloak, he would have taken her for a serving girl.

"Dash it, Persephone, been meaning to pay a morning call." Gregory's wide mouth curled up into a smile. For which young lady did his friend feel such an attachment? "Must have you meet Lord Andrew Finchley. Drew and I served together on the Peninsula, you know. These are the Ladies Athena, Minerva, and Persephone Cummins, Lord Finchley."

He inclined his head slightly. The quiet third female a sister to this lively pair? Now why should that strike him odd?

The child, Persephone, craned her head toward

the open window. "My lord, we are so pleased you have brought Gregory back to us for Christmas."

Lady Minerva, not to be outdone, nudged her sister back to take her place. "Oh, Lord Finchley, I am *so* pleased you will be attending the Christmas ball this year."

It took all his effort not to smile at the heavy-handed hint that she felt herself deserving of his attention. Still, the oldest sister remained silent and muffled to the gills.

" 'Tis hard to believe you're of an age to attend, Minerva." Long acquaintance made the familiarity acceptable. The squire reached in to chuck Minerva's chin while a deep chuckle rumbled up in his barrel chest. "And you, my lady"—the squire's eyes settled on the mummy in the corner—"will you be gracing the ball this year, Athena?"

The carriage's silent occupant shook her head, muttering something so low, the words were lost on the cold wind.

" 'Tis a shame." The squire shook his head. "Mayhap next year. Pray give our regards to Lord and Lady Cummins. We look forward to their attendance at our ball tomorrow."

"And I promise faithfully, I'll be by the day after the ball, Persephone!" Gregory laughed. "Have Cook make me some macaroons."

"Word of a Randolph, you shall come?" The child's voice held a light musical note, and her face lit up, making her cheeks blush a pretty rose.

"Word of a Randolph!"

Suddenly Gregory looked nearly as young as she did. Nineteen was no great age; certainly it was too young to die in the mud and blood of the Peninsula, as many had done.

To forget that Drew had returned to London and lost himself in women, drink, and cards, firmly putting the horror behind him. All the talk of war and heroics he'd experienced since venturing down to Burnham-on-Crouch was bringing back too many memories. Once his obligation was fulfilled, he would return to London and get back to the good life. And that couldn't be soon enough if the highlight of the upcoming ball was to be an overstuffed chit practicing her wiles on him.

When they had taken their leave, Gregory's face fell back into the somber lines etched by illness and war. "Has Persephone's condition improved at all? She was such a taking little thing."

" 'Tis sad for the family." The squire's normally jovial face paled. "But there ain't nothing to be done. The sawbones say she'll be in that rolling chair for the rest of her life."

That pert little thing with the enormous brown eyes, confined to a chair? Curious at last, he inquired, "What happened to her? She appears to be in the pink of health."

"Crippled," the squire uttered baldly. "A terrible fever weakened her limbs. Lord Cummins had Prinny's own physician to Essex to examine her. But there ain't no hope. They say the Lady Athena ain't taking it so well; refuses to let the little miss give up hope."

These people meant nothing to him, so what difference could it make? But after two years on the Peninsula, he understood pain and hopelessness. And there had been something of innocence and wonder in the child's eyes that reminded him of all that he had lost.

Lost in daydreams, Persephone gasped when her mother climbed into the carriage and a draft of icy air rushed up her woolen skirts.

Lady Charity Cummins's long face, framed by an ocherous bonnet, was the mirror image of Minerva's, but her hazel eyes were hard and discontented. She surveyed the three girls. "Was that Squire Randolph I saw who stopped to speak with you?"

"Yes, Mama," came one dutiful and one muffled reply.

"Mama, the most exciting thing occurred!" Minerva clapped her mittened hands together. "Gregory introduced us to Lord Finchley! He is ever so handsome and just as dashing as rumor predicted. He seemed particularly pleased when I said I was to attend the ball!"

Persephone wrinkled her nose. "I think him not so handsome as Gregory. What do you think, Athena?"

Before she could reply, Minerva laughed. "Everyone knows Athena is on the shelf and has no opinions of handsome gentlemen." She sneered, "Your precious Gregory cannot be compared to Lord Finchley. He is one of the greatest catches in the ton!"

"And what do you know of the ton?" Persephone snapped. "You should not even be going to the Christmas ball. You are not seventeen until spring!"

"Girls!" Mama exploded, her eyebrows lowering to a single line across her forehead. "Stop your bickering at once! Of course Minerva will be attending the masked ball. She has the most beautiful shepherdess costume, and today I purchased a matching feather and ribbons for her hair."

"Then why can Athena not attend?" Persephone protested, knowing full well the reaction she would receive.

As expected, Minerva looked smug and Mama angry, but Athena smiled gently. "And who would stay home with you, goose? Besides, you know I have no costume. Perhaps next year."

Minerva might look relieved, but anger coursed through Persephone's veins. Athena had spoken the same words every year since her seventeenth birthday. She could still hear Mama telling Papa Athena was too young for a Season, too young for the Christmas ball. Then she had fallen ill, and every year after Athena had given the same excuse.

But this year it would be different! She was thirteen, and she knew how important this ball was. Why, Athena would never get off the shelf if she didn't get about to meet some eligible men.

On her twelfth birthday, after sneaking one of Minerva's books from the circulating library, she had vowed to change things. Her good, kind, beautiful sister should have wonderful adventures and romance, too.

For one whole year she had plotted and planned. Now, keeping an eye on her oldest sister's profile all the way home, she could remember the night of the Christmas ball a year ago without getting angry.

As usual, Athena had come to her at bedtime to massage her legs with warm oils before wrapping them in flannel and tucking her under the covers. She had fallen asleep, but in a little while she woke to a strange sight: Athena, holding her cat, Morgana, to her breast, while she hummed and danced around the bedchamber. The firelight had flashed apricot in her nearly colorless hair, for once flowing freely about her face. Athena had looked beautiful and happy, not shy and withdrawn.

Persephone wished above all else to have the world see that side of Athena. To that end she had hatched her plot. Come tomorrow night, she would unveil it.

But when the carriage rolled to a stop before the impressive facade of Charybdis, Persephone had other things on her mind. She protested as she was being handed down. "I don't wish Stephens to carry me into the small parlor. I want John Coachman to carry me through the kitchen garden in to Cook. I must speak to her about baking macaroons for Gregory."

"Suit yourself!" Mama huffed, urging Minerva in from the cold. "I shall send someone to fetch you before tea."

Athena cast her a quizzical look. "I will bring your rolling chair myself, Persephone."

A sudden ache of love for her sister made her blink back tears. Only Athena guessed how she hated to be carried about by the underfootmen. Only Athena treated her like a real person, with feelings to be considered, and didn't talk down to her or about her as if she weren't there.

John Coachman swung her up in strong arms and whirled her about, as if she were three again and hanging about the stables. She smiled up into his broad, ruddy face. "Do you remember my asking you for a special favor?"

"Aye." His lips, cracked from the cold, lifted at the corners. "Aye, little miss, you know you have but to ask and I'll be doin' your biddin'."

"That would be ever so wonderful. I hope Cook feels the same."

"Feels the same about what?" Cook placed her fists at her ample waist and glared at her husband. "Don't you be carryin' mud into my kitchen, John Harris! Here, I have a nice cozy chair pulled before the fire for Miss Persephone."

She allowed Cook to help her out of her bonnet and coat and to pull her slippers from her frosty feet. With gentle hands Cook lifted Persephone's useless legs onto a stool and covered them with a warm rug while John poked up the fire to a roaring blaze.

"There now. What can I be gettin' you?"

"Gregory's coming the day after tomorrow. He particularly asked for your macaroons." Persephone saw a pleased smile suffuse Cook's genial face.

She turned away to brew a pot of tea, but not before a telltale blush crept into her cheeks.

"Do you think I am like Athena or Minerva?" Persephone's abrupt change of subject made Cook's mouth fall open as her husband pointedly turned his attention to the fire.

Cook looked to the ceiling for inspiration. "Lady Athena is the image of her dear mama, God rest her soul. You have the look of the Cummins family. But both you and Lady Athena have the same good heart, although she never be the minx you are, young lady!"

Cook's scold made Persephone smile. "I believe there is another side to Athena none of us has ever seen. Would you not like to discover it?"

Cook's eyes narrowed while John Coachman turned a suspicious gaze upon her.

"Would you not like to see Athena go to the Christmas ball this year?"

"That mother of yours won't be allowin' that to happen!" Cook declared with a huff. "Even if she be a vicar's daughter and her name's Charity."

"Aye, without a tuppence of charity she is," John Coachman chimed in. "Your father, good man that he be, all buried away in that library writin' a history of the ancient world, don't have no notion of the way of things. What be you askin' us, little miss?"

With a glance toward the door, she motioned them closer. They must finish their plotting quickly before Athena appeared. "Cook, have you not wondered why I asked you to secretly procure me so much fine muslin?"

Cook met her husband's shrewd eyes and shrugged. "You're such a good needlewoman, I thought you be making gifts for Christmas."

"That is precisely what I have done. But this gift is only for Athena. And you must both help me with the rest. If we all do our parts, Athena shall not miss the Christmas ball this year."

2

The day of the Christmas ball dawned cold and crisp. By afternoon the sun sparkled diamonds off the frosty windowpanes. Persephone sat ensconced before the fire in her father's library, as she usually did each day for two hours after tea. This was the only room in the house that did not have fir boughs decorating the mantel for Christmas. And it was the only room in the house where Mama's or Minerva's frantic demands did not ring out to spoil her concentration.

"Dear Papa, would you mind ever so much if I took your volume on Greek statuary to my room to study tonight?"

Lord Cummins carefully removed his spectacles from his nose and gazed at her with eyes remarkably similar to her own. "My dearest daughter, I am delighted at your thirst for knowledge. You have been studying this tome for weeks now—what do you find so interesting?"

He sprang to his feet, removing the book from the shelf above his desk. But before he could give it to her to keep, the door burst open.

Her mother stood there quivering with anger. "My lord, the servants may be terrified to disturb you in your library, but I am not. A light repast is now being served, as supper at the ball will not be until the unmasking at midnight. Pray join us at once, for then you must dress. We have only an hour in which to don our costumes and be on our way."

"I believe I will take a tray in my room. May I, Papa?"

"Of course, dearest. I will carry you up myself, and then, dear wife, I will be down to join you."

Being swept up by her father's strong arms made her feel much younger than her thirteen years. Usually she didn't like to be pampered, but on occasion, especially tonight, it was nice to get her way without questions. She hugged the statuary book to her chest as Papa carried her from the rolling chair downstairs to the one in her bedchamber.

Gently he tucked a coverlet around her legs. Although he tried to hide it, she saw the pain in his eyes.

"There you are. I will ring for your maid."

"No, not just yet. I have a confession." She leaned closer to him, whispering as if they were conspirators. "Cook herself is bringing me a tray with a sample of the macaroons she is baking for Gregory's morning call. Do not betray us."

Pleasure replaced pain in his eyes, just as she had hoped. He tapped the tip of her nose with one finger. "Your secret is safe with me."

She waited until she heard him on the stairs before propelling the chair out of her room and across the hall to Minerva's door. At that moment Cook appeared around the corner, carrying a tray with several silver covers.

"Is everything ready?" Persephone could barely contain her excitement.

Puffing from exertion, Cook declared stoutly, "Ready!" She positioned herself in the hallway as Persephone rolled into Minerva's room.

Just as she had expected, Minerva's costume hung from the top of the wardrobe, and her powdered headdress sat on a hat form on a side table.

With it were a puce loo mask with the matching feather and a plain white half mask.

Persephone snatched up the white one and slid it into the folds of her coverlet. She rolled herself as quickly as possible back to her own chamber, Cook watching the hall carefully.

Cook pulled the door shut. "Did you get it?" she gasped, placing the tray on the low rosewood table in front of the fire.

Persephone pulled the mask from its hiding place and waved it happily. "Do you have the roses?"

Cook raised one silver cover to reveal a wreath of white roses. Their centers held a hint of the apricot that would exactly match Athena's hair when she brushed it free.

"I picked them from the conservatory and hid in my chamber to weave them together," Cook declared proudly. "None of the others saw it."

Little shivers of excitement made Persephone's heart beat faster. "Is John Coachman ready?"

"Aye. One hour after he drives his lordship to Willowwood in the fine carriage, he'll be at the latch gate, waitin' for Lady Athena. We figured he should use the old landau with the crest covered by a dark cloth."

"Capital!" Persephone sighed with satisfaction. "Now I fear the most difficult task is ahead of me."

The words were barely spoken before she heard Minerva's shriek. A moment later a knock came on her door; then Athena peeked in. She gave Cook a sweet smile of surprise.

Flustered, Cook thrust a small plate of macaroons toward her. "A special treat for the little one."

"Save me one, please, Cook." Athena's low chuckle was nearly drowned out by Minerva's cries. "I fear Minerva has misplaced one of her masks for this evening."

"Isn't she wearing the puce one, which matches her costume?"

"That was her decision *before* dinner. But now that the white is missing, she is sure she must wear it. I will be in to tuck you up the moment I have helped her into her finery."

Refusing to feel guilty, Persephone snatched up a macaroon and bit into it. "The puce befits the costume, and well Minerva knows it."

A half hour later she had finished her dinner and was waiting for Mama, Papa, and Minerva to show off their finery. She was not surprised to see that, except for the color, Mama's and Minerva's costumes were identical. Dressed in gowns of the last century, more elaborate than any self-respecting shepherdess would ever have worn, complete with crooks and overpowered by towering powdered headdresses, her mother and sister would take the ball by storm. She smiled. Most of the neighborhood wore dominoes or some simple costume. But Mama felt she had to be in competition with the squire's lady; the competition seemed to be escalating rapidly. In contrast dear Papa wore proper evening dress with only a black loo mask in concession to the spirit of the evening.

"You look magnificent!" Persephone clapped her hands in appreciation.

"Thank you." Her mama sniffed. "Athena will see to it that you get to bed at a proper time."

"Persephone, tomorrow I shall regale you with our triumphs!" Minerva crowed, traipsing out into the hall after her parents.

Laughing softly, Athena shut the door and leaned against it. "I feel sure we will hear about nothing but the ball until spring."

"It is my fondest wish!"

Surprise widened Athena's eyes. "Persephone, you look flushed. Are you well?" A worry line marred her high forehead, below the colorless hair braided tightly into thick ropes and knotted at her nape to keep it out of her way.

"I have something for you." Persephone rolled her chair to the chest under the window, opened it, and lifted out a package. "Here. This is for you."

"What . . . whatever is this?" Athena unwrapped the package, lifting out a simple muslin gown fashioned into the robe of a Greek goddess. She held it up in awe.

Persephone met her sister's incredulous expression with determination. "I designed it by using the drawings right here in Papa's book. See the way it drapes across this statue of the goddess Athena? I have even made the rosettes across the bodice and to hold the gown at the shoulders."

"But . . ."

Persephone lifted one of the silver covers, revealing the wreath of white roses. "You must let your hair down and wear this wreath as a crown." Lifting another cover, she revealed the pilfered white mask. "And you must wear this at all times. No one will know you. Isn't it famous?"

"I cannot . . ."

"Don't give me cannot, Athena. This is your costume for the Christmas ball. I have been working on it all this past year." When she gazed into Athena's eyes, she was struck by the sadness she saw.

"Persephone, my dearest sister, I am overwhelmed by your achievement. But I am so sorry. I cannot attend the ball."

Knowing in her heart there was only one way her dream could come true, Persephone broke into loud, gulping sobs. Never had she wept: not during her illness nor the painful examinations performed by physician after physician, not even during the nightly massage of her legs, which made them tingle and ache.

Athena knew this. Tears streaming down her own cheeks, she knelt before her. "Persephone, please, I—"

"No!" she cut her off, swallowing a sob. "I do not wish to see the Christmas ball through Minerva's eyes. I wish to see it through yours! I will never be able to dance myself. You could give me a little of that joy if you do it for me."

"You will walk again!" Athena insisted, gripping Persephone's clenched fingers. "I promise you."

"Perhaps. Until then, you must do this for me."

"I have no way to travel to Squire Randolph's," Athena argued.

"Cook is waiting to let you out through the kitchen garden. John Coachman will be waiting with the old landau. I have arranged everything, Athena. It needs only your consent."

Athena's chin rose defiantly, it seemed, and deep emerald lights shot through her green eyes. Persephone knew she had won.

"I will go, but only for a short time. If I leave before the unmasking at midnight, no one will ever know of this. No one *must* ever know of this, Persephone. For you, and only for you, I will go to the Christmas ball."

Athena felt naked. She was wearing her flimsiest chemise, and the muslin floated over her body as if she wore nothing. The gown was unlike anything she had ever experienced. It flowed freely from rosettes of fabric at each shoulder down over her breasts, and yet somehow it silhouetted every curve as it fell in sweeping lines to brush her ankles. She was uncomfortable, but before she could voice her hesitation, she caught sight of Persephone's reflection in the mirror.

Persephone was in her rolling chair, petting Morgana, who rested on her lap and gazed up with an unblinking stare, a satisfied smile on her face. How could she disappoint the child?

She loosened the tight pins from her hair and fingered through the braids before leaning forward to brush the flowing mane into some semblance of order. Loose, it sprang to life, taking on color and vibrancy. When she threw her head back, it fell in gentle waves to her hips. The instant she pinned the rose wreath into place, her hair took on the delicate shade of their centers.

A strange stirring inside her made her suddenly afraid. She twirled to her sister for one last attempt at reason.

"I saw you last year on the night of the ball dancing by the firelight with Morgana in your arms." Innocent wisdom shone from Persephone's enormous eyes. "I want you to dance for real, with someone real. Be that Athena this Christmas, if only for tonight."

The gravity in Persephone's voice stopped her last protest. She stared at the stranger in the mirror, and suddenly this beautiful goddess looking back at her *was* someone else. And for this one night she would *be* someone else.

"I will, dear Persephone." She knelt, looking into her beloved sister's thin face. "I will do whatever you wish this night if you make me a promise. Never give up hope that you shall walk again."

Persephone hugged her close for one moment. "Anything is possible tonight, Athena. Make it your dream come true."

Flinging her old black cape around her and pulling the hood up to cover her head, Athena crept out into the hallway like a thief, looking both ways. From the servants' staircase Cook motioned her forward.

Silently they stole through the house and to a side door that faced the garden. Cook seemed almost as terrified as Athena was herself. She squeezed Cook's hand. Then she was gone.

A swirl of icy wind entered the landau before John Coachman pushed the door closed. But with the top closed and a warming brick at her feet, Athena felt reasonably comfortable. The horses sprang forward. Excitement mingled with some unsettling sensations tingling through her veins.

Moonlight brushed the familiar landscape in shades of white and shadow, making it seem a fairyland. The stillness intensified until she heard only the beating of her own heart.

She felt alive in a brand-new way. Laughing breathlessly, she tied the mask over her eyes. Tonight she *would* be someone else. Not the Athena who spun dreams alone at her bedchamber window, not the dutiful daughter, the sacrificing sister. Tonight she would dance not with Morgana but with a handsome stranger in her arms.

As John Coachman helped her from the landau behind a copse of trees at one side of the drive, she gazed up at him. "I shall return before midnight. Be ready," she whispered, and stepped away from him toward the manor.

The squire's majordomo did not recognize her as he removed her cape and placed it in a small anteroom. Relieved, she mingled with other guests. Recognizing the vicar and his wife, she stayed behind them as they moved toward the ballroom up the grand staircase.

Willowwood had never appeared more beautiful. Fragrant greenery, bows, and wax tapers filled every room. Fir boughs decorated the mantels and wound through the balustrade up to the next floor. On every chandelier was hung a kissing bough, lavishly beribboned and festooned with mistletoe.

Music and laughter enticed her into the ballroom. It was aswirl with color, costumes, and dominoes, fans, feathers, and masks everywhere. Minerva danced by in the arms of the vicar's oldest son down from Oxford, dressed like a bishop. Off to one side her stepmama sat with the ladies, all chattering as if they had not seen one another for months. At the other end of the room, the gentlemen huddled, lost in talk of hunting and cards.

It was exactly as she had imagined it would be.

But even in her deepest dreams, she hadn't realized how the excitement would catch her and set her free. Across the room a gentleman in a plain black domino turned, and she looked straight into Lord Andrew Finchley's sapphire eyes.

Drew was engrossed in conversation with Gregory and two young bucks who questioned him endlessly about London fashions. Then one of them drew a startled breath, and he turned to see what had caught his attention. An otherworldly creature had descended from the heavens to grace this ball.

"By God, what a ravishing creature! Who is she, and why have you kept her hidden?" Drew plucked Gregory's cup of rum punch from his hand and took a quick swallow.

"Dash it, never laid eyes on her before." Gregory fixed him with a bright stare, a smile twisting his lips. "Lay you a monkey you can beat out the field. Go, discover who she is."

Indeed the vision had become surrounded by eager suitors. Drew gave his friend a salute and, moving swiftly across the floor, cut through the circle of admirers to pluck her out of the arms of a rival and lead her onto the floor.

"My lord?" She hesitated, drawing away from him.

He found himself staring down into frightened green eyes. A pulse beat at the base of her slim throat above the diaphanous folds of fabric skimming her lithesome body. The sight of the soft curves so cunningly hinted at shot desire through his blood.

She cast a long, desperate glance toward the door, but before she could bolt, Drew placed his hand over hers.

She went utterly still. Boldly he turned her hand over and raised her open palm to his lips. "All *your* dances tonight are mine."

3

Athena gazed up into the clearest, purest, bluest eyes she had ever beheld. She could neither move nor breathe. Then his lips touched her palm, sending waves of response to regions of her body that were unmentionable.

"All *your* dances tonight are mine," he repeated.

Somewhere back in her mind where she could still think properly, she knew she couldn't possibly give him more than two or it would cause a scandal. But, to her horror, she felt herself nod in agreement and followed him onto the dance floor. The musicians struck up a waltz; his arms slipped around her, drawing her close—this was nothing like whirling about with Morgana.

She stared up into his face, made mysterious by his simple mask. How could she, who had never waltzed before, match him step for step? How could he, who knew her not, generate such feelings within her?

"I am Lord Andrew Finchley. What is your name?"

Tonight she could be whoever she wished. She laughed, deep in her throat, and teased, "I cannot possibly reveal myself until the unmasking at midnight. You must guess."

One black eyebrow rose above his mask. "I've told you my name."

"You have told me nothing, my lord." Deliberately

she kept her voice husky and low. "I knew who you were the instant I arrived."

She couldn't believe what was happening to her. To flirt and have some admiration returned—it gave her a feeling of power.

"Then tell me who you are supposed to be."

She almost blurted out the truth before realizing it would be her undoing. "I am most certainly a Greek goddess."

"Yes." A smile curved his mouth. "You are a goddess."

She had never felt more vulnerable in all her twenty-one years. But she could neither hide her nervousness by burying her face in his chest nor by fleeing, for a promise was a promise.

So she decided to play her role properly. She flung back her head confidently. "Do you wish to charm this goddess?"

Her action caused him to draw a long, deep breath. "I think you play with me, my goddess," he drawled, leading her out of the circle of dancers.

Only then did she realize the musicians had finished the waltz and a country dance had begun. Athena saw her sister whirl by with Gregory leading her. Frantic lest she be recognized, she ducked her head behind Lord Finchley's shoulder, and her hair became tangled in the frogged fasteners.

"I fear we are entangled, my lord. Is there a quiet corner where I might extricate myself without embarrassment?"

He drew her through a curtain into a small window embrasure where they could be alone. She hadn't realized how dark, how secluded, how overwhelmed she would feel. Trying to disentangle her hair quickly, she only made it worse.

His hand reached to still hers. Suddenly she was aware of the candles in the kissing bough hung above them.

"Be still, my goddess, and I will free you." He removed his mask, and his hands gently worked the strands of hair. "So soft, so radiant, like moonbeams," he whispered. "Ah, free at last."

Her body trembled in response. This could not be happening to her! She spared a glance at the beauty of his face, and her fate was sealed.

Perhaps it was only this man who would ever make her feel so. But she was more aware, more in tune with the beauty around her. His smile was entrancing, the cut of his clothes perfection. He even smelled wonderful; a clean hint of soap rose from his skin, making her think of the freshness of the woods in springtime.

Steady on, her mind said; but her body swayed toward him. "Why is Lord Finchley spending Christmas in Essex at the squire's ball instead of at some wonderful ton house party?"

"Tell me first who you are, my goddess," he urged.

There was no retreat, so she sat in the window seat, leaning against the icy window, anxious to cool her heated blood. He needed no invitation but sat beside her.

"I will tell you only that I did not travel far to be here tonight. Now why have you come here, my lord?"

"Because of a promise."

Her eyes widened; her reason was the same. On impulse she touched his arm. He needed no more encouragement to take her hand between his long fingers.

"Because of a promise to Gregory," he repeated. "We were on the Peninsula together. It is not a story I can tell a lady, or a goddess. Suffice to say Gregory fell in battle, and when I turned to save him, a ball caught me in the arm."

She gasped in fear.

"My injury was the merest scratch, although if I had not turned, it would have killed me. I carried him to the surgeon, who managed to spare his leg, but a fever ravaged him. During the worst of it he talked of this ball. I rashly promised that if he lived, I would attend this year. And I am now glad of my promise, for I have met a goddess."

She should not say what she felt, she thought, or she might spoil the magic of this evening. Yet she must take the chance, for the shadow of pain in his eyes could not be denied.

"I think, my lord, there is much you do not say about the war, yet you feel it still. My father once told me that war scars a man's soul. Mayhap now, in this season of peace, it is time to put your memories in the past, celebrate that you and Gregory are alive, and take your joy from the simple pleasures, like the smell of roast goose, or a waltz beautifully done, or the touch of a loving hand."

He gazed into her eyes so intently, she felt he burned away the mask and could see straight to her heart. Instead of an answer he lowered his head and kissed her.

His lips rested so lightly against hers that she felt no fear. They were soft, gently caressing. She could not help parting her own lips to more fully enjoy the delight.

When he raised his head, his mouth curled at one corner. "You mustn't blame me, for we are sitting beneath a kissing bough."

"I am not angry, my lord." How could her voice sound so calm when she trembled inside?

She knew little of men. Papa and John Coachman. What she had discovered with Lord Finchley's touch shook her to her core. She was twenty-one years old, and, as Minerva had stated more than once, on the shelf. The delights hinted at by Lord

Finchley's kiss tempted her beyond all reason. This was a side to herself she did not recognize.

"Perhaps we should return to the dance, my lord," she said quietly.

"Yes, I want to feel you again in my arms."

He drew her through the curtain to the edge of the dance floor. The ball was in full swing, and no one was there to watch her. She had not been missed by a doting mama. This time she leaned her head into his chest, fearing not what others thought. This was her night of romance and adventure; tomorrow she would be plain old Athena again.

"I must see you again. Tomorrow," he demanded.

Oddly enough she did not feel panic at such a request, only sadness. Tomorrow she would no longer exist. Not wishing to spoil the little time she had left, she smiled into his eyes. "After you see my face, you may rue your words, my lord."

"The mask hides very little of your charms, my goddess."

At his low murmur she stiffened, endeavoring to pull away. He must never recognize her! He allowed her no quarter, keeping his hand low and tight at her waist.

"You go too fast, my lord." She felt the heat rise in her body and could not keep it from her voice. "A goddess must set her own pace." She forced a laugh, terrified of the game she played, yet more terrified to end it.

"You have set the pace from the moment you entered this room. You were looking for me, were you not? And I have sought you forever."

Although shocked by the boldness of his words, she realized they were true. She had come for her sister, but also for him. And she would pay a heavy price. But not just yet.

She slipped her hands up to his shoulders, barely

able to resist the urge to slide her fingers into his hair. "I fear you have found me out, my lord," she teased breathlessly. "Are you quite shocked?"

"What I am, my goddess, is enchanted." He whirled her into a corner, bent over, and pressed a fleeting kiss to the corner of her mouth. "I think we may both have found more than we had bargained for. And I promise, goddess, I won't let you go."

She wished to go nowhere.

They danced through the night, ignoring the others around them. The hours flew by as she learned not only the feel of Finchley's strong body but also the complexities of his intellect.

At last they could ignore Gregory no longer. Pointedly he continued to place himself at Finchley's shoulder.

"Dash it, know I'm de trop. Must tell you the whole place is abuzz about you, my lady." His friendly grin was so familiar and so beloved by Persephone, she couldn't help smiling back at him, despite the chill of fear coiling in her chest. "Thought I should warn you that every busybody in the room will be staring at you for the unmasking."

The room came back into focus, no longer just a whirl of sounds and colors through which only she and Finchley moved. She saw her stepmama and Minerva whispering together as they cast her speculative glances. They were not the only ones—even the squire and the vicar's lady seemed to stare at her. Gregory had spoken true. She had sunk herself beyond reproach.

"How soon until midnight?"

"A few moments. Is something wrong?"

"Of course not." She began to shake. She couldn't leave him in the middle of the dance floor, but she had to get away. No one must ever know the brazen goddess of tonight was she.

Her eyes searched the room and found no escape.

"I am suddenly parched. If you would escort me to a corner and then procure me an eggnog?"

His arm tightened around her as he led her toward the far wall. "Stay here. I'll return shortly." He turned to cross the ballroom.

She waited until all eyes were on him, then quietly slipped into the window seat. She had to get away, but where, how. . . .

The curtain parted, and he returned empty-handed. "I turned to look, and you had disappeared. You must not frighten me like that, my goddess."

She could not let it end like this. The kissing bough swayed, flickering with candlelight. This was neither the time nor the place for what she felt, but it was all she would ever have. She tangled her fingers deep into his glossy hair, found his lips, and kissed him with all the endless longing in her soul.

Only then did her normal good sense flood back into her wanton body. Slowly she pushed herself out of his arms. He raised his head and looked down at her, his eyes unfathomable.

"Your goddess wishes only a moment of peace and an eggnog, my lord," she reminded him gently.

"Wait for me!"

The curtain closed behind him. She couldn't think, but she had to act. She unlatched the mullioned window and climbed through to a balcony from which she could access another room and disappear. She raced down the staircase, her gown flowing behind her, and demanded her cape. She snatched it from the majordomo's hands, flying out the door without even putting it around her shoulders.

As promised, John Coachman waited for her, ready to return her swiftly to where she belonged.

In the silence of her own chamber, she sadly offered the roses to the fire and then carefully removed her gown. A pang of fear pierced her when she discovered a rosette was missing, but there was no way it could be traced to her. She would have John Coachman search the grounds and the landau tomorrow just to be certain.

She folded the gown, rewrapped it, and hid it at the bottom of the chest at the foot of her bed. Sometime she might retrieve it from its hiding place and relive this night. But she would need no reminders, for the image of Lord Finchley, the feel and the taste of him, were imprinted on her forever.

Trying not to give in to her feelings, she donned her night rail, stole into Minerva's room, and placed the mask beneath the dresser as if it had fallen there by accident and not been seen. From there she went to Persephone's chamber. The child was sleeping peacefully, her face soft and achingly young. Morgana curled contentedly into her side.

She knelt beside her. "Persephone, you do not know what you have done this night," she whispered, kissing her sleep-warm cheek.

Bloody fool! he cursed himself again and again, his lip curling cynically. Fool to have left her side! Fool not to have learned her name!

Gregory called to him, and he swung around eagerly. The rest of the party had gone in to supper, all their chatter centered on the disappearance of the unknown beauty dressed as a goddess. It would be a nine day wonder for them.

"Dash it, Drew, not a trace of her. Charles says she fetched her cape and made her escape, but he caught nary a glimpse of her carriage."

"Who is she, Gregory?" He slammed his fist into the mantel, and the candles quivered with his anger. "She said she had not come far. How could no one know such a beauty?"

"A mystery, my lord, and the makin' of this Christmas ball." The squire approached them, his hands folded across his stomach. "It'll be the talk of the county. But there's naught to be done until morning. Come partake of supper, my lord. A full stomach always helps a man solve a riddle."

He did not need food! He needed her!

He wanted her. No one had ever kissed him with such innocence and desire mingled together with a sweetness he could still taste.

He swung away, his gaze searching the empty ballroom for answers. He strode to the embrasure and pulled the curtain aside, once again hoping against hope that she might reappear.

He stepped through the window, tracing her route. Just outside the French doors that led to a small retiring room for the ladies, he spied something white on the terrace. He picked it up, excitement coursing through his veins. It was a rosette of muslin from her gown.

"What is it, Drew?" Gregory asked from behind him.

He held it up in the moonlight. "It's from her gown."

" 'Tis not much to go on."

Not for most men. But for a man of his determination, it would be enough. His family would have to wait. The delectable demirep awaiting him could offer her favors elsewhere. He would not leave Essex until he found his goddess. And when he did, he would never let her out of his sight again!

4

To Persephone's dismay it was Minerva, not Athena, who burst into her room as she sipped her morning chocolate.

"My dear little sister, the Christmas ball was wonderful! Too bad you will never be able to go." Minerva danced around the room, her fat curls bouncing against her cheeks. "I danced with Edwin, who said he came home just for me, and Gregory, as well as all the gentlemen my age. . . ."

Persephone heard no more, lost in daydreams of dancing in Gregory's arms. Her affection was of long standing, for seven years ago, when he was twelve and she six, he'd climbed the apple tree in the kitchen garden to fetch Morgana down safely. She kept her feelings hidden, though, even from Athena. She glanced down at her lap, at the heavy coverlet wrapped around her legs, and shut the door firmly on her thoughts.

After a deep sigh she interrupted Minerva's recitation of her triumph. "Did anything unusual happen at the ball?"

Minerva blinked. "There was a mystery lady. If she hadn't been there, I would have had all his lordship's attention—"

"Mi-*ner*-va!" Mama's call interrupted her complaint.

"I must fly. Mama and I are making morning calls. The gossip should be delicious!"

Minerva went haring off, leaving Persephone more confused than ever. The mysterious guest must have been Athena. And she had obviously attracted Lord Finchley's attention, which had been the whole point. So why hadn't she come to tell the whole tale this morning?

Persephone rang for her maid, and when she appeared, she asked about her sister.

"Lady Athena is not yet up."

Shocked, Persephone glanced at the clock on her mantelpiece. Athena *never* slept late. Desperate to discover what had gone on, she ordered two footmen to carry her down to the kitchen. The surprise at her demand sent everyone into a flurry.

"What could have occurred to overset you so?" Cook made another pot of chocolate to calm her and prepared a cozy chair next to the fire, then dismissed the staff to their duties.

"Can you tell me what has happened? Athena has not awakened."

"But she has," Cook corrected, her eyes open wide as saucers. "At first light she came down and asked me to have John look for a piece of her gown that be missing."

Persephone stared up at her, realizing something must have gone wrong with her wonderful plan. "But how did she look last night upon her return from the ball?"

"Like the most beautiful creature I've ever laid eyes upon." Cook busied herself with the roast for lunch. "Never knew Lady Athena could look like that. Always thought her hair be colorless. I never seen anything like it."

One of the downstairs maids poked her head in the door. "Beggin' your pardon, ma'am. Lord Finchley and Mr. Randolph have presented their cards. With her ladyship out Mr. Stephens be having an apoplexy. What's to be done?"

Persephone straightened up immediately and took charge. "Nothing to it. Please have Stephens bring my rolling chair to me at once. Then ask Lady Athena's maid to inform her I need her in the front parlor. We have guests to entertain."

Athena stiffened at the soft knock on her door. She wasn't quite ready yet to talk to Persephone. She hadn't been able to sort through her feelings and tuck them away. Persephone's bright, inquisitive mind would pick out the truth in the tales Athena had spent the morning concocting.

"Enter!" she called softly from the window seat, where she had spent most of the night sitting, staring up into a starry sky. She turned a wary eye to the threshold. "What is it, Sally?"

"Lady Persephone has requested you to join her in the front parlor. You have morning callers, and Lady Cummins and Lady Minerva have gone out."

"Who are the callers?" she asked, already moving across the room, patting her braids into place.

"Mr. Gregory has brought that lord with him."

A hot flush of fear made her stop suddenly and run damp palms over her gray morning gown. She stared dumbfounded at her maid. "Are you quite sure?"

"Aye." Sally gazed at her as if she belonged in bedlam.

Of course there was no mistake. And even if somehow they had discovered the truth, she couldn't leave Persephone alone to face them down. But truth to tell, catching sight of her plain reflection in the mirror, she knew there'd be no way for them to connect her to last night's goddess. Her hair was pulled straight back, making her look older and colorless. *He* would never recognize her as the woman who had kissed him so passionately beneath the kissing bough.

. For just a moment at the parlor doorway, Athena froze. He might not know her, but she remembered every detail of his chiseled face, his hard, muscular body, his beguiling voice. She could hardly take her eyes off him. Then he turned to look at the doorway and stared right through her. Certain all must see the longing in her eyes, she glanced down and entered the room, taking the place beside Persephone on the rose velvet settee.

"Athena, Gregory has just been telling me the most exciting tale of last night's ball."

Her eyes flew to her sister's face. Persephone knew; her eyes gave her away.

"Go on, Gregory, tell us more," Persephone urged, turning back to him.

"Dash it, Persephone, it will be the tale of the county for weeks. Before long you will be bored silly with hearing how this beautiful creature comes to the ball, but no one knows her. Drew here scandalizes the county by dancing every dance with the beauty. Then at midnight she vanishes, leaving us all at sixes and sevens." His enthusiasm did not seem to be duplicated in Lord Finchley.

"Drew has me riding *ventre à terre* all over the county looking for her. And we have nothing to go on, except the fact that she revealed she lived nearby, *and* he found this."

Her pulse pounded wildly as Lord Finchley pulled the missing rosette from his inner coat pocket. Persephone, beside her, started. Did she make the same interpretation? Was his lordship keeping the rosette close to his heart?

When had she turned into a romantic?

"This was part of her gown." His deep voice caused heat to seep through Athena's pores, and she feared to meet his eyes. "Perhaps you know her, Lady Athena? She is tall, slenderly built, and has the most unusual hair. Very fair, with a touch of apricot moonbeams."

Athena shrank back on the settee, trying to steady her breathing before she forced her eyes up to meet his polite gaze. His eyes looked upon her with indifference, but the sapphire light burned with an intensity that was at once both frightening and bewitching.

Last night she had deliberately kept her voice low and husky. Today she would speak in her normal cool tones. "It appears to be a beautifully made rosette of muslin, my lord, but the lady and the gown it comes from are unknown to me. Perhaps she would appear different by the light of day."

"Dash it, Lady Athena's right! You saw only half her face, Drew. Could have a long nose and a squint!" Gregory laughed, stuffing one of Cook's macaroons into his mouth.

She continued to study Lord Finchley from under her lashes just to see his reaction. His mouth shaped a rueful grin. "Lady Athena may indeed be correct, yet I find I wish to discover the truth for myself."

He rose to take his leave, and Gregory pulled a cane out from under his chair. "Overdid it a bit last night. Feeling the effects today." He bent over Persephone's hand. "We're off then. Next time I'll stay for a longer visit, and we can play piquet. Tell Cook her macaroons are still unexceptionable."

"Come back soon, Gregory. And bring Lord Finchley with you." Persephone smiled brightly, not a trace of guile on her face.

The men were barely out the parlor door before Persephone rounded on Athena, her face blazing with excitement.

"Athena, his lordship is searching for you!" She grabbed her hand and squeezed tight. "He is mad for you! It is the most romantic tale I have ever heard. At last everything I dreamed for you has come true!"

Athena went utterly still. How could she possibly make her young sister comprehend the disaster that was last night? "Persephone, you cannot understand—"

A commotion in the hallway stopped her. Her stepmama and Minerva had returned from their round of calls. Quickly she made her escape, unable to deal with what the gossip mill had to report. She hid in the conservatory, so restless that she felt she might break apart and scatter to fly with the wind. She picked at the plants until it seemed she might strip them of all their foliage. Finally she clipped two of the roses she had worn in her hair last night and carried them to her room. For hours she sat in the window seat, dreaming the day away and watching the snow fall.

When Athena prepared for tea, Sally came in with her cloak.

" 'Twas wrinkled and mussed, my lady, so I sponged and pressed it. By the by, Lady Persephone's not feeling well. She's taking a tray in her room.

Horrified at her selfish isolation, Athena flew from her bedchamber across the hall.

"Persephone, are you not feeling well? What ails you?" Athena cried, rushing to her side.

"I am simply tired of waiting for you to confess all."

Athena stopped short, noting for the first time the pugnacious lift to her sister's chin and her arms folded tightly across her chest. "Well, now that I am here, you should do your exercises." The little minx—worrying her. Not waiting for a reply, Athena started the nightly massage and the stretching and bending movements she felt sure would help Persephone walk again.

"It was a beautiful evening last night, dearest," she said quietly, finding it easier to talk about it while her head was bent over Persephone's legs. "The manor never looked more delightful, decorated with fir and bows and candles. The smells were delicious."

Persephone remained silent. Athena massaged her ankles and tucked flannel around her feet. Finally she looked at her sister. Recognizing the stubborn set to her mouth, Athena smoothed the coverlet and sighed.

"Persephone, I know you are wise for your years. However—"

"Are you hiding the fact that you gave yourself to Lord Finchley last night?"

"Persephone!" Shock brought Athena to her feet, heat blazing to her cheeks. "Of course I did not! How could you think such a thing?"

"Short of that, there is nothing you could not confess to me," Persephone declared, her eyes alive with excitement. "You fell madly in love with Lord Finchley last night, did you not?"

"I am not sure it was love I felt for Lord Finchley last night," she replied, being as truthful as possible.

"Wanton thought and love, I think, go hand in hand on occasion."

Athena sank down beside her sister, overcome by the workings of her young mind. "Wherever have you got such ideas?"

She patted Athena's arm as if she were the older sister. "There are many books in Papa's library, and he notices not *what* I study, just that I *do*. Now we must face the facts. Lord Finchley is looking for *you.* He must be madly in love, and you . . . you must reveal yourself."

"No, dearest, he is looking for the woman I became for a few brief hours last night. The woman you helped create. She said and did things I would never dream of doing in the light of day. She no longer exists."

"Of course she does! Inside you." Persephone sat straight up in bed, her rich, dark hair falling over her thin shoulders. "You must let her out, so all can see her and love her, as I do."

"Look at me." She cupped her sister's small face with shaking palms. "Truly look at me. Not as my dearest sister but as a stranger might. Do I look like the woman you sent off to the ball last night?"

"No." The answer came out in a strangled whisper.

Athena released her and backed to the door. "That is why I do not reveal myself to Lord Finchley. I could not bear to see the disappointment in his eyes."

Persephone stared at the closed door for long minutes after her sister had slipped from the room. "No, you do not look like the goddess," she repeated into the silence. "Yet you could, Athena. You could if you would only allow it to happen."

She cast a long, exasperated look at her rolling chair across the room. She had to get to her writing desk. Flinging back the covers, she pulled her useless legs over the side of the bed. She braced them apart and, using a bedpost, pulled herself up. For one breathless moment they held her weight; then she fell. Angry, she pushed herself up again and rang for her maid.

Though the heavy parlor draperies had been drawn against the night, Drew flung them aside to gaze out at the countryside. Where could she be hiding? Despite the snowfall they had ridden to all the nearby estates today to no avail. His goddess still eluded him. He drew the rosette from his coat and rolled it between his fingers, imagining it carried the sweet scent of her.

Gregory made a noisy entrance. "Dash it, Drew, you have the look of a lovesick pup. Not yourself at all! Want a brandy?"

Drew allowed himself to be coaxed to a chair by the blazing fire. A glass was pressed into his hand before Gregory dropped into the chair opposite him.

"Sorry, Drew. Think the beauty has eluded us."

A sharp knife of disappointment made him tip all the fiery liquor down his throat.

Gregory poured him another. Swirling this glass between his fingers, Drew studied the amber liquid as if it held the answer he sought. "I have two more days until I must leave for Finchley Park. I cannot delay longer. It would displease my father. So there is still time. And if we don't find her now, I will be back."

"That's more like it. Dash it all, want to help you, but I'm promised to Persephone on the morrow. Received a missive she wants a sleigh ride now that we have snow. Bringing Lady Athena along, so she suggested you accompany us."

He looked up and shrugged. "Persephone is a delightful little minx, and her sister appears pleasant enough, quiet yet with a quick mind." Remembering her swift deduction about his quest, he lifted one eyebrow quizzically. "She definitely put me in my place today, and without calling me a besotted fool."

"Both sisters are smart as whips. Minerva can be, too, when she's not being so selfish. Their father is a brilliant scholar. Been writing a history of ancient Greece as long as I can remember."

The brandy glass at his lips, Drew paused. "I suddenly realize the sisters are all named for goddesses. Athena and Persephone are Greek, but Minerva is Roman."

"Due to that mother! Picked Minerva 'cause she is the equivalent of Athena. Didn't want her first-born slighted." He sighed. "Never met such a woman. Can't think how Lord Cummins puts up with her."

Rejecting the thought before it was even fully formed, Drew sipped at the second brandy. There had been nothing in the plain Athena to remind him of his goddess—a woman who had melted into his arms with such passion, he became aroused merely by the memory.

He started up and opened the draperies again. She had not been a figment of his imagination. She had to live somewhere, and he would not rest until he found her.

5

Persephone waited until her mama and Minerva had gone out to purchase the last of the Christmas gifts before she rolled herself into the conservatory, where Athena sat reading beside the fountain. "Will you come on a sleigh ride with me?"

Looking up, Athena smiled. "That would be lovely. I will have John Coachman hook up the sleigh at once."

"He has already done so." Lifting her chin, Persephone braved her sister's startled eyes. "Gregory and Lord Finchley will be arriving at any moment to escort us."

Athena shook her head, and her eyes dilated like Morgana's at dusk. "Persephone, do not do this thing."

"I fear I already have. Minerva has gone out with Mama, and I will not bring a maid along to be seated next to Lord Finchley. Fortify yourself. If the goddess he seeks no longer exists, you have nothing to fear."

Turning away, Persephone frowned. Of all the people in her world, she loved Athena the best; she would never hurt her. Devoutly she hoped she was not now doing so.

Somewhat bemused, Athena stared after her sister's retreat. Persephone, despite her words, did not understand the terrible pain she felt when Lord Finchley was near her.

The temptations. The temptation to discover the pleasures his lips and hands had promised. The temptation to once again have him look at her with desire.

Her stepmama had reported smugly that in two days he would be gone, she reminded herself. All she must do was survive until then.

Then, if she tried very hard, she could put him behind her and once again pick up the threads of her quiet life.

John Coachman had brought the sleigh around to the front door. She wore her drab cloak, the one that clashed with her hair and complexion, while muffling Persephone up in bright red kersey wool. When Lord Finchley and Gregory arrived by horseback, they were ready and waiting. Gregory carried Persephone to the sleigh, placing her carefully on the front seat and tucking a rug around her before leaping up to take the reins.

Lord Finchley very properly handed Athena into the backseat. She found herself snuggled up against the very man who filled her every waking thought and invaded her dreams. Even though they were separated by layers of rugs, cloaks, and clothing, she could feel his heat seep into her and undermine all her courage.

The bells jingled and the sleigh runners swooshed, and they were off. Persephone demanded the reins, and Gregory's merry laughter as he denied her that privilege echoed through the frosty air.

Lord Finchley smiled at Athena. "They are very fond of each other, I think."

She nodded. "When they were children, Persephone was his shadow. Lately, of course, they have not seen so much of each other."

He shifted in his seat uncomfortably. She did not want to betray her nervousness by shrinking away, yet she was certain she bored him. She sat utterly still, clenching and unclenching her fingers beneath the warmth of the rug.

"You and your sisters all have the names of goddesses. Tell me why." His eyes searched her face as if seeking an important answer.

"Our father is a scholar." She said it quickly, then changed the subject. "I am freezing."

A perfect excuse to lower her bonnet and bury her face in the rug. At once concerned, he rearranged the rugs, going so far as to put an arm about her.

Gregory pulled on the reins, and the sleigh stopped abruptly. Persephone turned to them, longing in her eyes. "Gregory and I always made snow forts here. He is willing to do so again."

Hating to disappoint her but knowing she must, Athena shook her head. "I am sure Lord Finchley—"

"Would love to build a fortress," he interrupted, laughing. "Used to be quite good at it."

At Persephone's shouts of joy he glanced down at Athena. "Let the child have some fun."

His kindness added to her feelings, already racing out of control. Her fingers trembled within her mitten as he took her hand and helped her down into the gleaming field of white.

Following Persephone's shouts of encouragement, Lord Finchley plowed off through the snow to make a fort while Gregory built his next to the sleigh.

"I shall be on Gregory's team. You, Athena, shall help Lord Finchley!"

Really, Athena began to fear that her dearest sister had become too bossy for her own good. At least out here, in the crisp, cold wind, she was free of the overwhelming closeness of his presence.

Knowing her duty, she rolled huge masses of snow along the ground to build up their fortress.

She felt a snowball thud against her back as she bent over the front wall, smoothing it to perfection. Gregory's laughing face told the story.

Lord Finchley retaliated for her and struck Gregory in the shoulder. She ducked into the safety of the fort and began rolling compact balls for ammunition.

Swearing vengeance, Gregory returned fire. Snowballs began flying in all directions. As quickly as he could make them, Gregory tossed snowballs to Persephone, and she pelted Lord Finchley and Athena with an accurate eye from her perch in the sleigh.

Laughing, Athena jumped up and began her own assault. She had true aim, managing to just miss Persephone, making her shriek with delight. But then a snowball splattered against her bonnet, knocking it off. Trying to catch it, Athena tripped and tumbled into a snowbank.

Lord Finchley ran to her and reached down a hand to pull her from the snow. Suddenly he froze, gazing at her wonderingly. Warmth tingled along her skin as she rammed the bonnet back in place, tying it firmly beneath her chin.

"What is wrong, my lord?"

He blinked and his eyes refocused. "I fear you will catch your death of cold sitting in the snow." Effortlessly he pulled her to her feet.

In truth Athena shivered, but not from the cold.

"Quickly, Athena, we must return home!" Persephone shouted. "I saw Mama's carriage drive past on the road. They have returned early, and there will be the devil to pay."

The gentlemen very properly paid their respects to Papa while Athena and Persephone confronted Mama in the parlor. Minerva was in a towering rage.

"What is the meaning of this nonsense? Why was Minerva excluded from your sleigh ride, Athena?" Her stepmama's voice when communicating with her never varied from a sharp demand, even at five, when she'd first met her and had read her right and true. But this time a quiver of outrage warned her she was in over her head.

"Gregory took us as a treat to me," Persephone piped up, trying to protect her. "It is not our fault Minerva was out shopping with you, Mama."

"See that you are more thoughtful in the future," she sniffed. "Tush, Minerva, I will see to it that you go on the next outing. Now I must see what is keeping the gentlemen."

The instant her back was turned, Minerva stuck out her tongue at her sisters. "Oh, you think you are so clever, leaving me out of your fun. Well, you shall be sorry this time! I put Morgana out in the snow, where you'll never find her." She turned and flounced out of the room.

All the color drained from Persephone's face. "She is wicked, Athena. Morgana is too old to be out in this weather."

"Never fear, I shall bring Morgana home." Athena, while terrified for her beloved pet, felt she should project confidence in front of her sister. She quickly donned her cloak and bonnet, tying a scarf over it to keep it in place and provide some extra warmth. She had to be gone before the gentlemen returned. Truth to tell, as much as she regretted Minerva's foolishness, she did not regret absenting herself from Lord Finchley's presence.

She walked along the drive, staying in the ruts the carriage wheels had made, calling to Morgana. But she reached the main road without a sign of the cat.

Morgana usually came when she called, but the cat had not been outside for two or three years. She was probably terrified, as well as cold and wet. Athena stoutly refused to think the worst and kept trudging forward even though large, wet snowflakes began to fall.

Trying to keep cheerful as the temperature dropped, she pretended to be delighted with the snowfall. Perhaps it would continue—she always loved when it snowed on Christmas Eve as they came out of church. Perhaps Lord Finchley would attend services.

"Morgana! Kitty, kitty, kitty," she called, trying to keep all other thoughts at bay.

A shaft of disappointment lodged itself in Drew's chest when he returned to the parlor to find Lady Athena gone. He assumed that she had quit the tea table on some trivial errand and would soon return.

He found himself eager to observe her. For one moment, due to some trick of the light in the snow, her hair had displayed a tint of apricot. The thought that he had rejected out of hand yesterday now refused to be dismissed.

Noting Persephone's distraction, how often she glanced toward the door, he set his teacup firmly on the table and asked politely, "Will Lady Athena be joining us?"

The swift glare Persephone shot toward her other sister could hardly be missed.

Gregory's brows drew together in a frown. "Is something amiss, Persephone?"

"Nothing to concern you, Gregory." Lady Cummins, a woman he found hard and cold, favored them with a frosty smile. "Let me pour you more tea, gentlemen."

Drew swung toward Persephone, effectively blocking her mother's view. "Where has your sister gone?" he whispered.

"She has gone out in this dreadful weather to search for our cat, Morgana."

He smiled at her. "Never fear, I shall return them both to your safekeeping." He bounded to his feet, made Lady Cummins a graceful bow, and started to the door. "I fear I have misjudged the time. We must be on our way. Thank you, my lady, for a delightful tea."

Gregory hesitated but was too bright to tell him nay. He surged to his feet, bowing correctly over Minerva's and her mama's hands but clasping Persephone's small one warmly. "Dash it all, we must be off. My compliments to Cook, and I'll see you Boxing Day."

Drew ran down the front steps of Charybdis Hall, where a groom held the reins of both horses in the falling snow. He whipped a blanket off each of their saddles.

"Dash it, Drew, where are we off to in such a hurry?"

"To find Lady Athena. It seems she is out in this storm, searching for Persephone's cat." Drew threw himself into the saddle and took up the reins.

"Morgana! Used to be Athena's cat, very old. Since Persephone fell ill, the creature spends most of the day on her lap. How did the old tabby escape?"

Remembering the look Persephone had sent her sister, Drew thought he knew. "That is of no importance. Must find Lady Athena before the snowfall worsens." He dug his heels into his mount and galloped forward.

Swirling snow clouded his vision as he crisscrossed the grounds. Gregory called Athena's name, and the wind caught the sound, blowing it away across the fields.

The road dipped, separating him from Gregory. Drew topped the rise, and his sharp eyes caught sight of a dark figure struggling toward them against the wind. Cursing, he galloped toward her, feeling the bite of the icy snow against his cheeks. Utter foolishness to risk going out on such a night. Foolishness and love for her sister, he realized with a pang of understanding.

He reined ruthlessly in her path. She gasped, gazing up with eyes suddenly as green as her cat's. A memory sucked all the air from his lungs.

"Dash it, Lady Athena, catch your death out here," Gregory declared, pulling up behind him.

"I found Morgana; that is all that's important." She smiled up at them, clutching the fat black cat to her bosom.

Of a sudden Drew envied the tabby. "Come, Lady Athena, we will return both you and Morgana safely home. Gregory!"

His friend needed no other encouragement to leap down and carefully boost Athena up before Drew. She kept a tight hold on Morgana, who began to protest at the prospect of riding a horse. Drew put his left arm around Athena and settled her back against his thighs, then stroked Morgana's fur comfortingly. "Hang on, little one."

Deftly he turned his mount back the way he had come. A scent of roses emanated from her cold skin. "Do you like roses, Lady Athena?" He tried to see her face in order to gauge her reaction to his odd question but couldn't get a glimpse around her bonnet.

"I spend much of my time in the conservatory, my lord."

He listened carefully to her voice for a hint of husky charm but failed to hear any. Sooner than he wished the lights of Charybdis greeted them. Before he could help her dismount, the Cumminses' majordomo had opened the door and sent two footmen to assist her.

Snow glistened on her eyelashes as she turned her face up to thank him. Still cuddling the cat, she swept into the house, leaving him to stare pensively after her.

"Dash it, always thought Lady Athena a quiet creature. She's as full of fun and valor as Persephone!"

"Yes, there is much to admire in Lady Athena, and many things to learn about her." Drew turned his horse toward Willowwood.

Gregory flicked him a grin. "Not quite in your style, I should say."

"I agree. A woman who possessed Lady Athena's intelligence, warmth, and humor, coupled with the beauty and passion of my lost goddess, would surely be more to my taste."

"But such a creature don't exist!"

Smiling to himself, Drew urged his horse to an easy canter. "I am no longer so sure of that," he murmured to himself.

6

On the afternoon of Christmas Eve, snowflakes drifted lazily down outside the window as Persephone sorted through her sewing box. She had promised the vicar to make bows that would grace the boughs over the altar during the special service tonight.

Minerva burst through the door, dancing across the room. "Oh, I love Christmas! The presents, the roast goose!" She stopped at Persephone's side and fingered the ribbons spilling out of the lacquer box. "What are you doing?"

"Getting ready to go to the church to decorate. Don't bother me now; I must finish this last bow." She was still angry about Morgana and tried to ignore her sister, who perversely kept rummaging through her workbox, tangling her silks into a bird's nest.

"What is this?"

Persephone glanced at the muslin rosette, and her heart gave one hard thud against her ribs. "Nothing!" she snapped, snatching it away and burying it under a pile of bows.

She had forgotten all about the practice piece. Now she had to hope Minerva wouldn't remember she'd seen one like it before, or where.

"It's pretty. Can I have it?"

"No!" Persephone glared at her sister. "You were

so wicked about Morgana, I shall never forgive you."

When she heard her name, Morgana's ears twitched, and she blinked sleepily from her place on the hearth.

"See! There was no harm done to your old cat."

"There could have been," Athena said quietly, standing in the doorway. "That is the point you miss. But enough of that. It's Christmas, and we should all be in good spirits. Persephone and I are going to the church early to decorate. Would you care to join us?"

Looking somewhat smug, Minerva nodded. "Yes. I shall run to tell Mama we are all going."

"She is up to something," Persephone fumed, closing her sewing box and putting it safely away.

"Persephone, we should think the best of Minerva. I know it is hard at times, but try."

Looking at her sister's sad face, Persephone felt a pang of remorse. She had tried her best to make happiness for her sister, but now she didn't know what else to do. Her only hope was that Lord Finchley would attend the service tonight before he left for his family seat in the morning. She would have one last chance, and she vowed she would make the most of it.

"Dash it, Drew!" Gregory grumbled as he pulled his hat lower to combat the combination of wind and snow. "Thought this foolishness about the rosette was at an end," he continued to complain as he trailed down the front steps of the manor. "Where are you dragging me off to now?"

"I feel the need to pay one last call at Charybdis."

Gregory's face lightened considerably. "Why didn't you say so in the first place? Always happy to visit Persephone."

It was not Persephone Drew had an overwhelming urge to see but her sister, that delightful mix of contradictions. As much as he tried to dismiss the absurdity that the quiet, pale Lady Athena Cummins and the glorious goddess of the Christmas ball were one and the same, he could not. In fact, the idea that one woman could embody so many different yet appealing sides fanned his interest into a raging inferno of contradictory emotions.

He felt an overwhelming sense of disappointment when he learned the young ladies were not at home. Trading on his long-standing acquaintance with the family, Gregory ascertained they had gone to the church and would be staying for services.

"Nothing to do but follow them!" Drew announced, springing into his saddle.

"Dash it, Drew, are you feeling quite the thing?" Gregory asked, an anxious note in his voice. "Thought you didn't care about attending the service tonight."

"You are quite wrong, Gregory," Drew declared, determination firming his jaw. "There is no place I would rather be."

Athena eyed Minerva whispering with Edwin, the vicar's oldest son, at the rear of the sanctuary. She came to the uneasy conclusion that Persephone was correct—Minerva was up to something.

She turned back to the fir bough above the altar, where she hung the last bow, making certain the tails were well away from the candles, which would be lit during the service.

Admiring her work, she backed to the narthex where Persephone sat in her rolling chair, weaving boughs together to festoon the walls. Minerva was glaring at her, in her usual superior way.

Athena sighed. "What is wrong now?"

Minerva turned away, hiding something behind her back.

"What do you have there, Minerva?"

Minerva threw a defiant look at Persephone and tossed her curls. "It is mistletoe. Edwin is attaching it to the boughs all over the church."

Athena should have been scandalized, yet the memory of the kissing bough at the Christmas ball made her smile instead. "Kissing boughs in the church?" She shook her head. "We shall have to ask—"

"I think it a wonderful idea."

Athena started. Lord Finchley filled the doorway, a greatcoat flung over his broad shoulders, his eyes sparkling, his cheeks flushed from the wind. He looked like every girl's dream come true. If she had not felt Persephone take her hand and squeeze it, she would be certain she *was* dreaming.

Last night, being held in his arms, was the culmination of a fantasy, a lapse in judgment she could not allow to continue. She turned her head away.

"What a wonderful surprise to see you, Gregory. And you, Lord Finchley." Persephone jumped into the breach. "What brings you here so early?"

Lord Finchley stepped closer, too near for Athena's peace of mind. Her heart quickened, and she felt a flush begin to spread over her cheeks.

"Dash it, Persephone, I thought Drew was dragging me out to search for the owner of that muslin rosette. He surprised me wanting to find you and Lady Athena," Gregory said.

"A muslin rosette, you say, my lord? May I see it?" Minerva asked sweetly.

Athena's embarrassment quickly changed to panic. The look on Persephone's face warned her Minerva was awake on all suits. She watched warily as Minerva took one glance at the rosette in Lord Finchley's palm, then lifted wide, knowing eyes to Athena before twirling on her heel and fleeing the church.

Persephone gasped. "We must go after her, Gregory!"

Immediately he swept her up in his arms and followed Minerva out.

Athena was alone with *him*. She had imagined this so often the past few days but never thought it might happen. She felt light-headed but knew she had to keep her wits about her.

She backed away as he leaned down to pick up the mistletoe, which had scattered on the floor when Minerva ran out. Laying the bundle on a table, he retained one small sprig between his fingers. Quickly he followed her retreating steps, closing her into a corner.

She had tried so hard not to wish for another moment such as this. Yet now, having him gaze at her, a look of desire in his eyes, she could not regret it.

He framed her face with his long fingers. "A Christmas kiss, Athena," he whispered so softly, she might only have imagined the words.

She tried to stand stiffly apart, denying her feelings, but she could not. As he pulled her into his arms, she leaned into him, her lips softening, warming, parting for him. A deep sigh forming in her body, she knew this was where she wanted to be; this was right. . . .

"Athena!" Her stepmama's horrified voice separated them. She felt Drew's confusion, but before she could react, cruel fingers grabbed her and tore her out of his arms.

Drew felt as if he were moving in slow motion. For a moment his world turned upside down and inside out.

He strode into the church, his eyes searching for her. It was already filling for the service. He saw

Lady Cummins pull Athena down beside her in a front pew. Short of making a scene by rushing up and sweeping her into his arms, there was naught he could do but wait.

He folded his arms across his chest and propped himself against the back wall. His mind raced.

Athena and his goddess—one and the same. No two women could taste so sweet. No two women could bring to him the same innocent, eager passion.

Why had she not revealed herself to him at once? Could it be that his regard was not returned? His natural arrogance and his instincts as a man told him one thing, but her actions told him another.

Now that it truly mattered, was it possible that he would meet rejection?

"Will this interminable service never end!" he bit out through tight lips.

Gregory turned from the back pew, where he sat next to Persephone's empty rolling chair, and gave him a startled look. Ignoring it, Drew pushed his way toward Athena as the last prayer ended and the pump organ began playing the postlude.

There seemed a conspiracy to keep them apart— village children overcome with excitement, ladies showing off their Christmas finery, gentlemen yawning after their naps during the sermon.

The squire stopped him to introduce the vicar's brother, a baronet visiting from Devon. By the time he had done the pretty and reached the Cumminses' pew, there was no one left. All he saw was Persephone's frightened face over her father's shoulder as he carried her out a side door.

"Fear something is amiss with little Persephone. Think her mama took a dislike of something?" Gregory asked, a frown twisting his mouth.

Drew knew precisely what she had taken a dislike of, and he had a plan to rectify it at once.

* * *

Athena threw a protective arm around Persephone's shoulders as they huddled together on the low daybed in her chamber. Mama was on a tear. She paced back and forth, casting a large shadow from the flickering firelight.

She clapped her hands together. "Such wanton behavior is beyond belief! Kissing! In the house of God!"

"Here, Mama! I told you so!" With a triumphant smile Minerva lifted a muslin rosette out of Persephone's sewing box.

"That belongs to me!" Persephone protested, struggling to reach for it.

"Where did you get this, young lady?"

"I made it." Persephone lifted her chin, braving her mama's glassy stare, unwilling to admit more.

"You . . . you . . . *made* it!" Charity clutched her hands in front of her heart and sat down heavily on the chair near the fire. "And what else were your busy little hands about?"

"It is my fault." Athena tried to deflect attention away from Persephone by crossing to the fireplace. "Persephone made me a costume. I knew it was wrong, but I went to the squire's ball anyway."

A few days before she could never have admitted the truth. Now she was prepared to face her stepmother's wrath. Now that he had kissed her again.

Charity gasped, her face turning a bright scarlet as she surged to her feet. She lifted her hand and struck Athena across the cheek.

The sting brought tears to her eyes, but she held them back for Persephone's sake.

"You wicked, wicked girls! You shall both pay for this deceit!"

A sharp rap upon the wood heralded Stephens's appearance. "Lord Finchley and Mr. Gregory are in the library with Lord Cummins. He has asked for Lady Athena to join them."

Her heart bounding into her throat, Athena took a step toward the door.

"Not so fast, young lady. You have not been dismissed!" Charity waved Minerva away and commanded Stephens to carry Persephone to the morning room. "You will remain in your room until Lord Finchley is long gone, Athena." She slammed the door in her face and turned the lock.

Athena covered her face with her hands and wept. Why had she not revealed herself to him at once? All the dreams her heart had been fashioning scattered around her.

She yanked on the bell cord. Surely someone would come in answer!

"You must help me, Minerva!" Persephone cried, straining toward her sister.

"Why should I? Stay out of this. You have done quite enough." Smirking, she pushed Persephone's rolling chair through the door to the hallway. "*Now* you will stay where you belong."

"Minerva, no!"

Her cries ignored, Minerva swept out, shutting the door firmly behind her.

Persephone had to do something. If Mama sent Lord Finchley away, he might never return. She looked toward the bellpull across the room and thought of her chair right outside the door. One way or the other she must reach them.

Over and over Athena had told her she must try to walk. Secretly she'd been standing by her bed, even tried a step, but she'd always fallen.

If Athena believed in her, she must believe, too.

Gritting her teeth, she pushed to her feet, holding on to the low couch. She let go and with all her strength tried to move her legs. One step. Then another. Just enough for her to fall forward and catch the edge of the wing chair. She pulled herself into it, her heart pounding and heat prickling along her skin.

Taking a deep breath, she pushed to her feet to try again.

One tiny step and she crashed to the floor. She used her arms to pull herself across the carpet to the door.

Panting, her hair hanging damp on her neck, she flung open the door. There was her chair! She pulled herself toward it, reserving the last of her strength to clamber into the seat.

Whatever happened, she *would* stop Lord Finchley from leaving Athena!

Drew had come here for reasons he did not fully understand. He started by attempting to apologize to an uncomprehending Lord Cummins, but it all came out a jumble.

Gregory looked at him, perplexed. "What game are you up to?"

No game, this! "I wish to ask for Athena's hand in marriage," he blurted out, not in his usual fashion.

Gregory paled.

Like any good father, Lord Cummins shook his hand and rang for his daughter.

He waited with anticipation to see her lovely face again. The door opened.

"I am sorry, my lord. Lady Athena does not wish to see you," Lady Cummins announced as she entered the library.

His arrogance refused to accept the words. "I wish to hear it from her own lips, my lady."

Looking uncomfortable, Lord Cummins cleared his throat. "Perhaps you should return tomorrow, my lord. Athena is a gentle soul. The suddenness of your attentions may have overwhelmed her. Confess they have me."

His lordship's attempt at kindness did not prevent the disappointment ripping through him. What a fool he had been at the church! He had seen how this woman cowed Athena. He should have swept her up in his arms and made a dash for Gretna! Crazy thoughts, he knew, yet a certain madness seemed to have come over him since he first laid eyes on her.

"Dash it, Drew. Nothing for it but to take our leave," Gregory muttered, urging him out into the hallway.

He went because he had no choice. Stephens held the front door open in readiness, as if he'd been listening. Lord and Lady Cummins stood to bid him farewell. Still he hesitated.

"Wait!"

Persephone's cry stopped everything. She rolled toward him from the back of the house, tears streaking her cheeks, her frock jumbled around her in the chair.

"Don't leave, Lord Finchley! Mama and Minerva have locked Athena in her room!"

"What?"

Lord Cummins's roar became lost in the pounding relief that spurred him into action. He took the steps two at a time. "Which room?" he called.

"Second on the left!"

A maid stood there, her apron over her face as she wept.

"Open this door at once!" he demanded.

"I shall do so, my lord." Lord Cummins, his pride a mantle around him, stepped forward and inserted the key.

The look of wonder in Athena's eyes as Drew stood before her banished any lingering doubts. He pulled her fiercely into his arms. "Why did you not tell me at once?"

"I did not wish to see disappointment in your eyes," she whispered.

"My goddess, I could never be disappointed with this." He bent over her tenderly, but the kiss soon became a fire, consuming them both.

Epilogue

Persephone sat in the front parlor, Morgana resting on her lap. Through the mullioned windows she could see the carriage that would take Athena to Finchley Park this morning, Christmas Day. Sally was already dressed for the journey and bustled around the footmen, making sure all the baggage was packed properly in the second carriage.

No member of this house had slept peacefully last night. Athena's whirlwind engagement and precipitate departure had been her heart's desire. But, here alone, Persephone wondered who could take Athena's place. Who would be her friend?

Through the parlor door she could see Papa in the hall, making arrangements with Lord Finchley. After the disaster of yesterday Lord Cummins had vowed to spend less time in the library and more time taking up the reins of his family.

Mama was absent, sulking in disgrace in her chambers. Minerva had been sent to her room for a fortnight, all her novels removed from sight, with only "elevating books" and selected sermons to keep her company. Papa felt sure they would improve the tone of her mind.

Smiling, her hair newly fashioned in loose curls, Athena skipped down the staircase to Lord Finchley's side. Even from here Persephone could see the love that radiated from his eyes. He couldn't stop looking at her.

Hand in hand, they came to Persephone and knelt by her chair, each kissing her cheek.

"I shall return in one week, Persephone." Athena held her hand in tight fingers. "We will continue your exercise and massage. See how much better you are already."

"Yes, I now have hope of improving even more." She squeezed her sister's hand one last time and released her, for in truth she must let her go in more ways than one. "You will marry Athena soon, won't you, my lord? Perhaps she can teach my maid the exercises before that time."

"Yes, I will be taking your sister away from you soon, Persephone. Perhaps the shortest engagement the ton has ever seen."

She had never noticed before what kind eyes Lord Finchley possessed.

"But you may come to stay with us as often and for as long as you wish. We owe you a great debt, my dear new sister."

"When did you fall in love with Athena, my lord?" She liked very much that he did not appear shocked or angry at her question. It had become a matter of great importance to her.

"At the Christmas ball. When she first let me see into her heart. It happens like that for some people."

Athena blushed, making her even more beautiful. The look in her eyes conveyed a special kind of message.

She kissed Papa good-bye, and Lord Finchley helped her into the carriage. As it pulled down the drive, Persephone caught a glimpse of them wrapped in each other's arms.

That made her smile.

For years to come all would talk of the squire's masked Christmas ball and the mysterious beauty who had won the heart of a great lord. Persephone was most happy to have been a part of it. Most happy indeed. Her hand stroked Morgana's fur, and the cat rumbled in contentment.